Anjali Joseph was born in Bombay in 1978. She read English at Trinity College, Cambridge, and has taught at the Sorbonne, written for the *Times of India* in Bombay and been a Commissioning Editor for *ELLE* (India). *Saraswati Park* is her first novel.

SARASWATI PARK

Lakshmi and Mohan live in Saraswati Park, a quiet suburb of Bombay. While Mohan spends his days in the city, working as a letter writer and collecting his beloved second-hand books, Lakshmi passes her time with small domestic tasks and her favourite TV soaps. Until, into their settled life, arrives Mohan's nephew Ashish — an uncertain nineteen-year-old, struggling with himself and his place in the world. As Ashish becomes entangled in a risky affair, his aunt and uncle start to question the quiet rhythm of their lives . . . and discontents — left unspoken for many years — begin to break the surface.

ANJALI JOSEPH

SARASWATI PARK

Complete and Unabridged

ULVERSCROFT
Leicester

First published in Great Britain in 2010 by
Fourth Estate
An imprint of HarperCollins*Publishers*
London

First Large Print Edition
published 2011
by arrangement with
HarperCollins*Publishers*
London

British Library CIP Data

Joseph, Anjali, *1978 –*
Saraswati Park.
1. Letter writing- -India- -Bombay- -Fiction. 2. Families- -
India- -Bombay- -Fiction. 3. Gay college students- -
India- -Bombay- -Fiction. 4. Bombay (India)- -Social
life and customs- -Fiction. 5. Large type books.
I. Title
823.9′2–dc22

ISBN 978–1–4448–0860–5

Published by
F. A. Thorpe (Publishing)
Anstey, Leicestershire

Set by Words & Graphics Ltd.
Anstey, Leicestershire
Printed and bound in Great Britain by
T. J. International Ltd., Padstow, Cornwall

This book is printed on acid-free paper

To my grandparents

1

He held out the book and pointed to the margin. 'Do you have more like this?'

The bookseller looked distracted. It was nearly five: a tide of commuters would soon spill past the stalls, towards Churchgate and the trains that would take them home. The heat lingered but already the light was changing: it was finer, more golden. From the sea, at the end of the road, there spread a pale brightness, as though the street and the bookstalls were a mirage that would disappear with the sunset.

The thin young bookseller glanced at the open page, where handwritten notes in blue ink danced next to the sober type. 'You'd have to check,' he said. 'I can't say.'

'What's your name?' the customer persisted. He was a tall, broad-shouldered fellow in his fifties, grey-haired, with steel spectacles on which the last light glinted; there was something pleasant about him.

The bookseller raised an eyebrow. 'Uday,' he said. He turned to stare past the customer's shoulder. At the Flora Fountain crossing, they had started to flood this way:

the white-shirted, briefcase-carrying tide. The traffic light held them back.

'I work just nearby,' the customer went on. 'At the post office, the GPO, near VT station. I'm a letter writer, Mohan Karekar. You're new here, I haven't seen you before?'

The bookseller grunted, his eyes on the approaching crowd. 'I'm looking after the stall for my brother,' he said.

Mohan put the ten-rupee note into his hand. 'If you see more like that, with the writing on the side, keep them for me,' he said. He walked into the pressing wave of commuters. He was taller than most; the bookseller saw the back of his steel-coloured head for a moment. Then a fat man with a briefcase stopped at the stall. He took out his handkerchief and wiped his face all over.

'Da Vinci,' he said urgently.

The bookseller bent and picked up two copies of the pirated book, each with a slightly different cover. 'Complete,' he responded. 'Every page is there.'

★   ★   ★

Mohan walked through the crowd, crossed the wide junction, and passed under the long porch of the American Express Bank. The arcades were a nightmare at this time of day,

2

but he navigated his way through the continuous stream of people.

Where the arcades ended, outside the McDonald's, he waited for the traffic to pause. There was an extraordinary sky today: a bright, deep blue like butterfly wing, with streaks of orange that reached towards the west; it was framed by one of the arches. No one seemed to have noticed; there were trains to be caught.

He crossed the road and walked between the stalls selling office clothing — consignments of white shirts, spread out helplessly on tables — past the bus stand and the side entrance of the station, to the tarpaulin and the gnarled, mythic-looking banyan tree where the letter writers sat, next to the pigeon shelter. It was all right; their tables were chained and padlocked in place, and one of the others would have left his things — sealing wax, muslin, packing needles, the directory of postal codes — at the shop nearby. He patted his shirt pocket, where his train pass was a reassuring flat surface; in his back pocket his wallet was undisturbed.

A group of pigeons flew out of the old tree and into the sky, their wings making the sound of wind on the sea; they crisscrossed each other and made for the west. He tucked the new book under his arm and returned to the station, where a Harbour Line train was pulling into platform two.

★ ★ ★

When he woke in the morning his wife was still asleep. In the half-light he saw the back of her neck, a few inches away. At the nape, fine hair curled; one shoulder rose under the sheet into a hillock that sheltered her face. The perfume of her neck, which had astounded him when they'd been newly married, was unchanged: intense, overripe; lotuses mixed with ash.

He extricated himself gently from the cotton sheet, which seemed to have become needy during the night. He padded into the bathroom, switched on the water heater, and went to the kitchen. It was good, this moment of silence before the machinery of the day began. It had been different when the children were young: Lakshmi would be up early, making tea and breakfast, and sending them for baths. There would be regular catastrophes: someone needed card paper; someone else had a form to be signed. Now all he had to do was float to the kitchen, still in his kurta-pyjama, and make his tea, and a cup for his wife. The habit irritated her, because she wouldn't wake for another hour,

4

but he hadn't been able to come to terms with making tea just for himself, as though she didn't exist.

In the gloom he moved about, putting water to boil, adding sugar, then crushing a chunk of ginger with the kitchen pliers. At this time, soon after he'd woken, incongruous characters moved through his consciousness: his elder son, Gautam, aged about sixteen, rushing out and saying he didn't have time for breakfast; the man from yesterday's book, Lambert Strether, who had just arrived in a foreign city with a vague but important task to execute. The water hissed. Mohan reached for the tea leaves.

Birds were singing stridently outside; the grey covering over everything was slowly being plucked away as the light came. He strained the tea into two cups and covered one, which he took into the bedroom and left on the table next to his wife's head; he opened his mouth to say 'Tea', but thought better of it and went to the living room. Amid the clutter of the big table, the old alarm clock, whose pale green enamel paint had broken into rust spots, said six o'clock. It continued to tick, a loud, busy noise, as he moved towards the window.

He sat in the cane chair; from here he'd be able to watch the lane awake. The boys who took in ironing were opening the door of their blue tin hut, at the mouth of the lane, near the watchman's shack. One of them brought out a kerosene stove to make tea; another, bare-chested and holding a plastic mug, went off in the direction of the empty plot. The first of the morning walkers appeared, a middle-aged man in white t-shirt and navy shorts. He began to march doggedly up the lane.

Mohan went to the bathroom and emerged half an hour later, quietly happy after the usual encounter with the white tiles, the morning sunshine, and the clear, warm water. Lakshmi got up when he opened the cupboard to take out a clean shirt.

'Every day,' she observed. She picked up the covered cup of tea and regarded it at arm's length. She sighed. Mohan began to do up his buttons. The shirt was crisp; it hung at a polite distance from his body. He started to roll up his sleeves, and followed her to the kitchen to point out, 'But I didn't wake you.'

She poured the tea into the saucepan and lit the gas. Her eyes were still heavy. 'That's what you think,' she said. 'You think I don't hear you, clanging about in the kitchen.' She covered her mouth and yawned loudly, a cry of weariness at the tiresome nature of the world.

'I don't clang,' he said.

His sleeves were neatly rolled; he felt

satisfied, clean and ready for the day; his mind moved ahead to the train, where he might get a seat, feel the breeze on his face, and be able to read.

The tea began to bubble; with a faint expression of distaste Lakshmi removed it from the fire and strained it into the same mug. She drew her housecoat about her and went into the living room.

★　★　★

When the train pulled into VT the station was alive but not yet swarming. Mohan walked away from the grand building and its light, high-vaulted hall. At the bus stand he moved through the queues and made for the GPO. How strange it had been, years earlier, when the letter writers had been forced to shift from its shaded colonnade, first to the pavement outside, and then under the tarpaulin at the kabutar khana. He had missed the shapes of people passing through the stone arches all day and the light as it changed — by afternoon, the figures in the colonnade became shadows with bright outlines. But he'd grown attached in turn to the sound of the pigeons when they took off and landed; their little kurr! kurr! of protest and, he sometimes thought, happiness.

He wasn't the first to arrive. When he returned from the stationery shop with his possessions, Khan, the oldest of the remaining letter writers, had already unlocked the tables and sat drinking the first cup of tea, the *Urdu Times* spread in front of him. He was an irascible, balding man with tiny spectacles; although dark-skinned, he often seemed to redden in the sun. Mohan sat down, stowed his tiffin under his table, and arranged his pen tray; he put the torn red postal ledger into the drawer in the table and laid out the stack of electronic money order forms and a small pot of gum. He opened his book. Soon, to the sound of kurr! kurr! above him, he was deep in an elliptical, drawn-out conversation between Lambert Strether and Maria, a woman Strether had just met. The flow of commuters outside the tent increased.

'Uncle.'

He recognized the woman, who was in her early thirties. Today she wore a bright green sari. She beamed at him; he smiled, and took up a money order form. Two thin gold bangles on her arms chinked among the glass ones.

'Uncle, two thousand five hundred rupees.'

He uncapped a pen. 'Name of the addressee?'

'Ganesh Solanki.'

'Name of the village?'

'Bhandari.'

'Chhota post?' She named a town that no one in the city would have heard of. 'Bada post?' A slightly larger town.

Mohan opened the directory to check the postal code. While he flipped through the torn, closely printed pages, she wrapped the free end of her sari around her right shoulder, and swayed on one foot, looking into the crowd. It was hot now, full mid-morning sun. The flowery, synthetic scent of her talcum, mingled with perspiration, drifted to Mohan, and he looked up for a second before lowering his eyes again. Got it: 811 307. She would be a different person at work, he thought, copying the code into the form: heavily made up, standing in a doorway and calling out to the men who passed, but this morning, up early and neatly dressed, she was a figure of efficiency, a working woman.

He gave her back the form, which she would have to take to a counter inside. She smiled and took out a roll of notes from her blouse; she held out a twenty-rupee note. He nodded, but her bright green sari was already bustling its way into the sun. As it receded the flash of viridian made him think of the parrots that used to come in a sudden swoop at dusk and roost in trees near the old house at Dadar.

For a while he sat and watched the world,

framed at the upper edge by the fringe of the tarpaulin — hairy bits of rope and a jagged piece of packing plastic, once transparent, now grey, hung down. Beyond this, all around the letter writers, life persisted at its noisiest. A fleet of cockroach-like taxis in black and yellow livery waited at the junction outside the GPO. When the lights changed they all, honking, took the u-turn. A man on a cycle passed; he carried a tangle of enormous red ledgers, each wrapped in plastic, atop his head. The gold on their spines flashed in the sun.

A luxury coach lumbered by; it was bound for Rajasthan. Mohan read the inscription on its side: Pushpa Vihar. The bus was nearly empty — it'd pick up returning Rajasthanis throughout the city before it left in earnest — but a few curious faces peered out at the start of their long journey. There was a small silver altar on the dashboard, and strings of black pompoms hung from the rear bumper to protect travellers from evil looks. A young man hung out of the doorway, enjoying the breeze on his face.

The morning was always so beautiful here. The location of the shelter, which hid under its dirty tarpaulin and the gnarled, ancient-looking banyan tree, meant that only those who knew about the letter writers came to find them. The workers in the offices, hotels and restaurants in Ballard Estate, Horniman Circle, and the inside streets of Bazaargate passed every day and were used to seeing the writers. But disoriented-looking white tourists, their belongings trussed to their backs and their money strapped to their waists, would pass, stand near the shelter, which served as a traffic island, and peer in; they'd be affronted because they couldn't work out what was going on inside. Khan would call out to them, showing off: 'Hello? Yes, Madam?'

And there were the pigeons, who spent their day moving with apparently frantic urgency from tree to tree. They'd suddenly all take off from the banyan here and rise, wings flapping madly, before heading either to the taller banyan outside the GPO, or the trees in Bhatia Baug in front of the station. If you looked up you saw the birds themselves — in passing, one or the other would casually drop a chalky blot on the road below. But if you remained gazing ahead, you saw only their shadows, which fluttered and moved with even more delicacy and life than the real birds: their silhouettes would rise, flap their wings and return to roost in the shadow of the tree.

He was starting to feel pleasantly hollow

— that meant it would soon be time for lunch — when a small, familiar figure with a pot belly hailed him cheerfully. Kamble worked as a peon at the sessions court; he had been to deliver an order at the municipal corporation building. He sat on the stool next to Mohan, smiled, and took out his handkerchief to mop his face and the top of his head, which glistened in the humidity. Mohan passed him the water bottle; the other man leaned, in a friendly way, on one wooden arm of Mohan's chair, a thing of tubular steel and disintegrating plastic webbing.

'Getting hot now,' Kamble observed. He tilted his head back to pour the water directly down his throat; a gold ring on one fat finger winked at Mohan.

'Busy day?'

Kamble put down the bottle and wiped his mouth. 'Not really,' he said. 'Summer session. Just a few cases: anticipatory bail, chain snatching, one foreigner who got caught' — and here he waved in the direction of the GPO's enormous dome — 'posting marijuana to herself.' He raised an eyebrow. 'When it didn't arrive she came back from abroad to ask what happened to the parcel. Strange how people always think they won't get caught.'

Mohan chuckled. Kamble replaced the lid

of the water bottle. He relaxed and leaned back on the chair arm, and his eye fell on the book on Mohan's table. 'Hey, the BMC is moving the booksellers today, you heard?'

'Moving?'

'Evicting them. Part of the anti-hawker thing.'

'But what are you saying?' Mohan held onto the small desk as though it was about to fall.

'Come, you want to come and see? I'm walking back. One of the peons in the BMC was telling me. The trucks went this morning.'

Mohan stumbled up. He looked around; most of the letter writers had arrived. Khan nodded at him. 'Yes yes, you go.'

'I'll go and come,' he muttered. He reached for the book, then left it where it was.

'Don't walk so fast, re!' Kamble ran after Mohan, who had shot out in front of a taxi. The driver was outraged; he braked, gave the horn a long blast and leaned out of the window to question Mohan's relationship with his family. The letter writer ignored him and hurried on. They crossed the road and headed into the arcades, which were shot with hot strips of sun.

'Look,' said Mohan suddenly. 'None of these people has a licence either.' He stopped

13

and waved at the hawkers, thin young men in tight shirts and jeans, belts with exaggerated buckles; they folded their arms and eyed him in return.

Kamble shrugged. 'It's part of what they're doing everywhere, they say it's to clear the main roads so people can walk more easily in the morning,' he said apologetically. He put a hand on Mohan's arm and smiled at one of the more aggressive looking hawkers.

'Corruption. The booksellers have been there for years — people who take the train stop there on their way to office.'

'Well — '

'Quickly!' Mohan had seen a bus, rolling to a halt a few yards ahead; he pulled Kamble after him through a white stucco arch and they dashed for the stop.

'You want to take the bus? But — '

'It'll be faster.' They climbed aboard as the bus began to move, and pushed their way down the narrow aisle between the humid bodies of the other passengers.

The bus took an age to cover the short distance. Finally it reached the stop just before Fountain: they pushed their way to the front and jumped down. Mohan was sweating; the back of his neck prickled. 'Come on,' he said. His head pounded. They darted across the first road, waited at the crossing, and started to cross the second, but as he hurried he felt a small release at his right foot: the strap of his sandal had broken.

Two green municipal trucks were parked near the junction. Mohan's hand flew up to clutch his head. Men in dusty blue uniforms were picking up books by the armful and throwing them into the back of the nearer truck. His broken sandal flapping, he ran towards them.

'What are you doing? You can't do this! Stop! Wait!' The man ignored him, and grinned at the drama. Mohan saw the thin bookseller from the day before. 'Where are they taking them?' he asked wildly.

'Some warehouse or godown, I don't know where. I don't know how we'll ever get them back.' The young man stood still, his arms full of thrillers; he looked adrift, as though he had no idea what to do next.

'Here, I'll take some.' Mohan started to scoop up the volumes scattered around them.

'Oye, you can't do that,' the BMC man said. 'They're being confiscated.' He picked up another armful and walked to the truck. A policeman, smacking his stick into his palm, strutted up. 'Come on!' he shouted. 'Move on!' He was bored, Mohan noticed; probably he wanted his lunch.

'Come on, re,' Kamble said. He took

15

Mohan's arm and tugged at it. Only a few books remained, lying on the ground and beside the railings. Mohan handed those he held to the young bookseller. One fell from his arms and Mohan stooped and picked it up, touched it to his forehead in apology. It was a business book, with confident red letters on the cover: *Master of Your Own Fate*.

Mohan, still clutching the book, allowed Kamble to pull him towards the crossing. 'My sandal's broken,' he muttered.

★　★　★

He went home early, feeling dazed and unreal. The outer door was closed because it was the afternoon and a time of rest; the flat was warm, silent, and sleepy. His wife opened the inner door.

'I thought it was you! You're not well?'

'Don't attack me right at the door,' he said wearily. He came in, and closed the outer door with a soft click.

'Another book,' she said.

He walked past her and deposited the books on one of the jars that covered the old table in the living room. He went to the kitchen, reappeared with a steel tumbler of water and sat down heavily; he rested his elbow on the small fringe of available space on the table and drank. When he'd finished he set down the tumbler, rubbed his forehead, removed his spectacles, and pinched the top of his nose.

'Are you feeling unwell?'

'No.'

'Then what happened?' Her voice had become sharp, but she hovered close to him.

He waved towards the books. 'The BMC moved the booksellers away today — took all the books and threw them into a truck. They're taking them to a godown somewhere.'

'Just like that?'

He nodded.

She went into the kitchen, came back with a bottle of cold water and a jug and refilled the tumbler, half with the iced water and half with room-temperature water. He closed his hand around the tumbler.

'Maybe it's for the best,' she said thoughtfully, and put one hand on her hip. 'We're running out of space for all these books anyway.'

He stared across the landscape of clustered jars. The table was old, from the house at Dadar; it was good Burma teak, and beautiful when polished, but they'd never used it properly. Over the years it had become a receptacle for jars of pickle, bottles of sauce and squash, tins of drinking chocolate, papers, paperweights, and all kinds of other objects that, someone had reasoned, were about to be in use. What a waste, he thought.

'Oh, I had to tell you,' she continued. 'Your sister called.'

He looked up. 'Vimla?'

'How many sisters do you have? Milind's transfer order has come through. They'll have to leave in a few days.'

'Oh.'

'And they just found out that Ashish can't take his exams this year, he has to repeat.'

'What? Why?'

'Attendance,' she said.

He put on his spectacles again, diverted for a moment. 'Always something new with that boy,' he said, almost admiringly. Fecklessness was not a quality one had been encouraged to develop, or that one celebrated in one's offspring; still, it cut a certain dash.

'So they were wondering if he can stay with us till next year.'

Mohan smiled. 'Of course, where else will he stay?'

'With your brother?' However, she smiled.

'Ha!'

Lakshmi sighed. 'It's going to be a lot of extra work. And also expense.'

'But we have the money from the printing shop. And what Megha's been sending, we haven't even touched that.' His income from his daily occupation had never been considerable; in recent years it had dwindled to a trickle.

She nodded, then frowned. 'You know that I'm fond of Ashish. But it's a big responsibility. We'll have to make sure he studies, attends regularly when college starts. You'll have to speak to him. Make him understand he needs to be sincere.'

Mohan snorted. 'I'm sure his mother's spoken to him comprehensively,' he said. He drained the second tumbler of water, put it into his wife's hand, and went inside to change his clothes.

2

Seven in the morning, Ashish thought he must be dreaming. He stood under the big notice boards and read the names of suburbs he had rarely visited: Belapur, Titwala, Vashi, Panvel, Andheri. It was too depressing.

Most of his possessions were in a large suitcase at his feet; he clutched a cardboard box filled with books, cassettes and compact discs that he had rushed around retrieving when his uncle arrived at six. His parents had been too harried to become sentimental; they would be flying to Indore in the afternoon and some of their things had already been sent by road. Ashish, with similar efficiency, had been plucked out of his life and sent to live with his aunt and uncle.

Now he stood inside the grand station, which was light, quiet, and almost cold at this hour. Pigeons fluttered in the sunlight, high above the vaulted ceiling. A few red-coated porters passed at a brisk little jog; a long-distance train must have been arriving. Mohan had gone to buy a ticket for Ashish. He came back, put a hand on the boy's thin shoulder and slipped the two-inch rectangle of yellow pasteboard into his shirt pocket. 'Come, that's our train. Can you run?'

They began an awkward trot. The elder man ran easily, despite the aged VIP suitcase he carried, and the boy skipped lopsidedly behind him, trying not to spill the contents of the carton, which slithered, skittish, and threatened to make a leap for freedom.

The wide platform was clear; the horn sounded; at the same magical moment the train began to pull out. Mohan heaved in the suitcase, jumped on, cried, 'Here!' He took the carton from Ashish and pulled him on by the wrist.

The heavy train was already moving fast. It drew away from the station and into the warm, bright sunlight just outside. Ashish looked down: this was the place where the tracks intersected, then separated again.

★   ★   ★

Saraswati Park was settling into its Sunday. A few people were outside the vegetable shop; a woman negotiated with a man who stood behind a handcart covered with large, green-striped watermelons; the rickshaw turned into the lane.

'Take a right — up a bit — no, stop. Yes, here.' Mohan dragged the suitcase out and

21

paid the rickshaw driver, who stared unabashedly at the four-storey building. Its yellow paint was peeling. The name Jyoti was stencilled in dark red letters on the gatepost. Ashish staggered out of the other side of the rickshaw, still clasping the carton, and followed his uncle into the small entrance with its wall of pierced tiles. He had come here regularly as a child, but not recently; the last occasion he recalled was his cousin Gautam's wedding three or four years earlier. Now everything came back to him: the names on the plate at the foot of the stairs (Gogate, Kulkarni, Gogate, Gogate, Prabhu, Kamat, Karekar, Dasgupta) and the double doors — the inner ones were open and the outer doors had a large ornamental grille from which Sunday cooking smells came into the stairwell. Withered garlands of auspicious leaves hung from the lintels, and, outside several of the apartments, pairs of sinister looking red footprints marked the time, years before, when the lady of the house had arrived as a new bride.

When they reached the third floor, panting, Mohan put his hand into the grille of number 15 and opened the catch. He turned to beam at his nephew. 'Come,' he said.

Lakshmi appeared, in her post-bath outfit of clean salwar kameez, her hair still loose.

'Wait!' she said dramatically to Ashish, who paused at the door, taken aback. She held a comb in one hand and raised it like a ceremonial item. The scent of her hair oil, amla, floated to him. 'Now,' she said, 'with the right foot.'

Ashish grinned foolishly and rebalanced himself. He stepped over the ledge, right foot first, and his aunt smiled and closed the outer door behind him.

'You never made me do that before,' he mumbled.

'But then you were only visiting,' she said.

Mohan had melted into the passage with the suitcase; he now reappeared. 'Come,' he said. Still holding the carton, Ashish followed him. The peculiar smell of the dark corridor returned vividly: a mysterious amalgam of old calendars, dust, and superannuated cockroach repellent sachets, with their intriguing round perforations. The room at the end had been Gautam and Ashok's. Ashish strode towards it with a new-found audacity, Gulliver in Lilliput. A collection of his cousins' comics was neatly piled on the lower shelf of the bookcase; a cricket bat, badly cracked, leaned against the desk.

His aunt opened the steel cupboard proudly. 'Look,' she said. 'I cleared it out for you.' The cupboard seemed to have shrunk;

the stickers welded to the mirror in the door were now at Ashish's eye level. One showed the West Indian batsman Viv Richards making his famous on-drive; the other was a logo of a red fist, thumb pointed perkily upwards. Behind them, his reflection wavered: knife-thin, suspicious looking. He tried to smile at himself. The effect wasn't reassuring.

Mohan patted him on the shoulder. 'Come on,' he said. 'Take off your shoes, wash your hands and have some breakfast.'

They left Ashish in the room, the door open, and he sat on the bed and untied his shoelaces. The cold floor felt smooth and clean under his feet. He looked around the room, so familiar and yet new.

From the kitchen, he heard the rumble of his uncle's voice.

★ ★ ★

After lunch his aunt and uncle disappeared into their room where, with the door open, they lay on the bed, immobile. His aunt slept curled to one side; his uncle lay like an Egyptian embalmed under a sheet. The fan, on a high setting, made the pages of the book on Mohan's chest flutter.

Ashish fidgeted, and fiddled with his mobile telephone. He pressed, repeatedly, the

24

key that cleared the display: each time it illuminated anew, a bright green. There was no message from Sunder. What was he doing at this moment? Ashish imagined him eating lunch in a hotel coffee shop, or playing a computer game; watching a movie on an enormous flat-screen television. It was possible that Sunder was bored too, but even his boredom was exotic: it would take place in a vast, air-conditioned flat.

Ashish wandered, examining the well-known apartment with a detective's eye. The flat had its own, specific virtues that he couldn't imagine Sunder appreciating: the cane chair with a high back, where his uncle liked to sit and read in the evening, in the bright circle of light emitted by a hundred-watt bulb; the woven rope footstools, which had a piece of old tyre at their base; the reading table piled with books and papers; the bookshelves. There were Marathi novels and short stories, pirated thrillers from the pavement, translations of Sherlock Holmes into Marathi (the action had been transposed to Bombay), P.G. Wodehouse, Agatha Christie, Charlotte Brontë, George Eliot, Nancy Drew, Henry James, and, on the bottom shelf, behind the cane chair, a few more esoteric titles. He pushed the chair aside and squatted to look at them. The shelves here smelled pleasantly musty, of an organic, reechy dust. He pulled out a volume with a yellow spine: *I'm OK, You're OK*. Another, with a black cover: *The Silva Method*. A third, battered-looking, with only a few vestiges remaining of the original red jacket: *Become a Writer*. He carried them off to his room; they'd help to pass the afternoon.

★　★　★

He woke up later, drooling on his arm. His feet were cold. Why was it so quiet? Then he realized: the noises of water pipes gurgling, of feet running up and down the corroded cast-iron stairs, and the whole building rattling around him every time a bus or truck passed on the road outside; these had been left in Esplanade Mansion. Here there was only the sound of birds chirping, implausibly cheerfully. He sat up and examined the phone. Still no message. Was it because of what had happened on Wednesday? The servant, coming into the room with glasses of cold lemonade on a tray, had given them a funny look. But they hadn't been doing anything, just lying on the bed and reading the same book. When Ashish hadn't seen Sunder in college for three days he'd called him, but there had been no answer. He ached to know what had happened, what would happen; during the last year, their friendship, so odd and circumstantial, had been hesitating on the edge of something else — but he couldn't be certain. Surely it wasn't all in his imagination?

There was a shout from outside. He wiped his mouth and went to the window. Boys were playing cricket in the lane. A small child ran up to bowl a tennis ball at a much older boy, who whooped and hit it hard; the ball landed, making a joyous thump, on the bonnet of a car halfway down the lane and the watchman got up and began to walk, with the detached enjoyment of someone playing a well-known role, towards the cricketers.

Ashish rubbed his eyes, turned off the fan, and went into the living room, from where he could hear voices.

'Tea?' His aunt came out of the kitchen and smiled at him.

'Hm.'

He sat down, still half immersed in the dense warmth of afternoon sleep, and peered at his aunt and uncle. Mohan was drinking a steaming cup of tea and reading the newspaper. Ashish leaned his elbow on the edge of the table and allowed himself to re-enter the world.

'Here.' Lakshmi mami put a cup in front of him. He recognized it: it was tall and had a blue handle; a fey character called Little Boy Blue danced about on the front. All his cousins and sometimes he had been force-fed milk with protein powder in this cup, in the belief that it would make them strong.

Mohan grunted and folded the newspaper.

'Anything interesting?' Ashish asked.

'Nonsense,' said Mohan dispassionately. He brightened. 'Shall we go for a walk?' Ashish smirked; he recalled this meant his uncle wanted to visit the snack shop at the edge of the market, and buy hot samosa.

'Let him finish his tea at least,' Lakshmi mami intervened.

Ashish immediately adopted a hangdog expression and put the cup to his mouth. 'It's hot,' he whimpered, making for the television. He found the remote, put on a music channel, and began to watch the video of a new song that blared, cancelling out the birdsong and the cries of the cricketers outside.

'No hurry,' said Mohan. He got up and began to drift around the living room in a conspicuously bored way.

★ ★ ★

The last light was golden, like something in a film; it fell carelessly across the dusty leaves of the old banyan in the empty plot, here and there picking out the new, shiny green ones. Television aerials cast extravagant shadows.

A chubby, frizzy-haired girl whom Ashish thought he recognized was pretending to walk for exercise. She dawdled down the lane, her mobile pressed to her ear.

'I know,' she said into the phone. 'Seriously!'

As they passed, she smiled at both of them, and Mohan reached out and patted her head with the flat of his hand.

'Madhavi, Dr Gogate's daughter. Do you remember her?' he asked Ashish quietly.

'She used to be a little fat girl?'

'Well, a little healthy maybe.'

'That's exactly what he said!' Madhavi said. Her voice followed them for a yard or two after they rounded the corner. They crossed the small roundabout, where Ashish saw two stray puppies play-fighting, rolling in the dirt next to a heap of rubbish.

'We'll go to Matunga one Sunday for dosa if you like,' Mohan said.

'Mm,' Ashish agreed. He had changed into his Sunday clothes, a t-shirt and shorts made comfortable from much washing. The evening air was soothing on his skin.

'Your parents will reach this evening, we can call them when we get back.'

'Okay.' He scuffled along. He didn't miss his parents; he wasn't sure if he would. But already he missed town: on a holiday like today, outside Esplanade Mansion the streets were as quiet as the inside of a cup, and at such times the city always seemed to belong to him alone.

'So,' Mohan cleared his throat, 'college doesn't start for a month, a little more than a month?'

Ashish's ears pricked up at the mention of college, but he kept his head prudently down. 'Yes, in June,' he said.

'Ah. Hm.'

They continued to amble along the second lane, where the bungalows and apartment blocks were low-rise and set back from the road. Next to a broken culvert, bright green weeds flourished illegally.

'Your parents were surprised about your attendance record,' Mohan said.

Ashish looked at him. Mohan looked away, and waved at an unattractive grey bungalow on the left. The gatepost was marked Iyer. 'Famous doctor lives there,' he remarked. 'Heart surgeon. Son is also a doctor. Dermatologist.'

'Hm.'

Mohan frowned. 'I don't want to lecture you about your studies,' he said. Ashish,

30

holding his breath, flapped on in his rubber slippers. A rickshaw, containing two laughing young people, went past; the exhaust made explosive, farting noises.

'It'll be nice for all of us if you have a good year,' Mohan said finally. He sighed, laughed, and pulled Ashish closer to him so that he could perform a familiar manoeuvre of affection and exasperation: he put his left hand on Ashish's head and clouted it with his right. This was the only punishment he'd ever managed to inflict when his children, nephews and nieces reported each other's misdemeanours to him.

Ashish grinned, but not too much. 'Yes Mohan mama, don't worry,' he said obligingly.

His uncle snorted. 'You have no idea. You should have heard your grandfather talk about studies, doing well at school . . . Vivek mama had it worse than I did, of course.' He smiled.

They were passing a dilapidated beige bungalow. 'He used to write, your grandfather,' Mohan said suddenly. 'Did you know that?'

'No,' Ashish said. His uncle was smiling, as though he had pulled a forgotten rabbit out of an old hat. 'Do you mean stories?'

'Stories, essays, little things. I don't know

what you'd call them. On Sundays he would get up early in the morning. When we woke up, he would be writing and he'd carry on all day.'

'So he didn't take you all out, you didn't do things?'

'It was his writing time.'

Ashish tried to digest this image of his grandfather, whom he mostly knew from photographs; there, he seemed like a grimmer, more stolid edition of his uncle: white shirt, trousers worn somewhere around the nipples, those small spectacles, slicked-back hair. 'Did he publish anything?' he asked.

'No. One of his friends was a writer of short stories, a very clever fellow, Nandlal Gokhale. My father showed Gokhale some of his stories once and he took them away to read. But he said that they weren't good enough to publish.'

Ashish frowned. 'But I've never heard of this Gokhale.'

'He's not so well known now,' Mohan said.

'So how does anyone know that he was right about grandfather's writing?'

Mohan's pace seemed to slow. 'Well — he was a man of letters,' he said.

Ashish was still mildly indignant. 'Do you have any of grandfather's stories?' he asked, though he was a slow and reluctant reader of his mother tongue.

Mohan shook his head. 'No, re. It's possible that there were some papers and they got lost when we left the house at Dadar. But I think he burned them, some time before he died.'

★   ★   ★

Later in the evening Ashish was sitting at his desk when there was a knock at the door. His uncle came in. 'Your aunt says dinner's ready,' he said. 'Come soon. Oh — you found this book.' He wandered further into the room and picked up *Become a Writer*.

'Yes, what is it?' Ashish asked. 'I haven't really looked at it, I started these ones.' He pointed to the pirated copies of *I'm OK, You're OK* and *The Silva Method*. They were near-perfect facsimiles, but their thin paper and flimsy covers made them seem interestingly insubstantial, as though they belonged to a more temporary world to which they would one day return.

'I bought this a few years ago, from a man sitting outside the Museum,' Mohan said slowly. 'He was next to the other hawkers, you know, the comb-and-keychain guys. But all he had was three peacock feathers and this

33

book, in the same state as now.'

'How much did you pay?'

'I don't remember. Too much. I didn't bargain, he seemed in a bad way.'

From the other room came the cry, 'It's getting cold!'

'Come on,' Mohan said.

Ashish scrambled up, and stuck a ruler in his textbook. He had the disconcerting feeling that someone with immense, vacuum-black eyes had stared at him for a moment from the darkened window of the empty flat opposite.

'So did you see the man again?' he asked, following his uncle down the dim passage.

'See him? No, I don't think so,' said Mohan vaguely.

It was nearly dark; the in-between of dusk had been replaced by the bright electric light of indoors, and it was as though the lane outside had completely disappeared. By chance, Mohan was still holding the tattered paperback, and when they reached the drawing room he put it down on a chair. Food was already on the table; they sat down.

3

In the train, Mohan sat as usual, hands resting on his knees, his arms straightened like cantilevered posts. Tilak Nagar came and went, with the coconut palms near the station, and GTB Nagar, where there was a school, and shacks next to the railway line. At Kurla, something or other was always going on — children chasing each other across the tracks, or a ticket collector who'd caught three defaulters, tied their wrists together with cord and was making them walk behind him in a line so that they didn't run away laughing.

Mohan sat on the left of the compartment; the morning sun flooded through the window and onto his face. It was hot and humid, the summer coming to a peak. Though he wasn't next to the window, a vestige of the breeze reached him now and then; it was warm and had that city smell: a mix of rotten flowers, fish, and laundry drying in the wind. The house in Dadar returned like a presence, an early memory from the days before he'd started school. After his bath, wearing nothing but his shorts, he would be put to sit on the landing in a patch of sunlight. It was always there at that time of day; it seemed to wait for him. He would sit there, warming his legs and looking out towards the front room, where the sun paused in a panel of the window. The light played in the blue and yellow glass and came through to him, undisturbed and liquid. He could hear his mother's voice in the kitchen, and felt his hair drying in wisps; in the street, the wastepaper man called out.

There was a rising and falling sequence of clicks, like the rattle of an insect. 'Twenty rupees, twenty rupees,' the voice had the unignorable nasal timbre of the train vendor. Mohan opened his eyes. It was a boy of about thirteen — he was thin, with dusty skin, enormous dark eyes and gummy lashes; a dirty cloth bag was slung over his shoulder. He had a pair of elliptical magnets that he was throwing up in the air and catching again. The magnets attracted and repelled each other as they twisted and fell; their surface was too shiny for them to stick, and the friction produced the insect noise.

'Go away,' said another passenger. 'Who's going to buy things like that at this time of day?'

It *was* early for such toys: they normally appeared in the evening, when the mind

36

turned more naturally to leisure, and to one's family. But he watched the shiny magnets flying up, and twisting around each other as they fell, and wished that he could think of a child for whom to buy them. Ashish was too old; there was no one, really. 'Twenty rupees, twenty rupees,' urged the boy; he'd seen the interest in Mohan's eyes, but Mohan shook his head regretfully. This was a new toy, its arrival another movement in the life of the city. The fashion in these toys, or the ones sold on the street, the narrow advertisements pasted under the luggage racks, these had their own seasonality; they marked the passage of the year as clearly as a change in temperature, the appearance of lanky red flowers on the gulmohar, or yellow bloom on the rusty shield bearer.

At Sewri the boy jumped out of the carriage. Mohan watched him run along the platform, barefoot and jaunty, on his way to another compartment. He thought of Ashish, who'd asked the previous night to be woken early; he was going to start studying in earnest. Two hours after Mohan had put a cup of tea on Ashish's desk this morning, he'd been about to leave the house. Ashish had emerged into the living room, hollow-eyed, and sat at the table drinking a fresh cup of tea; he'd looked exhausted and appalled, like a child born too early. He'd get into a routine, no doubt. But despite himself, Mohan began to worry. Things had a way of happening; in his case it had been his father's death just when he was finishing school. The family business wasn't in a great state then, and he'd had no choice but to start work.

The train was moving again, drawing near the dusty yet magnificent Cotton Exchange building, marooned in the middle of an empty plain. The big textile companies still had offices here, but no real dealing took place — the trade, which had swept into the city like a tide, bringing with it mills, factories, and jobs more than a hundred years earlier, had receded some time ago. Now, construction work went on nearby. As the train passed, he saw the stall where thin, sunburnt workers stopped for tea.

The printing shop, which his brother had taken on, made a reasonable profit. It specialized in minor work: the annual reports of clubs and associations, wedding invitations, jobs for the small businesses in the area where they'd grown up. Mohan's share of the income and the money from the sale of the old house had made it possible for him and Lakshmi to buy the flat in Saraswati Park, then a new colony in a part of the city they hadn't really known existed. And it had allowed him to persist with his work, the point of which no one in the family saw. 'You had to do those odd jobs when Baba died — messenger in that agency — then this strange letter-writing thing,' his brother said. 'But when we started the business again you should have joined in, taken responsibility.'

He frowned; Vivek had phoned yesterday while he and Ashish were out. When Mohan called back his brother reminded him they hadn't met for several months. 'Come and see us some time,' he'd said, and Mohan murmured something about Saturday next week; it wasn't an obligation he could avoid. This weekend, too, a visit from his brother-in-law loomed; it had been a few weeks since Satish had come over, and this Sunday was his birthday.

The train stopped at Reay Road. The wide platforms were nearly clear and a bare, scrubby field stretched out beside the station. There were a lot of empty spaces in the city that people forgot, and in them, forgotten people carrying on their lives: the dockyard and mill workers, or the port trust employees, who were part of the city's story but nearly invisible now.

Mohan sighed and thought of his earlier Saturday routine, which had often included a wander through the bookstalls between

Fountain and Churchgate. This, so different from his children's studies, had been the way he'd educated himself. There was a special magic that operated in the books he found; the thing he needed frequently came along without his having to look for it. His mind went covertly back to his other existence, the one in his chair, at home in the evenings, under the naked bulb. He sometimes felt he left himself there, unseen, while an automated version of him went about the daily routine. Those people and emotions, the ones from the pages he turned, were always so clearly present. And there was the feeling of following in the footsteps of other readers, those who'd scribbled in the margins; he'd many times come close to doing the same.

The next station was Dockyard Road, a rather charming stop on the crest of a slope that looked as though it belonged elsewhere, in a hill station perhaps; then dusty Sandhurst Road, and Masjid, filthy and busy, right next door to VT.

★ ★ ★

He was a little late this morning; when he sat down at his table most of the others were there. There had been fourteen of them in better times; now there were, on and off,

40

eleven letter writers, of whom at any given time perhaps eight were at work, ranged round the old fountain.

Soon after the boy from the Sainath Tea House made his first round with a small metal plate on which he carried hot glasses of tea, another regular appeared. This was a cripple, with maimed legs and shortened arms. He looked as though he was in his twenties, and crawled surprisingly fast on his hands and knees; his pelvis, the only part of his body that was clothed, lurched between his legs like a cranky motor between twisted pistons. He skirted Mohan and came to a halt, smiling expectantly, in front of Bablu, the youngest letter writer. Bablu was a mere child, in his late thirties; he had been at the job only twelve years. He looked over the top of his table, saw the cripple, and passed a few coins down; the other man took them and, satisfied, went away wordlessly. This happened every day at the same time but none of the letter writers commented. Mohan sometimes amused himself by spinning out scenarios: the two boys were brothers, but by different mothers; the more fortunate one knew that only his good luck had saved him from his brother's fate ... the baroque suppositions made him smile, mostly at himself.

He'd been thinking again about the woman in the green sari, partly with a simple fascination, as when a particular face, or a gait, something alluring about a woman walking past, caught his eye. But then he'd begun to think of her in a different way, giving her a name that wasn't the one he'd written on the money order form, and picking up a thread in his mind about her story, where she'd come from, how she'd arrived in Bombay, what she felt about her life, the kind of room she might live in. These details lingered in his head, and he looked up absently into the traffic to see two green parrots shoot past the GPO and towards Bhatia baug, making an elegant arc of speed through the air, their feathers flashing electric green as they corkscrewed. They were gone before he could be quite sure he hadn't made them up, but he smiled again, suddenly feeling luckier.

The day extended, shapeless, because the usual bookstall excursion wasn't there; the thought of the blank pavements between Fountain, Churchgate and the University made him feel strange, as when in a dream you open a favourite volume only to find page after page unaccountably empty.

Soon enough customers came along — first, a man who wanted to fill out a passport application. When he had taken the completed form and gone, Mohan leaned back in his chair and watched the shadow pigeons take off, wheel wildly, then land in the shadow tree, and merge into its substance. Later, a shadow leaf would seemingly tear itself out of the tree and fly up, into the sunlit sky.

★　★　★

That afternoon he was coming to the end of his lunch — its components neatly laid out on his table, three different small boxes for daal, vegetable and chapatis — when a familiar figure, knife-thin, appeared in his field of vision.

'Eh, Ashish!'

The boy approached, slowing as he got nearer the tarpaulin. Four men looked at him interestedly. He smiled in a measured but general way and came to a stop near his uncle.

'Come, sit here.' Mohan patted the stool next to him.

'No, I just . . . '

'Sit!'

Ashish sat down, reluctantly. But when he'd moved into the world under the tarpaulin, only a metre distant from the road, he began to look about him with curiosity.

Mohan waved towards him for the benefit of the other letter writers. 'This is my nephew Ashish, my sister's son. Studying at Elphinstone College.'

Khan smiled at Ashish and examined him closely through his tiny glasses. 'You are studying . . . '

'Yes.'

'Which stream? Which year?'

'Um, third year BA.'

A doubtful look passed over Khan's face. 'BA?' he repeated incredulously, as though it was hard for him to believe anyone could be such a malingerer.

'Arts,' muttered Ashish.

'Literature,' said Mohan firmly. 'He's studying English literature.' He put a hand on one of the boy's thin shoulders.

'Um, Mohan mama, can I have the key?' Ashish murmured rapidly. 'I don't have one yet, mami said to get it from you in case she was still out.'

The boy from the tea house reappeared with another round of glasses.

'At least stay and have tea with me,' Mohan said. 'Have you had lunch?'

Ashish looked embarrassed, and also unencouraging. 'I'll eat at home,' he said.

Mohan hadn't yet eaten his puran poli;

he'd been saving it till the end because it was his favourite sweet. 'Here,' he said, putting it into the boy's hand. 'Eat this and have some tea. Anyway, I shouldn't have all these things at my age, I'll get fat.' He patted his stomach and grinned.

Ashish, now that he had been forced into staying, sat quite contentedly and munched the puran poli.

'You don't know how busy it used to be, earlier. People coming all the time, we didn't even have time for lunch until four o'clock,' Khan told him. Ashish sipped his tea and nodded sagely.

'Hm.' Mohan cleared his throat. The boy, even as a child, had had a gift for sitting still and doing little that had easily allowed them to be close. Mohan watched a couple of buses turning the corner from the GPO towards Ballard Estate and seemed to see them as Ashish did: big harmless animals, something like oversized water buffaloes, their engines breathing and hydraulic brakes hissing as they turned. The boy looked at the curved frontage of the nearby buildings and Mohan's eyes followed his and noticed, today, how the air conditioners were suspended from the façade in metal cages, like strange, rusting offerings.

'So, what work did you have in town?' Mohan asked.

'I had to check something in the library,' but he wasn't carrying any books, 'and I met a friend.'

'Hm.'

Ashish's tea was over, and his reverie had passed. 'Well,' he said, standing up, 'I'll go.' He nodded at the other letter writers.

'See you at home!' Mohan called, and waved. He continued to look after the thin figure as it receded towards the station.

'So you think he'll pass this year?' Khan asked. He pushed his spectacles up his nose and reopened the morning's paper.

'Definitely,' said Mohan resolutely. 'Very intelligent boy. And he's studying hard, now.' He cleared his throat and remained staring into the brightness for a while.

★ ★ ★

He reminded himself as he dressed that Sunday that lunch should go well no matter what. Satish was coming over for his birthday; Lakshmi had for days been planning what to cook, muttering to herself to use less salt since her brother suffered from high blood pressure; a present had been bought and wrapped. Mohan pulled out his Sunday clothes — a sort of t-shirt with a collar that Megha had given him, and old, comfortable trousers — and resolved not to be provoked by Satish. He put on his sandals without disturbing his wife, who lay sleeping under the fan. It was turning so frenetically in the early morning high voltage that the sheet covering her stirred, and exposed the instep of one foot.

As he went down the stairs he noticed the smell and coolness of the air. Sunday morning in Saraswati Park and all over the city was a time of languor. The routines and efforts of other days were performed, but at a smaller scale and a slower pace; suddenly, there was time to live.

He padded into the lane. The usual figures emerged from their gates, coming towards the shops for bread and milk; today they were dressed not in neatly pressed trousers and shirts but in voluminous t-shirts and shorts. An older man wore white kurta-pyjama. A couple of ghostly forms still promenaded at the end of the lane, taking their morning walk, but there was absenteeism, and a sense of festivity even in the movements of the stalwarts.

As he crossed the circle he remarked again the bizarre advertisements for the limb replacement clinic that sponsored the garden in the middle of the road. Three other men were waiting at the tiny snack shop that had recently opened and begun to sell idlis in the morning. Because it was the first Sunday since Ashish had arrived he bought jalebis too. When he got home, the brittle coils of fried translucent dough, sticky with syrup, sat in a tangle on a plate at the edge of the table, waiting for Ashish to wake up. Mohan boiled the new milk, hummed, and made tea for three.

★ ★ ★

Satish's fingers were precise and long. They undid the package, carefully detaching the tape from the paper, which was dark blue with golden stars printed on it. He was sitting in the cane armchair; in this moment it had come to resemble a throne.

'Oh, an alarm clock!'

Lakshmi's face shone and then trembled slightly. 'You said yours had stopped working,' she said.

'Oh, that old thing,' Satish said. His voice conveyed that the clock had been incalculably precious to him, and was irreplaceable. He held up the plastic box that contained the new one, which was silver and sleek, with a white analogue face.

'Such a nice new clock,' he said. The glow from his sister's face returned. 'Looks expensive,' he went on.

'No no,' said Lakshmi, rather proudly.

'So many functions.' He turned the box at arm's length to peer at the lettering on the back. 'What's this: snooze?'

'Yes, and you can also set it to ring at the same time every day.' She reached out to indicate a button on the side.

'Almost too nice to use,' said Satish decisively. He seemed to be talking to himself, but his voice was quite audible. Mohan, who had been standing near the chair to witness the small ceremony, felt the familiar mix of emotions that his brother-in-law so easily aroused: he wanted to hit him, but he also felt like laughing, so neatly had Satish turned the situation around. But then there was his wife's face. Mohan became aware of an insect buzzing increasingly loudly as it banged against the glass of the balcony door; he reminded himself not to speak, and drifted towards the kitchen as though to check on something.

Behind him, he heard Satish's soft, educated voice: 'Yes, it's too good for an old bachelor like me. You'd better keep it here, I wouldn't know how to look after it.' As Mohan went into the kitchen he turned and saw his wife's face, which was shocked, like a child's after it has been slapped. Ashish had

49

gone to the balcony and was using his slipper to try to flick the insect, still buzzing irately, off the glass door and into the warm afternoon.

★ ★ ★

'The daal is interesting,' Satish said. Lakshmi began to smile. 'Completely tasteless,' her brother mused. 'I wonder how you managed it.' Her face darkened, and she looked down at her plate without appearing to see it.

It entered Mohan's head to say, 'If you don't like the food, get out of my house and don't come back.' He didn't, though; such a spat with Satish's elder sister's husband had left him unable to visit her house until she died five years later.

'Give me the daal,' Mohan told Ashish instead. He helped himself to more and continued to eat in silence, thinking about Satish and what had become of his early promise. He'd been exceptionally bright as a young man, but his father had favoured the elder children, and Lakshmi, who was the youngest. The crowning injustice had been when Satish, after graduating, had got a job with a British-run textile company. His father had told him to give the job to the eldest brother, Bhaskar, who hadn't, anyway, kept it for long; he was indolent and good-natured and had married and moved to Nagpur, where he became a college lecturer. It was an incredible story, Mohan reflected, working the daal into the heap of rice on his plate. It was hard to imagine such a thing happening today. Which employer, for one thing, would hire one brother but accept another as substitute? He squeezed a little lime onto the rice and daal mixture, and sprinkled salt over it. At some point Satish's hopes had given way to sourness; he had never married, and after he retired from his own post as a lecturer in law, seemed to spend his time devising small ways of upsetting his siblings.

To Mohan's surprise, Ashish began to talk. The boy smiled at Satish who, caught off-guard, smiled back. 'Satish uncle, I was reading in the newspaper about that case of a Hindu Undivided Family where one of the married daughters changed sex to become a son, what do you think about it?'

Satish laughed; his face became quite attractive. 'So you read the newspapers, is it? That's more than many law students seem to do. Well, it's an interesting case, since there doesn't seem to be a precedent at this level. But if we go back to the basic concept of the HUF there are two main considerations — '

and he went on talking for some time, while Ashish nodded, his face intelligent.

Mohan chewed a mouthful — the daal wasn't tasteless, it was comfortingly bland — and thought of the flat in Grant Road where Satish lived. This was where he'd return after spending the afternoon and early evening with them. Mohan had been to the place some years earlier; it was in a dingy building, not very far from the post office, and more resembled a chawl, a workers' tenement, than a modern apartment block. The main room contained some books, jostling for space in and on top of the shelves, and a steel cupboard for papers and clothes. There was a desk, and a dusty wooden chest of drawers topped with a newspaper, a comb, a hair brush, Satish's steel watch. The bed was narrow. There had been a sense of monasticism in the place, but without any of the rich stillness that might imply. 'This is a room a man might kill himself in,' Mohan had thought, surprising himself.

There was a pause in the conversation. Satish had rounded off his explanation, Ashish had made a joke, and both their faces were flushed with amusement. Mohan pushed a jar towards his brother-in-law. 'Lime pickle?' he said. Their eyes met.

Satish smiled — he had, after all, a

charming smile — and reached out a thin hand. 'Thank you,' he said.

★ ★ ★

In the evening, Mohan sat in the circle of light from the hundred-watt bulb above the cane armchair. *Become a Writer* lay on his lap, unopened. He remembered the pitiable face — dark, thin, desperate — of the man he'd bought it from. A few days later, Mohan had been in a bus on Marine Drive when he'd seen what appeared to be the same man, standing on the parapet and looking down at the waves. The wind blew the white clothes around his thin figure. Noon: it was blindingly hot. As the bus passed, the man had half turned. He'd seemed to see Mohan, and their gaze had held for a moment. Don't jump, the letter writer had thought. Then the bus hugged the curve of the road, and the man was no longer in view. There was no way of knowing whether he had stepped back, onto the pavement, or forward, onto the rocks.

When Mohan had seen the book last Sunday in Ashish's room he'd had the feeling that something big was about to happen, and with it, something bad. Neither of these things was negotiable, so it should have been obvious that it was pointless to think about them. He ran his mind over all the usual augurs: the train notice boards, the advertisements in the compartment, the faces of the other passengers and of his customers in the last few days, even the toys being sold on the street stalls. But he remembered nothing remarkable. Instead he found himself thinking of his father, at his desk on a Sunday, that inviolable time; his white shirt very white against the dim room, and books gathered on the table around him. Maybe Ashish had been right; maybe Nandlal kaka hadn't known what he was talking about; maybe Mohan's father could have published his stories?

That Sunday Nandlal kaka had come to lunch and afterwards the children had fallen quiet when their father brought out a manuscript, a bundle of pages tied up in a purple ribbon like legal documents. A week later, Mohan's father had left to meet Nandlal, but when he returned had simply gone into his study, quite silent, and closed the door. The incident had been so terrible, and yet never discussed, that it was as though it had slipped underwater, never to be seen again.

4

When Ashish ambled towards the grocer's at ten thirty the next morning the dosa man was already at his stall, under a tree near the roundabout. He was growling at two put-upon young men. One was sweating, and chopping onions; the other scrubbed the enormous griddle on which, at mealtimes, the dosa man would drop a splodge of batter, then, using a knife so large that it resembled a ploughshare, sweep it into a thin circle that sizzled while it crisped. For now, the lackeys sweated and the dosa man stood in the shade, arms folded; between blasts of sarcastic sounding invective he smiled to himself. He was very dark, with the brave moustaches, flourishing sideburns and bouffant hair of a south Indian film star.

Ashish walked back from the grocer's carrying a packet of semolina wrapped in newsprint. It was hot; the early freshness was gone and he smelled traffic fumes in the air and felt the sun on his face.

He was exhausted. The first time he'd woken it had still been dark; he'd been startled by a moment of dead silence and then by the screaming. It was birds, he realized after the initial horror, shouting about something; perhaps, incredibly, the dawn. Not just the crows, pigeons and seagulls that he was used to, but many more: mynahs, koyals, and another that let out insane, rising whoops then waited for an answering burst of mad laughter.

There was too much space in the room. He'd got up again, gone past the bookshelf, peered out of the window suspiciously and seen no one in the darkness below. This is where I live now, he'd thought, but it had seemed unreal.

When day broke and he saw the first figures in the lane, walking for exercise, he felt better. The crisis seemed to have passed, and he slept in the pale, early light, his body cool and soothed under the fan.

There was another memory of having woken, but this was more vague, like a dream one has when sleeping on a long-distance train: mashed memories of the sulphur-yellow overhead light, the swaying of the bogey, and the abiding sense of transit. When he woke it was with an erection, and in the middle of a confusing dream in which he and another boy, possibly Sunder, chased each other in the colonnade of the college.

From another room, he heard his uncle's voice, and his aunt laughing.

He ducked into the bathroom, locked the

door with relief and set about waking up.

By the time Ashish had bathed, Mohan had already left for work. Lakshmi had discovered that there were ants frolicking in the semolina and sent Ashish out for more; she was going to make him breakfast.

He let himself back into the house now, handed over the semolina, and sat at the table drinking tea and flicking through the newspaper.

His aunt came to talk to him. 'It'll be ready in five minutes,' she said, and her face lit up. She wiped her hands on the cloth she had been holding and sat down near him. He was fond of his aunt; unlike his mother, she had a soft face that seemed to crease easily. She was often vague, unless she was angry, and then she was extremely specific.

'It's changed a lot here, you must have noticed,' she began to tell him sorrowfully. 'Gopal building, that probably hadn't been reconstructed the last time you were here.'

'Oh yes, the white one.' It was almost opposite, a six-storey tower that stood out next to the small, faded 1960s blocks in the rest of the lane.

Lakshmi made a 'what can you do' grimace. 'These builders are offering a lot of money — they pay you to let them redevelop and take the FSI and then they put up a taller building and sell the extra flats.'

'Hm.' Ashish drained his tea and, slightly bored, covertly eyed the newspaper's city supplement, where the image of a popular film actress on the masthead had been misprinted; the blues and yellows were marginally separated instead of overlaid, and her famous smile, as a result, was scattered.

'We've also had offers,' Lakshmi went on. 'But luckily the Gogates, you know, they own three flats, they don't want to sell. None of us does really, at least not so far. You can't tell when these people start offering more and more. And then there'll be construction work going on endlessly — something's going to start soon, in the empty plot, a builder's already bought it. I don't know if they'll begin now, or wait till after the rains.'

A toasty, pleasant smell came out of the kitchen. She got up and hurried inside; there were sounds of the lifting of a lid, and the scraping of a spoon. She came back with a plate of the hot upma, which smelled delectably of ghee and a roasted red chilli.

'Here, eat well. You should, since you have so much studying to do,' she remarked, and, unsure whether the comment was pointed or just another part of her morning conversation, Ashish nodded and picked up the spoon. His aunt put on her spectacles, frowned, and went back to the kitchen. She reappeared with a cup of instant coffee, picked up the city supplement, and moved towards the living room window.

★   ★   ★

In his room, he half closed the door and wandered around, inspecting the drawers, the bookshelves, the old comics. Later, when lunch smells began to float down the corridor towards him, he panicked. His books waited officiously on the desk, next to a jumble of pens. He sighed and sat down. It was best to be methodical — first of all, he'd draw up a timetable.

Half an hour later, he'd wedged his shoulders and elbows at awkward angles, the better to concentrate, and found a ruler. He was nearly done with plotting out the grid, which accounted for each day in half-hour units from six a.m. to midnight.

'Ashish!'

He threw out a medium-distance grunt.

'Lunch!'

Carefully, he finished colouring in the last of the green squares that denoted time allotted to bathing and ablutions in the morning, from seven to seven thirty.

Lakshmi was probably a better cook than his mother; she was usually in a better mood, and that seemed to affect the food. And she was less stingy with the oil, salt and chilli; Ashish's father, though he had turned fifty only last year, already had cholesterol, and the doctor had hinted darkly at 'BP'.

Ashish had hogged slightly too enthusiastically at lunch, and now he sat slumped at the desk and eyed the bed and its handloom cover, which was striped, with a prominent slub. It would feel reassuringly rough against his cheek while he slept; but he looked at the bright squares of the study timetable and sighed.

He stared into the sun. A little later, some boys came out to play football in the lane. They seemed to be engaged in a strange dance whose purpose was to cover every inch of the lane with the ball, which slipped between them as though attached to their feet by lengths of elastic. It never got away, nor was it ever caught. Occasionally it flew up, and was knocked down by one of the players, who used his forehead; another dived for it. Ashish read:

The date is out of such prolixity:
We'll have no Cupid hoodwink'd with a scarf

Bearing a Tartar's painted bow of lath,
Scaring the ladies like a crow-keeper;
No, nor without-book prologue, faintly spoke
After the prompter, for our entrance:

It was enough. He couldn't understand, and had been a fool to try. At the same time as the words drew him in with their rhythm, they barred his passage. Lath? Tartar? Without-book prologue? He should have stuck to the books of notes that everyone else used to pass. His eyes wandered outside, where the football was making a lovely long curve towards the goal at the mouth of the lane. The watchman grabbed the ball and waved the boys out of the way; Dr Gogate's new car turned in.

Ashish bent his head down to the page.

The date is out of such prolixity:

His elbow leaned on the desk and his cheek found a resting place in the palm of his hand. He looked into the sun and wondered what had become of Sunder, but the question didn't seem as urgent as a few days ago. For diversion, he went looking for the book that his uncle had picked up.

★   ★   ★

'Aren't there any family photos?' he asked his aunt in the afternoon.

'Photos? You mean of your mother's childhood?'

'Yeah, from the old house.'

She paused, and blew on her tea. 'I'll have to see, they're probably in the chest here. You want to see them?'

'Hm,' Ashish nodded.

'We'll ask your uncle when he gets home.'

'Okay.'

But a little later, he heard her calling to him from the living room and left *Romeo and Juliet* to wander out. She had removed the ornaments from the top of the tea chest and opened it; bits of newspaper, cloth, and a few albums lay on the low table. Her face was amused. 'Come, see?'

He sat next to her on the floor, and they began turning the enormous pages, on which card-like black and white prints were affixed by decorative corners. Here was Mohan mama, about six years old, swinging on the gate of the house at Dadar: he looked small, skinny, and mischievous, but ultimately well behaved. Ashish's mother was in another picture, a young child, pugnacious in a frilly frock with a large bow at the waist. His grandparents, looking young and self-conscious; his grandfather wore a suit, his grandmother wore a

62

nine-yard sari and carried a baby, presumably Vivek mama, in her arms. Various other cousins, aunts and uncles; his aunt speculated about their identity.

They heard the door catch: Mohan was home.

'What's this?' he asked. He took off his sandals and came to stand near them, tentative but eager.

'He wanted to see some of the old photos,' Lakshmi explained.

Mohan reached down and took the picture Ashish was holding. It had a white border and scalloped edges, and showed a formal group. A plant stood in one corner; on a sofa sat a woman in a sari, now the ubiquitous six-yard variety, holding a toddler on her lap. Two boys stood next to her; at the side was her husband, his hand on the elder boy's shoulder.

'That's my grandparents with my mother, Vivek mama and you, isn't it, Mohan mama?' Ashish glanced up; his uncle's face was inscrutable.

'Yes, the three of us and our parents. Look at your mother's face.'

'Hm.' Ashish reached up for the photo. The toddler, fat-kneed, had the familiar aggressive expression. 'So Vivek mama was about twelve. You must have been six or so? Everyone looks so different.'

63

Mohan snorted. 'It was a long time ago.'

'That's not what I mean,' Ashish said. 'You all seem more serious or something.' The photographs were different, say, from those of him and his sister growing up. The figures here regarded the camera with greater intensity; they seemed more present than people in pictures today.

His uncle looked down at him. 'Well, these photos were taken in a studio, we had to pose. Best clothes, a lot of waiting. Your mother used to get very bored and start shouting.'

'I bet.' Ashish looked back at the photo. The elder boy, Vivek, already looked pompous; he was sticking his small chest out, and his brilliantined hair showed the marks of a comb. Ashish's grandfather seemed preoccupied; his grandmother was a definite entity, as though the photographer had drawn a thin black line around her. The middle child, his uncle, appeared to be elsewhere. His eyes were remote, and his smile engagingly goofy, as though he were gratified to have been included. Already, he looked like a person used to spending a lot of time on his own.

'Can I have this?'

Mohan looked startled.

'Can I keep it in my room?' Ashish modified.

'I suppose. There's no frame.'

'That doesn't matter.' He thought perhaps he should explain why he wanted it. 'I don't really have any old pictures of the family,' he said. It would be a warning, he thought, feeling a kind of self-doubting impatience towards the boy in the photo. Wake up! he wanted to shout at him. Get on with it!

'All right, take it.' Mohan started to put the other photos in an ancient envelope that he slipped into the back of the album. He wrapped it in a piece of old sari that acted as its shroud, and replaced it carefully in the tea chest; he shut the lid. Aha, thought Ashish: only people who've had truly happy childhoods can afford to forget about them. He went to his room and stood the photo on his desk, against the window ledge.

* * *

After dinner he prowled around his uncle, who was sitting in the cane chair reading.

'Mohan mama.'

'Hm.'

Ashish circled the chair. The light glinted through his uncle's steel-coloured hair and onto his scalp, which showed, oddly pale, at the crown.

65

'Have you ever thought of writing something?'

'Ha! Apart from letters and money order forms, you mean?'

'Yes.'

No answer. Ashish continued to hover about the chair, dragging one rubber slipper along the tiles until it squeaked. His uncle lowered the book and looked at him.

Ashish grinned. 'I was looking at that book, *Become a Writer*. You should try writing some stories, you know, short stories. You must know a lot of stories, from all the people you meet.'

Mohan's eyebrows shot up. 'That's a very different thing. It's difficult to be a writer, not everyone can do it,' he muttered.

'Yes, but you already write a lot anyway.'

'That's different.'

'And also you read so much.'

His uncle regarded him for a moment, frowning. Then his face cleared. Unexpectedly, he laughed. 'I was published once,' he said. 'Have I ever shown you?'

'No!'

'Hm, I wonder where it is now. It was in a magazine.' His face had begun to gleam. 'Come, I think it might be in your room.'

He bustled out of the living room and into the kitchen. Ashish had just begun to follow

66

him when Mohan reappeared with the stepladder. He went into Ashish's room and planted it between the bed and the window.

'Do you want me to do that?' Ashish mumbled, but he enjoyed the sight of his uncle hurrying up the pyramid-like stepladder, which creaked loudly under his weight. In the upper reaches of the shelves near the bed Mohan began to rummage in various piles of paper.

'Chhi,' he said perfunctorily. The dust here was thick and silky; it floated down to the floor in flakes. 'Got it.' He descended the ladder, his face triumphant, eyes bright, and a dirty smear on the bridge of his nose. Ashish, long-suffering, folded up the stepladder and carried it back to the kitchen. When he'd restored it to its dark corner he hurried to the living room. His uncle stood under the bare bulb; he had gingerly unfolded the ageing, brittle newsprint.

'See, here.'

Ashish bent, and read:

Dear Sir,

I am a faithful reader of the *Junior Diplomat* and I am writing to ask you print more short stories.

Yours faithfully,
Mohan V. Karekar (age 4½).

'Aged four and a half! Mohan mama!' Ashish crowed. He was still more entertained when his uncle removed the paper from his grasp. 'We used to get the *Diplomat* every Sunday, and I loved reading the *Junior Diplomat*, the children's section, it was very popular. Here, this paper's old, it'll crumble.' Carefully, he refolded the page and put it on the reading table.

'So you were already published at four and a half?'

Mohan smirked, and sat down in the cane armchair. 'There are a lot of things you don't know about me,' he said. He opened his book again.

Ashish had heard a familiar music in the distance; he listened, part of his brain thinking it might be a song he knew. Then he ran towards his room: it was his phone.

★　★　★

Later that night, he was about to go to sleep when an electronic shrieking began in the flat below; it was in the room underneath his. He cocked his ear and listened: an urgent trill of three rising notes. It must have been Madhavi, the plump girl: she was of the right age to have exams. Setting an alarm for revision, or to signal the end of a timed

68

question, was the kind of thing serious students did. But no one came to switch off the alarm; it shrieked itself into catalepsy and, with a squeak, died out.

Ashish sat at the desk and thought he would read a little more. He was thinking about Sunder, about his lazy, deep voice, and his inarticulateness, and about how they were to meet the next day; at the same time, he was reading, but too fast to notice any of the words that passed his eyes like long distance trains at night, noisy but unmemorable. At once he felt eyes fixed on him, and heard a gobbling sound. Very slowly, hairs rising on his neck, he looked up. Two round white faces, enormous, dark, knowing eyes, and a look of surprise modulated by the polite pretence of disinterest. In the open window of the empty flat opposite sat two white owls. They rocked slightly, their eyes scanning the darkness. As his eyes met theirs, one of the birds unfolded like a threat suddenly swept aside and Ashish's heart contracted; the whiteness of its wings flashed into a V, then a line; it swooped through the glow of the street lamp and was gone.

His aunt, who couldn't remember whether the apartment door had been double-locked, came out of her room after midnight to check. On her way back she saw the line of light under Ashish's door and was surprised; none of their children had studied this late, especially so far before the exams. He must really be serious, she thought. She went back to her room and quietly closed the door.

5

Her day held its breath until Mohan and Ashish had been safely eased into the world. When the morning's whirlwind was over — tea cups and clattering arrivals in the kitchen, departures for the bathroom, reappearances in different stages of readiness, last-minute forgetting of things — she felt like a sports coach who retreats into his private life between moments of crisis.

The cleaning over, she went to the bathroom, stripped off the old salwar kameez in which she slept, and watched the red light of the water heater come on. A good stream of hot water came out of the tap and filled up the bucket. She threw half a mugful over herself, flinched, and added more cold water. Her skin was still soft and pale below the neckline. She picked up the cake of citrus soap, streaked in yellow and green; its slight tackiness and the hint of steam, the scent of lemon and clean skin that lingered in the bathroom, were all signs that her husband and Ashish had been there before her.

She came out of the bathroom, wrapped in a towel, and considered what to wear. Her cupboard was full of saris, ironed, folded and stacked like important documents, but these days she mostly wore 'suits': long, fitted kurta, baggy salwar, and a matching dupatta. The suits were easier to look after. Unlike cotton saris, they didn't need to be starched, and they went uncomplaining into the laundry and then to the ironing boys' blue hut from where they were collected, pressed and submissive, by Mohan in the morning when he was on his way back with the bread and milk.

Still, the sari, and the ceremony of putting it on, retained some glamour. Today she stood in front of the open cupboard and thought she'd wear one. She scanned the shelves: her eye passed appreciatively but without great interest over the heavy silks, the practical synthetics, which in their way had been exotic years earlier, and the few chiffon saris that her daughters had given her, and which she rarely wore. It was hot today: she wanted a cotton sari. She put her hands in and pulled out a slim, pale blue spine. It was a simple one, with large grey dots and discreet embroidery on the border. The matching short-sleeved blouse looked saggy and depressing until worn, when it filled with the authoritative curves of upper arms, shoulders, and breasts. The petticoat too became more graceful, a vestige of a milkmaid's outfit in a painting, like the one they had hung in the bathroom, a fabric calendar picture of Krishna teasing the gopis. This was an unlikely gopi, of course — she regarded herself, in the latest instalment of the daily conversation with her own image, and checked the lines between her nose and mouth, and the grey hairs at the side of her head. She'd put on a little weight in recent years, and probably looked better for it. But the eyes gazed back, doubtful.

She unfolded the sari, shook it out and examined it for any rents or stains; then, with absent-minded grace, tucked it in so that it made half a round of her petticoated lower body. Her arms danced as cheerfully as the limbs of an automaton to pay out the fabric, pleat it, and secure it at the front. The neatly gathered folds made her think of the last letter they'd had from their youngest daughter, who was working for a computer company in America. Her life was unimaginable; she had no family of her own yet but no help either, and had to work long hours as well as manage her own food, laundry and cleaning, though she said that these were simpler affairs than at home. Lakshmi glanced in the mirror to check the pleats fell straight and her mouth curled; she liked this impudent daughter's freedom. Megha would find it difficult, though, when she married;

there were so many things — but all that was a later worry, and marriages, also, were different these days.

She wrapped a further length of the fine cotton about her body, stretched the remaining cloth along her left arm, scrutinized it for holes, and threw it over her left shoulder. Then she went to the small idol of Ganesh near the window, lit a stick of incense in front of the god, and said a prayer. It was a ritual she performed every day, though not because it was supposed to achieve anything; it was a counterpart of her bath, and created a quiet corner in her mind that might, with luck, survive the rest of the day.

The building was quieter; earlier there had been the sounds of office workers opening and shutting their front doors. Now it was the domestic traffic. Cleaning women were arriving at some houses. Here, too, the doorbell rang loudly; it must be the rubbish collector, a leering, dark, and cheerful youth who wore brightly patterned shirts. He came whenever he pleased between the morning and lunch time, except on Sundays, when he arrived promptly at eight; later, she or Mohan would see him out and about, nattily dressed and with brilliantine in his hair, so that he looked as if he were on his way to meet a girl.

She put her head into the passage. 'Yes?'

'Kachra!'

'Yes yes,' she replied, 'wait a minute.'

The kitchen basket already smelled ripe. She picked it up and went forward, her nose wrinkling; she was opening the outer door when something dark and solid, sensing its imminent danger, shot out of the basket, along her arm and off her shoulder.

She screamed.

'Oh, a lizard! Ugh!' She found herself trembling with disgust. It wasn't a pale green house gecko but one of the dark, shameless outdoor lizards that wouldn't take fright decently even at loud noises.

The kachrawala grinned; wretched fellow, he'd enjoyed the show. 'It's good luck,' he said. 'You'll come into some money.'

'Ugh!' She opened the door, and handed him the bin, which he emptied into his bag, knocking it so that the last vegetable peelings fell out. He pointed just outside the outer door. 'There he is,' he said. 'Looks like he's waiting to come back in.' The lizard skulked next to the jamb.

Lakshmi's neighbour opened her door and began to berate the kachrawala. 'It's after eleven. When are you going to start coming on time?'

He smiled and nodded, and gave Lakshmi back her bin.

Ashish had gone out; he said he had to go to college for something. Outside, it was hot and still: the last days of summer before the rains came. The empty hours stretched ahead. She thought of various things she had to do: change the sheets, put more camphor pellets in the cupboards before the monsoon started and insects multiplied; perhaps, in the evening, go and collect a new suit that she'd ordered two weeks earlier from a tailor in the market.

Instead, she sat near the window, looking out at the lane, which had come to a midday lull. The watchman had disappeared, probably for his lunch; the ironing boys were inside their hut; she heard their radio. She could do one of the more infrequent cleaning jobs — the shelf next to the stove, for example, where salt and other condiments were kept. But the idea had neither reality nor urgency. The crows on the electricity wires were quiet after their early morning exuberance; soon they'd find some shade to sit in until it was cooler again.

A single bird sang out: a falling sequence of four notes, with a cheep at the end. It sounded oddly familiar, yet she hadn't, she thought, heard it before. Maybe it was a bird that used to come near their childhood home, in Tardeo? Its song — she hummed it to herself — brought no specific recollection, only a vaguely poignant feeling.

It was hard to work out, sometimes, how she had come from that house, with a family full of loudly talking, cheerful people, into this one, where, often, each person withdrew into silence, nursing his or her own dreams, oblivious to everyone else. Only her elder son, Gautam, resembled her family; he'd also spent most time with his cousins from that side. He talked and laughed more loudly, didn't think deeply about every single thing, and, like her, seemed to exist most clearly when he was speaking. Like her, he narrated aloud to himself whichever action he was about to take ('Hm, I mustn't forget to get that CD for Alka'), a habit that bemused and irritated his father, who would wonderingly ask, 'How does saying it aloud help?' and privately, no doubt, add: 'And why are you intruding such banal reflections into *my* world?'

She ran through the rest of the day's tasks, murmuring some of the words aloud. 'Vegetables . . . ' No, she'd looked, there were enough for dinner. 'Newspapers.' Yes. She made herself a cup of coffee, and sat near the window where the light was good, the pile of last week's papers and the scissors next to her. She clipped out a picture of a polar bear, and a recipe for macaroni cheese with baked vegetables, the sort of thing that Ashish might like. It was nice, this process of revisiting the novelties of a few days earlier, which now seemed agreeably tired — it was a habit from childhood, though then the paper had been *Navshakti*, or old issues of *Stree* or *Kirloskar* that a neighbour provided for her scrapbook. There was something she had been meaning to clip, but she couldn't remember what — it bothered her for a few minutes, and she turned over the pages. Then she found it: a column on the edit page about Seema Kulkarni, a classical singer whom she'd admired very much when she was younger. The article was about the tradition of singers as divas, and the often extravagant caprices they displayed. Lakshmi had gone, more than once, to hear Seemabai sing; she always turned up a couple of hours late, while the audience sat patiently waiting. Finally the singer, richly dressed and made up, with kaajal, lipstick, and an enormous bindi on her forehead, appeared on stage; she smiled, did namaskaar to the audience, sat down, then snapped at the tabla player before closing her eyes and beginning to sing. Here an odd thing happened, each time: the woman of so much personality completely disappeared, and only the music was there till the raga ended.

The newspapers now addressed, Lakshmi piled them near the door, ready for the wastepaper man.

★　★　★

After lunch she found herself drawn to the television, though at this time of day there was nothing she wanted to watch; her favourite serials were aired much later, in the evening. There were two: one ran on Monday, Wednesday, and Friday, and the other on Tuesday, Wednesday, and Thursday. Both were about the travails of young women newly married into traditional families, and how they dealt with the women around them: their sisters-in-law and mothers-in-law. She preferred the first one, *Daughters of the House*. On Wednesday, when for fifteen minutes they overlapped on rival channels, she was distracted, flicking between advertisement breaks and trying to keep up with the stories.

She put on the television and waited with the usual tense expectation of pleasure as the screen flickered into a point of light, then animated. There really was nothing to watch

— some terribly dry cultural programme on a Marathi channel, endless cooking shows in English — and she turned the television off again and resealed its clumsy plastic wrapper; it was supposed to protect the set from the corrosive sea air, but made it appear to be a sort of cranky deity that had to be kept in check.

'Sheets . . . '

She went to get the clean ones from Ashish's room and became diverted while searching for a packet of camphor pellets that she was sure was in a bottom drawer of one of the big cupboards. Instead, among candles, ballpoint pen refills and curtain hooks, she found a thin envelope with four small pieces of paper inside: 'Baby boy, 8.34 a.m.', 'Baby girl, 5.21 a.m.' and so on. They were from the nursing home where her children had been born; though they were years apart, the writing was the same politely curling convent-school hand. They had carefully preserved each record relating to the children, in case the government, which might be omniscient in such matters, spotted and rebuked neglect; there was a vague feeling of contributing, by this scrupulousness, towards national housekeeping.

Four of Mohan's shirts, collected this morning from the ironing boys, lay on the bed. She looked at them in exasperation. It was still there, the mild ring of dirt inside his collars, like a smudged pencil line. It wasn't his fault; nothing could be done. She had scrubbed at some of them to remove the mark, but it had been the collar, not the stain, that had begun to despair and fray. It was in these things, which didn't talk or, strictly speaking, have lives, that her days played out: her relationship with the shirts, neatly ironed and folded, was so much more direct than any other interaction these days.

She changed the sheets, and decided to go to the temple; this was turning into an afternoon habit. It was partly a pretext to leave the house and take a walk; she saw other women there, who were probably bored, like her.

The apartment block was quiet and sleepy now: a hot diagonal strip of sun was the only living thing in the stairwell. She almost smiled as she recognized her state of mind. Often, on the way to the temple, she'd feel slightly irritated. It was perverse, after all, to go out in the afternoon heat and walk in the dirt beside the main road. As she went, looking down and treading carefully to avoid stepping in anything, she ran through the vegetables left at home and worked out what to cook for dinner. Ashish's expression as he'd been

81

leaving in the morning flitted through her mind. What had he been up to? He had seemed happy, pleased about something. Her thoughts turned to the most recent episode of *Daughters of the House*. The misunderstandings between the heroine, Shruti, and her daughter-in-law, Shreya, never seemed to end: it was deliciously vexing. Of course it was unlike real life; when she'd first been married and living with her mother-in-law and sisters-in-law, there'd been no dramatic arguments or cruelties, only ongoing frustrations: her sister-in-law's perpetual sniping, or Aai, their mother-in-law, with her rules. She'd been a traditional woman, not unkind, but rigid in a way Lakshmi's upbringing hadn't prepared her for. The two daughters-in-law had to serve the food and eat later, with Aai; though this didn't apply to Mohan's sister, who was a little spoilt. And Aai had a habit, when Lakshmi was slipping out in the morning after having done her chores, of saying, 'Make sure you're home in time for lunch', even when she was going to see her father and her brother.

She turned into the temple compound, a little door set into a wall. How she'd missed her brother in those first days after her marriage. They had been close when she'd been a young child, after their mother died.

The sister closest to her in age was envious of her; the elder brother and sister were aloof, already involved in their own lives. Satish had been there, though. He was doing well in college but he had time for her: he would come home in the evening and discuss school with her, or take her outside to play a game of badminton. Even now, those days seemed so near — they were just behind her elbow.

In the temple she said her prayers in front of each idol. At first, she felt slightly foolish doing this; by the end, she was relieved of something inexplicable. The cold stone floor under her feet became associated with handing over a slew of tiny troubles to the gods, who accepted them impersonally. She felt lighter afterwards, and was nearly playful as she circumambulated the inner shrine; she put the palm of her hand on each of the four rough stone walls as she passed. On the way home she'd feel calmer, more confident: she'd think about Shreya, Shruti, and the others, and imagine helping them solve their differences; she'd make them sit down (in her own house) with cups of tea and get them to talk through their quarrels. She saw them smile and relax at the end of these scenes, and though the fantasy made her laugh at herself, it was oddly delightful; the thought would accompany her for some time.

In the courtyard she blinked at the light. An older woman whom she'd often seen here was sitting on the bench where Lakshmi had been planning to rest.

The other woman smiled; Lakshmi smiled back and sat down. They looked towards the gate of the complex; then Lakshmi leaned back and gazed into the papery, shifting leaves of the banyan tree above, where two crows were having an amicably ill-tempered conversation.

'So quiet here,' her companion said.

'Lovely,' Lakshmi agreed. She adjusted her dupatta, and kept an eye on her slippers, which were near the four steps leading to the main Shiv temple; really, it looked like a low, square hut, except for the decorated roof and the small gopuram, which disappeared into the outreaching arms of the tree. The banyan seemed very contented here, and she thought of those in Saraswati Park, especially the one in the empty plot. It was a tall, handsome, spreading thing — but now it was surrounded by building debris and concrete dust.

The same bird, whose song she almost seemed to recognize, sang and chirruped above them. She hummed the sequence to herself, a fall of four notes in which the first was stressed: MA ga re sa, except that they weren't full notes apart, maybe half; a plaintive effect followed by a squeak of happiness.

The older woman laughed. 'Do you sing?'

'Oh no. No.' She smiled. 'Only when I'm alone. I always loved music, but my father never wanted me to learn. We lived in a small place, and he thought my practice would disturb everyone.'

The bird went into an extra trill of what appeared to be sheer joy.

The other woman disclosed, 'I'm fasting today. Until sunset, then I'll eat something, but without salt.'

Lakshmi nodded. One fasted for one's husband, or one's children, for good health or good exam results; one could fast in order to propitiate a particular god, or even to lose weight. Some people, and this thought made her raise her eyebrows, fasted in order to obtain the same husband in the next life. She'd never kept a fast, partly because Mohan hadn't encouraged it. This was one of the ways in which their marriage was modern; she also called him by his name openly, unlike many women of a previous generation. And fasting had always seemed peculiar to her, a specious way for women to add structure to the week; it was a voluntary trial that made them feel virtuous, but not for any reason that she understood. However, she knew her part in this conversation.

'So you take milk during the day?'

The other woman sighed. 'Water, milk, sometimes fruit; also Lay's.'

Lakshmi nodded. Potato wafers, not being made of grain, constituted fasting food.

The other woman turned to her. 'You don't fast at all? Not even on Mondays?'

She wondered if she should lie and claim to be diabetic. But she smiled instead. 'No,' she said.

The older woman shrugged. 'Well, I must go home and cook,' she said. She got up a little stiffly; she wasn't thin, despite, or perhaps because of, all the fasting. 'Good for you,' she said. 'These things are a pain when you start. You can't stop, and then it goes on, week in, week out.' Lakshmi smiled, and the other woman waved, an oddly masculine gesture, and began to walk slowly towards the gate.

Lakshmi sat on. It was only five forty-five or so; she'd go home in some time and do the cooking just before they ate. Ashish would be on his way back now, or perhaps he'd already arrived, but she relinquished the thought of hurrying home to make him eat something. She had worried, at first, that he was unhappy living with them, or that he didn't feel comfortable. He so often lurked in his own room. But then she recognized something in him: the pleasure in quietness, the curious interest in navigating his way through vast spaces of boredom. Anyway, he was quite capable in the kitchen, and if he wanted tea or a snack, knew how to help himself. His uncle would soon be home; the two of them could sit grunting at each other over sections of the newspaper or, as an adventure, make something to eat.

As sunset approached, she felt a small stinging, as though someone had stuck a tiny syringe into her forearm. She wiped at the skin. There was an angry whine: the first mosquito bite of the day. From the main temple came the sound of chanting and more people, some younger as well as the elderly ones, filed in hastily from diverse places, removed their footwear, and hurried inside. A good, strong smell of incense came out: it would soon be time for the aarti to start. She didn't want to go in and wait for the prasad, so she got up and found her sandals in the jumble of others and went out of the gate as the sky darkened and birds began to cry. More people were still coming into the courtyard.

6

Just when it seemed the temperature could go no higher and the weather become no stickier, there were storms. A crazed wind rifled through the house, knocking things over; Lakshmi and Ashish ran around trying to shut the windows, but the wind was too strong: it entered and left heaps of a strange, ash-brown dust in the corners of rooms. One night Mohan woke as though to a familiar voice in a dream. The air was cool and moist; outside, he heard the rain.

By morning the world had altered utterly. He looked out of the living room window and saw the grey sky and the rain; the lane was transmuted into mud. The watchman's hut had magically acquired a tarpaulin over the door; it was time to take out the umbrellas and raincoats. He went to look for them in the passage, where the air hung moist and heavy, as though a low-density cloud was passing through the house. The rain gear was in a plastic bag behind one of the shelves.

Every year when the rains came it was like returning to a well-known place after a long journey. The mind mercifully blocked out the recollection of how it really was: the sodden, dark days, roads full of water, the dirt; instead, as the summer heat built up, one waited impatiently for the rains, when, it seemed, new life would begin. Soon, it would be time for Ashish to start college.

Later in the morning, Mohan walked into the muddy lane. He wore dark trousers and rain sandals, and carried a sturdy black umbrella. When he saw the enormous old banyan in the empty plot he did a double take: the tree appeared to have grown fresher and younger with the new season. Two of the pi-puppies from the lane shivered, drenched, under its overarching arms. The construction workers who were laying a foundation in the plot had made a shrine at the bottom of the tree; they had plastered orange paint on part of the trunk, tied red threads around it, and put a couple of laminated pictures of gods at the base. Recently he'd seen one of them lighting a stick of incense and muttering a prayer there early in the morning. The banyan tree now looked serene and benevolent, the kind of tree village students sit under in a historical film.

He plashed his way to the train station. The back lanes were filling up with dirty water; the storm water drains were clogged. The smell of the first rain — fresh, leafy

— brought back memories: walking to school behind his brother, who was charged with Mohan's care and was impatient in the way of elder brothers, hissing, 'Come on! Hurry up!' When they entered the school lane he'd turn with a snarl to remind Mohan that from here onwards they were as strangers to each other. Mohan hadn't known what it was to have the favoured slot of the first child, so he found Vivek's resentment comical, even witty. Other memories: running around in Shivaji Park with friends, kicking a ball and getting filthy. One of his classmates had been a boy called Yezdi, whose father owned a bakery; he now wrote cook-books and food columns for the *Indian Record*. Yezdi had been fat, or at least what passed for fat in those days. Mohan had quite liked him, even admired his audacity. He remembered conversations with the other boy as they walked part of the way home together after a match.

'My father's going to scream when he sees my marks from the maths test,' Yezdi had said, swinging his school bag from one arm. He was never tired after games, mainly because, Zen-like, he attended them without really participating.

Mohan had grinned. 'Does he always ask for your marks?'

'Always. And he always screams.' Yezdi

chuckled. 'Last time he was going to clip me round the ear because when he said, Why is it that my only child can never get above sixty per cent in anything, I said, Remember, I get the highest marks of all your children.'

Mohan had giggled, scandalized but also impressed. 'What about your mother, what does she say?'

'Oh, she doesn't care.' They had reached the road where they would part ways, and they stood on a corner chatting under a gulmohar tree; tiny, petal-like leaves fell into Yezdi's hair. Mohan's shins ached from running. 'She just wants me to eat well and be happy.'

Mohan had reached out and grabbed a handful of the other boy's infinitely soft stomach at this, and Yezdi must have puffed his pregnant belly out in valediction; that was his habit. He grinned to himself at the thought. The fellow had been shameless. His face closed: later, they'd fallen out over a stupidity, though it had seemed to matter very much at the time — perhaps just one of those things, an awkwardness seized with relief by boys who silently realized that, as they grew up, they had little in common.

★　★　★

Because of the rain, everyone felt less like moving around. So in the morning, when it was quiet, the letter writers sat under the tarpaulin reading the papers while it poured outside. Legions of ankles and umbrellas hurried past, on their way to offices.

'Arre-arre-arre,' said Khan.

Mohan looked up. 'Hm?' he said.

Khan waved a page of the *Urdu Times*. 'Cinema projectionist Saleem Ansari, alias Munna, twenty-nine, from Albert Cinema, Falkland Road, held for allegedly raping and murdering a girl,' he said.

'Him? But we know him, don't we?'

Khan nodded. 'He's been in that area for ever. I remember when he started out at the theatre, he was just a skinny kid who used to hang around outside the projectionist's office, getting on his nerves.'

'Who's the girl?'

'It doesn't say — the victim was a twenty-four-year-old woman, that's all it says.'

Mohan opened his English paper. A short report, in more or less the same words, appeared in the Metro Briefs column that he read daily, a collection of notices and items taken from the police briefings:

Friends of the Trees announces its annual planting drive: saplings include

bakul, cannonball and tamarind . . .
Chain snatching in Wadala . . .
Maid arrested for theft, Bandra (West) . . .
Cinema projectionist arrested for rape.

But there was no further information. What could have possessed the young man? He thought of the woman in the green sari — these were the occupational hazards she and her colleagues faced. But perhaps the victim hadn't been a prostitute — the paper would have said so, surely. Some other young girl, then. Inexplicable things continued to happen, a fact to which the Metro Briefs attested. When the crime was sensational enough the reports would reappear in the afternoon paper, fleshed out and sporting a photo of the accused. The smaller items, though, flared and died in the briefs. He read:

Woman attempts suicide in Shivaji Park

A 34-year-old woman who had drunk a bottle of pesticide was found at about 8 a.m. by morning walkers in Shivaji Park, police said. The woman, who was not named, was taken to Hinduja Hospital and was reported to be recovering.

Things that happened near Shivaji Park always struck him because it was so near the area where they'd grown up (a shard of his mind pointed out that he'd yet to go and see his brother; he'd promised) and he thought, what a way to let a life leak out, poisoned, probably in a lot of pain, twitching in a dusty corner of the maidan and found by a man in shorts, or a woman, a little burly, in salwar kameez and sneakers.

It continued to rain; outside the tarpaulin the air was heavy and moist. Drips fell from the plastic sheeting into a small, reservoir-like puddle that had appeared in the road. Every third passer-by tramped heavily into it, and cursed when he or she realized how deep it was.

Lost lives, Mohan thought, and his mind returned, bleakly and then with forbidden excitement, to Ashish's suggestion and the book.

'I want a letter written in Hindi, please.'

It was a tiny, thin, undistinguished-looking man, who wore a clean but threadbare kurta-pyjama and steel spectacles; his hair was neatly oiled. He looked like a computer programmer but turned out to be some kind of guru.

My dear disciple Raju,
I am writing to you from Bombay. Hemant,

Kabeer and I are still in Goregaon. We think of you often and wonder how you are progressing at home.

'Your student?'

'My disciple, yes. He doesn't read English and I can't write Hindi. He has a lot of problems,' the man mused. Mohan looked up. Nervous energy seemed to buzz from the other man, as though he existed at a higher frequency than other people. He smiled suddenly. 'Actually he has no problems,' he went on, in his accented, odd Hindi, 'but it seems to him that he has a lot of problems. His father has died, he has to look after the family. He was working here in Bombay but then he went home. He's young, he worries about his life.' He cleared his throat and Mohan bent again to the inland letter card.

I hope that you are remaining calm and hopeful and that you find a little time each day to do your spiritual practice. Even if it is for five minutes before you sleep at night it will do you good. Do not worry about money matters, health or other things. We are all with you.

Nityananda.

'That's it?'

The other man's eyes, vulnerable and apparently enormous behind his thick spectacles, peered into Mohan's. 'You see, there is nothing wrong with him. His luck is very good. But he worries.' He sighed. 'I'm like his parent, his friend, his little brother. He feels alone, that's his only problem. But it won't be his problem for ever.'

'You are a yogi? You have a school somewhere?'

'Not a school. Just four young men who were studying with me in the evenings. I spend part of the year in Bombay, in a hostel. I'm a Jain. The other part is in Gujarat, where our order is based.' He smiled. 'How much do I owe you?'

Mohan hesitated. 'Let it be,' he said.

The other man began to waver even more than before. 'Please, that's not right. You must charge me,' he said.

'You'll need to send more letters to him, in any case. Pay me next time.'

A smile broke out over the other man's face. 'Thank you,' he said, and waggled his head. He was about to turn, then he enquired, 'Is there anything I can do for you?'

'Me? No, no.'

Mohan remained looking after the thin figure as it worked its way into the crowd.

After lunch the rain held off; he thought he'd take a walk. He headed through the arcades; they smelled damp and were slimy underfoot. The umbrella seller had new stock: umbrellas shaped like the faces of cartoon animals, or printed to mimic a Kanjeevaram sari. Mohan cut through Fountain and made for the university. He'd always been fascinated by the back of the severe, neo-Gothic cloisters, with their thick, unadorned walls and iron bars in the windows. As a child he'd taken them for a prison in which scholars were shut up and forced to produce works of learning. Now the rooms held nothing but steel shelves of periodicals thickly covered in dust.

The old stones were quiet here, polished by the footfalls of the years. Gandhi and Jinnah must have walked up this stretch, founding fathers of two quarrelling nations; the same basalt flagstones offered a place of rest to beggars and itinerant vendors of fresh lemonade, second-hand textbooks, and handled-looking postcards that showed ten famous views of the city. Walking here, he felt that he walked among the great and insignificant of the past; all, alike, hurried as he did, for in this city even idlers liked to look as though they had somewhere to go smartly. All the clerks and petty officers; in their stream, he imagined his father, hurrying along with a set of proofs in a large envelope; he'd been proud, at one time, to do some printing for the university. It hadn't been a lucrative job, but had seemed to confer a diffuse glow of learning over all his work. A hundred and fifty years earlier this had been the beach, before the land reclamations; perhaps it was the murmur of the waves one heard on the busiest of days, through the endless talking of peons and clerks and bearers and passers-by, and the rumble of the red buses, the taxi horns, the metallic steps of each person hurrying through the Fort.

Something was missing. He wanted to leaf through the pages of unknown books on a stall, and hear a title call to him from the stacks. There was a new bookshop on the other side of the maidan; he found himself walking towards it. At the same moment it began to rain. The people crossing the Oval flinched, suddenly exposed to the dark and heavy sky, the wind and the rain. Mohan had forgotten to bring his umbrella with him; he smiled as though the weather had made a joke. He looked out towards Churchgate: the maidan was muddy in places; a few wanderers huddled under plastic sheeting tied to the iron railings; behind him the clock of the university library rang the hour.

The bookshop was alive with brightness. Fluorescent light reverberated from every surface, and the red livery rang out here and there. Life-size cardboard cut-outs of famous characters stood in front of stacks of books; other volumes were piled on large tables, apparently by subject. One table bore heaps of a picture book called *How the Earth Works*, *The Lost World* by Arthur Conan Doyle, *Around the World in Eighty Days*, the Upanishads in translation, and a volume entitled *Save Yourself, Save the World*. A couple of slender south Bombay girls stood turning the pages of the picture book.

He wandered, finding nothing that spoke to him; even the classics were overpriced and oddly blank. The shop was organized in jagged alleys that reached towards the nave, where a small cafe served different types of tea in strange looking cups. When he reached it he paused. A pair of college kids, like Ashish except obviously wealthier, looked up at him in surprise and giggled. Mohan dived around the partition.

Against the terminal wall of the shop, there was the spirituality section; an illustrated *Dhammapada*, a pocket Bhagvad Gita, *Tales from the Bible*, four different editions of *The Prophet*. Crab-like, the letter writer kept to the edge of the room and followed the wall till he reached the entrance again. There he recoiled, for he saw now that one of the cut-outs, fatter, smugger than ever in laminated board, was his old classmate Yezdi Sodawaterbottlewala. The cardboard Yezdi was beaming, gap-toothed, and holding a book entitled *Easy Dishes for Busy Days*. His belly burgeoned over his trousers. Mohan walked around the back of the cut-out to make sure it was two-dimensional. What was the fellow doing here? Wasn't it enough that his mugshot appeared weekly at the head of that ridiculous column, or that Lakshmi had once acquired a copy of one of his books (which Mohan had tried to lose in the bookshelf)? Yezdi even had a television show, though not on a particularly popular channel; in it, he smilingly took viewers on a tour of the best places in the city to eat particular dishes, a subject on which he was, unsurprisingly, well informed.

The back of the cut-out was white card, with a stand at the bottom. Mohan had a fleeting urge to kick it away. Instead, he hurried towards the door. The rain was falling more steadily than when he'd come in, and the air outside was clammy and smelled of leaves and mud. He plunged into it at once.

★ ★ ★

That Saturday, the visit to Vivek couldn't be put off. Mohan left work early and took a train to Andheri. When he arrived, in a light drizzle that was almost a mist, his sister-in-law greeted him warmly. Her face wore the usual slightly anxious expression; it made her look vulnerable and belied the fact that she was a bit of a shrew. 'He's in the balcony,' she said, and cried in the direction of the balcony, 'Mohan's here!' There was no discernible response. 'What'll you have?' she went on. 'Tea? Something else? Juice?'

'Tea,' he said.

He went through the living room into the long, narrow balcony. His brother was wedged there, in one of the ridiculous plantation chairs from the old house. It always disturbed Mohan to see the furniture from that house here, which was illogical, since some of it was in Saraswati Park, where it didn't disconcert him at all. Vivek had a few news magazines next to him, and a right-wing newspaper. He wore reading glasses, attached to a cord around his neck.

'Ah, Mohan,' he said, as though his brother had merely been in the next room for a few hours.

Mohan grinned a bit and sat down in the less comfortable chair next to Vivek, who continued a conversation that, probably, he had been having with himself. 'It's too bad about these Biharis, Bangladeshis, UPites,

101

Mohan,' he said, staring at his brother accusingly over the top of his reading glasses. 'They're everywhere, building slums, contaminating the water supply, making the city dirty.' He waved an arm towards the balcony railing, through which Mohan could see a segment of the backs of other apartment blocks, a small, scrappy park, and part of a road.

'Hm,' Mohan agreed. He preferred to be thought a dreamy idiot than to engage in one of these conversations, which he couldn't bear. How had his brother, who had grown up in the same house as him, turned into this kind of idiot, he wondered sometimes. It wasn't just his political opinions, about which he tried to involve everyone that he met in conversations that, for his side at least, faithfully followed what he read in the newspaper: Vivek complained about everything; he only seemed to be interested in the rising price of grocery items, or how much better the old days had been. He doesn't even read, Mohan thought, except for thrillers, the ones with titles in shiny, embossed lettering, in which authoritative, excessively masculine men throw women around and beat up villains.

'How are the children?' he enquired.

'Very well,' said Vivek without interest. One

of his sons, like Mohan's younger daughter, worked for an American company. He had subscribed to *Time* for Vivek. 'Very good magazine. But a lot of the things they write about India are wrong,' he observed, pushing up his spectacles again, and flicking possessively through his stack of *India Today*, *Outlook*, and *Span*. 'When are you going to retire, Mohan?'

'I'm only fifty-eight,' his brother murmured.

'Still, you should think about it. Acquire some interests, other than sitting at home. Join an association.' Vivek was a member of two, and had fallen out with the committee of one because he was too pushy. 'The Lions Club, except that they're idiots, or the Rotarians. I could have a word with someone I know, see if I can get you in.' Now that he had a good manager for the printing business he rarely dropped in there, perhaps two or three times a week.

'Hm,' Mohan smiled. His sister-in-law brought tea, and some boxes of fried snacks: chaklis and sev.

They sat looking out at the rain. Mohan slid a sidelong glance at his brother. Vivek's face had chosen an unexpected moment to solidify into age. The lines that ran between his nose and mouth, the set of his features, spoke of decisiveness, a person rarely at a loss for a judgement. His eyes had tiny patches in the sclerotic; the whites had begun to be less white, in the way that pages of old books in Bombay yellow at the edge, because of the humidity: the books look as though they have escaped a terrible fire. Is this what happens? Mohan wondered. A young man's face can change at any moment, move into a different expression, but by our age it's different. He thought of the elder brother he'd idolized as a child. He'd loved, for example, in the afternoons when he was supposed to be napping, to root among Vivek's things, touch his pens and books, use his comb or try on his clothes, all activities that enraged Vivek, who would come home from school, discover the unwanted rummaging, and hold the young Mohan upside down by one leg. He'd thwack the seat of Mohan's pants, muttering through clenched teeth, '*How* often — smack — have I *told* you — smack — *not* — smack — to touch my — smack, smack — *things*?'

Mohan had then secretly vowed, tearily, to hit Vivek back harder when he was older. Somehow, this hadn't happened; instead, their fights had melted into a different relationship, one in which the elder brother liberally dispensed unsolicited advice, and the younger, wary, listened and said nothing.

Perhaps that was only fair; after all, Vivek, the elder, had had to manage things when their father died. He'd been the one who decided it was pointless, given the state of their finances, for Mohan to go to college. 'I got a degree and I have no use for it, better if he learns the trade straight away.' With their father's death a new era had begun: one of practicalities, and stubborn truths like those in the newspaper editorials Vivek admired.

The air was damp and chill; the rain continued to fall. The side window of the balcony, closed so that a rack of clothes could dry, had misted over. Mohan took off his spectacles and wiped the lenses with his handkerchief.

'King's Circle will flood,' Vivek said.

'Hm.'

'Will you have trouble getting back?'

'No no,' Mohan said. 'I'll leave soon. The train will be fine, I checked high tide, it isn't till later.'

Vivek's stomach, which wasn't enormous but was rounded, seemed to have made a semi-permanent crease in his shirt. His feet, unselfconsciously hairy and the heels a little rough, were propped on the long arms of the plantation chair. And I, what do I seem like to him, Mohan wondered. He imagined Vivek telling his wife later, 'Mohan's still the same, completely unrealistic. I made some suggestions to him, but he didn't listen . . . '

Near the door, as ever, his brother became more human. 'So, how's Ashish?' he asked.

'He's fine, he's doing well.'

His sister-in-law came out of the kitchen, wiping her hands on a towel. 'Stay for lunch and then go,' she said. 'It's nearly ready.'

He smiled. 'No, I said I'd be home.'

'How's Lakshmi? And Ashish? Tell him to come and see us some time.'

He nodded. 'He's busy studying, but I'll tell him.'

'About time he studied,' Vivek observed.

'Well, I think the rain's less now. I'll go,' Mohan said. He took his umbrella from his brother and went out; Vivek stood, the door ajar, watching him. When Mohan reached the street he felt gleeful, as though it would have been fun, suddenly, to kick through a puddle and splash someone. Birds were singing raucously; the rain had stopped. He hummed to himself as he walked up the muddy lane towards the main road and the station.

The house was empty when he arrived. He put away his umbrella, washed his hands and feet, then sat in the chair, surprised at the silence. The smell of damp had crept inside, and hung in the corners. He got up and found the volume whose pages he had for a while had his eye on. It was a facsimile edition of a book by Mark Twain, *How to Tell a Story and Other Essays*. The title had first interested him, and then, when he'd opened the book at the stall, he'd been struck by its generous expanse of margin, nearly two inches. He took out two new pencils, sharpened them, then set them on the table next to the book. He flicked through its pages, and sat there for some minutes, silent. Finally, just as he heard the putter of a rickshaw in the lane — it drew up to the gate — he wrote a sentence in the margin: 'Outside the house at Dadar were old, tall trees where, at sunset, parrots came to roost.'

Before they got to the door he had put away the book and was sitting in the cane chair. He smiled when they came in, with all the bustle and importance and joy of people who have been out in the rain and are home again.

'Ouf!' said his wife. She looked much younger, like a child who has been outside, doing unsanctioned things: eating street food, playing in the mud, or splashing strangers. Strands of her hair, wet, clung to her forehead; her salwar kameez under the raincoat had become limp.

'I'll make tea,' Mohan said. He took the umbrella from her.

'Go, wash your feet and come,' she told Ashish. He looked from one to the other of their faces and smiled; he went inside. Wet footprints followed him, shining in the dim light that faded into the passage.

'The market was really dirty,' Lakshmi said with enjoyment. 'We bought kanda bhajia. To have with tea.' She had taken off her wet dupatta and he took it from her hand.

7

He'd been here too many times, but still Ashish felt a surge of proprietorial affection as he pushed through the gate of the college and into the elegant stone courtyard. The first day of lectures, and he could easily categorize the people he saw: first-years in scared huddles, dressed in their best clothes and murmuring in Marathi while they eyed the older students and waited to be tormented; a couple of dazed looking north-eastern boys; and the more confident second- and third-years, who greeted each other in loud voices.

He looked around for but didn't see Mayank. They'd been at school together, though the other boy was a year younger; now they'd be in the same class. The bell was about to go — he hurried down the colonnade towards the stairs. No point waiting for Sunder who, if he arrived at all, would be late.

He slipped into the lecture room just as Mrs Sahasrabuddhe was beginning. She wore her spectacles and read from a typescript in a flat, precise voice: 'We will be dealing with the

Modernists in literature, as this is the English syllabus, but this lecture will give you an introduction to the Modernist movement overall.' She seemed to notice the small scuffle as Ashish slid into a middle row and she looked up, apparently burning his image onto her retina. 'I request you all to be on time for the lecture so that the class is not disrupted,' she said. 'You are?'

'Ashish Datye, ma'am.' She made a mark in the register and gave him a cold look. Hastily, he got out his pad and began to take notes: Modernist movement . . .

'Modernism is about discarding everything that stops progress, about doing away with old ideas about art . . . '

It was amazing how long forty-five minutes could last . . . already, after five, he felt weary, and the euphoria about his new start was fading fast. Four more classes before the day ended. No wonder he and Sunder had found it so easy to bunk last year, though Sunder had little incentive to bother; he would in any case take up a job in the family hosiery manufacturing company and work there for a few years before taking over from his father.

'In the nineteenth century we had the positivists who believed that art represents objective reality. Modernism is different: it says that life is chaotic and fragmented . . . '

For Ashish, who had no such prospects, it had felt daring, also a little insane, to be skipping classes. Education was a luxury for him, or should have been.

'The first world war, when millions of young men lost their lives and the world experienced killing on a scale that had never before existed, changed people's expectations of art also.'

He'd been sure, or nearly, that he'd fall on the right side of the not-very-stringent sixty per cent attendance rule. Who could have foreseen they'd change it to sixty-five per cent?

'Modernism became the new orthodoxy and was widely adopted where earlier it had been rejected.'

'I'm a victim of injustice,' he told Mayank, when his parents had found out; they'd been appalled that he'd have to repeat the year.

The class went on and on, Sahasrabuddhe droning about the modernists as if they'd been a cricket team; the lecture made it sound as though someone had decided on trends in intellectual history then picked sides, a moment in school that Ashish had hated. He was always chosen second-last, just before the stupidest or most unfit boy; he could run fast enough but lacked any will to win. Now he distracted himself, imagining a team huddle of the Modernists. Spectacled, nearly blind Joyce was the captain: he hissed, 'No linear plotlines! Reflect the confusion of post-war life!' and wily looking Eliot, his cheekbones gleaming, took the ball and went for his run-up, polishing it against his flannels.

Ashish sighed. Time dragged on. He scrutinized the neck of the boy in front of him; it was hairy, which was off-putting, he should shave it or something. He scanned the class and spotted his favourite pair of running shoes. They belonged to a boy called Ravi, a friend of Sunder's: they must have been bought outside India and were white and sleek, with small rainbow stripes on the side. He examined his own runners, plain and scruffy, with distaste, inspected his hands, stared at the steamed-up, dirty windows, the long-stalked ceiling fans, a puddle on the stairs leading down to the lecturer's podium. He also managed, to his surprise, to write down much of what Sahasrabuddhe said.

All the girls in the class seemed to be in danger of shoulder strain; they bent over their notebooks, swapping frantically between pens of different colours to take notes and underline. Maybe I should get a girlfriend, he mused, then she'd take notes for both of us, that'd be restful. His gaze skimmed the heads and shoulders below: perhaps one of the really shy, swotty girls, who wore overstarched cotton salwar sets in which the dupatta was so stiff it looked like a chastity protection device.

'In architecture,' the precise, monotonous voice went on relentlessly, 'the trend is for clean lines and functionality instead of decoration. Buildings are constructed in steel and glass, like the Crystal Palace, or the Eiffel Tower. In Mumbai we have Watson's Hotel, in Kala Ghoda, where the building's cast-iron frame is on the exterior as a design feature.'

Ashish stirred slightly at this mention of his former home — Esplanade Mansion had once been Watson's Hotel. But the lecture moved on, and his attention wandered. How would he manage to convince any girl, even a sad one, that he was desirable? How would he convince himself, importantly, that he cared what any of them thought about him? What if he had to kiss them, or hold their clammy hands?

'The advent of modern psychology,' Sahasrabuddhe pronounced the p, 'was heralded by Sigmund Freud who posited the existence of unconscious drives, primal urges, and self-imposed restrictions or repressions.'

Ashish scribbled, Freud. Had he spelt it right? He'd privately thought, most of his life, that he might be some kind of eunuch-in-waiting; in early adolescence, it wasn't that he hadn't had sexual urges, but these had been directionless. He liked particular girls, like his cousin Megha, that is, he liked spending time with them; but the images of desirable women that he saw — film actresses with pneumatic bosoms and attractively wobbly waists — left him uninterested.

'At the Paris Salon of 1863 Edouard Manet displayed his famous painting *Olympia*, which shows a naked lady, a prostitute,' Sahasrabuddhe's voice lowered, 'instead of the Greek goddess. The woman is depicted with an African servant and a black cat. The picture reverses expectations and shows us that the modern world is as much of a subject for art as classical mythology.'

He'd thought he might be a late developer, and ignored the various crushes he'd had on unattainable older boys. They'd always been exactly unlike him: conventionally handsome, popular, and brimming with 'team spirit' (it had been written in his eighth-standard report, damningly: 'Lacks team spirit'). Usually, he hardly knew them. Then, in what was to have been his last year in college, he'd met Sunder. Ashish had imagined that when he fell in love it'd be with someone appropriately worthy — handsome, kind, etc

— he hadn't expected someone like Sunder who, on paper, represented little that Ashish thought he valued.

'So we see that modernism embraces disruption and chaos as ways of organizing artwork.'

Sunder in his way was everything that Ashish could never be: rich, thoughtless, overprivileged; and Ashish found him completely desirable. Just a week ago, Sunder had called on his return from Switzerland, where he'd gone on holiday with his parents, and Ashish had gone to his house to hang out and play computer games. He'd dressed smartly, imagining that he might meet Sunder's mother, but she hadn't turned out to be home.

'Traditional forms of society are seen to hinder progress. We will be looking at D. H. Lawrence's *Women in Love* later in the semester.'

Now he wondered, when would they meet next? There was always this uncertainty and flakiness about Sunder, who didn't seem to control his own life, or have much idea where it was going.

'Pessimism about human nature also characterises the modernist movement, along with an interest in the primitive.' Sahasrabuddhe stopped and looked at the clock. Ah, she was running on time. 'For next week, read chapters three and four and look over *The Waste Land*.'

Class was over. There was a general scraping of feet and a cloud of voices rose to fill the room. Ashish filed out with the others into the damp-smelling corridor. He saw Mayank and they were just starting to chat when a familiar voice, deep, loud and unselfconscious, brayed as its owner heaved himself into view from the stairs, 'Fuck yaar, these stairs again, I can't believe they don't let us use the lifts. Ashish, what's up? What was first class?'

'Modernism,' said Ashish, grinning foolishly.

Sunder thumped him on the shoulder. 'You have the notes?'

'Yeah.'

Sunder was wearing sunglasses and new designer clothing. His shirt hung off his sloping shoulders and stretched at the stomach.

'It's not sunny inside,' Mayank pointed out. He reached towards Sunder's glasses. 'Oye,' the other boy protested, 'watch my Tommy's.' But he removed the sunglasses. His eyes were brown and uneasy-looking, innocent of intelligence and set in pouchy sockets decorated with smears of tiredness.

He looks like he jerks off a lot, Ashish thought, and liked the idea.

'Come on,' Mayank said; the five-minute break was over.

Ashish went home that day in an excellent mood. College was starting, he was utterly on top of his studies, and only slightly behind his timetable. Moreover, Sunder had asked him home for lunch on Sunday.

★ ★ ★

He told his aunt on Saturday, 'I'm going to a friend's tomorrow for lunch.'

'Yes, fine,' she said. And then, 'When will you be back? Take your key. We're invited to a wedding reception in the evening, six o'clock, you could come if you feel like. Or if you don't want to we'll say you're studying.'

'Where is it?'

'Ghatkopar.'

'Maybe I should use the time to study,' Ashish said hastily.

'Decide on Sunday if you feel like,' his uncle cut in. 'It doesn't matter, one more or less.'

'Well,' he revealed, 'I'll be going for lunch in Cuffe Parade, so I don't know if I'll be back in time.'

'Oh, Cuffe Parade?'

'My friend Sunder's house.'

'Achchha. Anyway, up to you.'

He was slightly annoyed that they hadn't been more impressed.

★ ★ ★

The next day he dressed carefully: he wanted Sunder's mother to like him. He imagined her, gliding around their enormous apartment and murmuring orders to the servants, all of whom stood continually at attention. So he put on his good trousers and, furtively, polished his shoes; he removed all his shirts from the cupboard before deciding which to wear.

'Wah!' said Mohan mama when he looked up from the newspaper.

Lakshmi mami looked him up and down and smiled.

On the way to the station Ashish rolled up the sleeves of his shirt; otherwise, he worried, he'd look like a bank clerk or a shop assistant, instead of a young film-maker or painter, one of the Top Fifty People Under Thirty that news magazines listed.

It struck him when he was in the train that he didn't have a gift for Sunder's mother. Ordinarily it wouldn't have occurred to him. But he had an image in his mind, perhaps related to the suave way that people behaved in English films; he saw himself carrying a bottle of wine and handing it over. No, that might give the wrong impression. Flowers, then.

He took the bus from VT, got off at Old Cuffe Parade, crossed the road towards the President hotel and saw the flower vendor near the milk booth. Ashish had spent the bus journey with his eyes closed, visualizing, as the book he'd read suggested, a perfect version of the encounter he was to have with Sunder's mother. It began with her opening the door, radiant and friendly. 'So this is Ashish — I've heard so much about you,' she purred, giving him her hand. The apartment was suddenly illuminated as though by Diwali lights; its vastness became cheery. They sat on a chair and sofa respectively and sipped watermelon juice, while they discussed college, Sunder, and Ashish's artistic ambitions; Ashish made astute remarks; Sunder's mother laughed tinklingly.

'Yes?' said the flower vendor. He glanced at Ashish, then resumed scraping lengths of metallic ribbon against the discoloured blade of a pair of shears; the ribbon squeaked in protest, then curled into coy ringlets. In the absence of rain, it was humid and still.

Ashish imagined Sunder's mother, smiling,

lipsticked, choosing flowers.

'These, how much are they?' he asked, and pointed to some massive pink and white lilies.

'Five hundred rupees.'

'Huh?'

The flower man paused, his thumb holding the ribbon against the blade. 'Why don't you tell me what you want to spend,' he suggested.

Fifty rupees? thought Ashish. Instead, after a moment of agonized concentration, he pointed to some carnations. 'And those?'

At the building, the watchman, who had probably seen him before, made a point of asking, with an aggressive lift of the chin, which flat he was going to. A maidservant, small and efficient in a Kanjeevaram-effect sari, was waiting for the lift. She held a lead; at the end of it was a tiny white dog who pattered agitatedly on diminutive legs. The presence of the dog appeared to mean she wouldn't take the servants' lift. She pushed the button with one finger and, bored, stuck her hand on her hip. When the elevator arrived she, without any token submissiveness, marched into it and stood expectant. Ashish followed, and the liftman, seated on a wooden stool under the panel of buttons, seemed to look at the bunch of carnations in their tissue wrapping with amusement.

'Which floor?' he asked Ashish.

'Fourteen.'

The servant, Hitesh, came to the door and opened it just wide enough for Ashish to sidle in. He stopped to remove his shoes, then decided not to; smiled at the servant, who remained impassive, and finally made a feint at shutting the heavy door. But the catch was stuck.

'Ek minute,' Hitesh said. He shoved Ashish lightly aside, and released the huge brass lock, which looked like it had been looted from a fourteenth-century temple, or the set of a television historical drama. 'Baba is inside,' he added, politely yet managing to convey that Ashish was an idiot.

'Thanks. Uh — please take these.' Ashish gave him the flowers and went down the quiet corridor to knock on Sunder's door.

'Yeeeah?'

Ashish opened the door and put his head in. 'Hey. Oh, sorry.' Sunder, clad in only a pair of boxers, stood peering into the cupboard; the room was dark and the air conditioner blasted. Crumpled clothes lay on the floor.

'Oh hi. Just come in. Shut the door, I'm nearly naked.'

Ashish nodded. He closed the door, and turned on the light. The room smelled as

121

though mild fermentation had been taking place in it. He hovered near the door, examining the shelves: *Junior Britannica* (looked untouched), a full set of Hardy Boys, their course books, all bought new, and a No Fear poster, which showed an unpleasantly sinewy man, wearing a low-cut vest and a strange pair of baggy leggings; he was abseiling down a cliff, while the view to his right disappeared in a chute of blue sky and, somewhere below, green fields.

Sunder came to stand right in front of Ashish, who tried to look casual. In the cold room, he could almost feel the warmth from Sunder's thin chest and hairy stomach.

'So what do you think?' Sunder enquired in his deep voice.

'Hmmm?' Ashish's voice went squeaky. He would have been turned on if he hadn't been so incredibly nervous; a sort of paralysis focused his mind and his eyes darted to the white-painted bookshelf, off whose edge the electric light glinted, then back to Sunder (*don't* look at his crotch). Finally, Sunder held the two shirts in his hands up again and repeated, this time with a touch of pique, 'So whaddya think?'

One was checked and preppy, the other flowered.

'Oh, that one.' He jabbed at the floral shirt.

His friend dropped the other shirt over the back of the desk chair and put on first a t-shirt vest, then the flowered shirt, and finally a pair of jeans. He kicked the remaining clothes into the bottom of the wardrobe.

Ashish wandered around the room. There was a wonderful desk, with shelves above it and concealed lighting that cast a bright, warm glow — a desk that someone who actually enjoyed studying would have loved. Next to it, a piece of paper was tacked to the wall.

Sunder's handwriting was childish and round; he wrote (in magenta ink) like a recent convert to literacy.

1. 50 crunches every day
2. 50 squatts
3. 50 dips
4. Learn five new words a day
5. Read *Wall Street Journal* online

God almighty, Ashish thought; then he smiled, thinking, the squats at least are a good idea, should I add something to the list? And Sunder wasn't even embarrassed. He, Ashish, had made countless such lists, but had he thought anyone might see them he would have been mortified.

The time before last when he'd come to Sunder's house, just before he'd moved to Saraswati Park, they'd sat in the room, on facing black leather armchairs, and talked in brief, scornful phrases about life and their plans. Then they'd lain on Sunder's bed reading a Calvin and Hobbes book. At a certain point they'd both started to laugh. Their heads, bent over the wide pages with their beautifully inked strips, were close together, and their hair touched as they shook with laughter. When Sunder's fringe mingled with Ashish's, the other boy had leaned forward slightly, and his lips, which had been dry, had brushed Ashish's. In the same instant, they'd heard the door catch, Sunder had drawn back quite naturally, and the servant had come in with cold, grey glasses of lemonade on a tray, only to see Baba and his friend reading the same comic and lying at an oblique angle from each other on the large bed so that they looked like the hands of a clock at some insignificant moment of the day: twelve thirty-five, or ten twenty-three.

As Ashish watched Sunder now, rolling up the sleeves of his expensive shirt and making a poor job of it, then squaring up to the mirror, putting a glob of imported gunk into his hair and spiking it, he found it hard to believe the earlier incident had taken place.

Maybe it hadn't. He threw a superstitious glance at the No Fear poster.

'Okay, come on. My dad hates to be kept waiting,' Sunder said. He snapped off the light and the AC.

The passage opened into a bright space that smelled of the sea breeze. Ashish was marginally aware of paintings and art objects at the peripheries of this room, which was so large that it was unreal, like a film set. In the sea of expensive white, a baroque sofa, all claw-like gilt legs and serpentine frame, made a tiny atoll. Here sat Sunder's father, a small, skinny man who appeared to have put a spherical clay pot down his polo shirt. He smiled, like a frog smiles when a chubby young fly bumbles towards its lily pad. 'Ah, hello, hello,' he called across the expanse, and waved a beringed hand.

They approached, and Sunder stopped en route to grab a magazine from a coffee table. Ashish proceeded alone until he was within a metre of Sunder's father.

'Hello uncle, I'm Ashish, I go to college with Sunder,' he said, smiling what he hoped was his ingratiating, clean-living smile.

'Hm, yes, you are studying?'

'I'm studying English as well, uncle.'

'English, mhmm!' remarked Sunder's father throatily.

Ashish shifted from foot to foot.

'Hm, what does your father do, Ashish?'

'Uh, my father is an engineer, uncle.'

'Very good. Does he have his own company?' In the froggy, affable face, the beady eyes were quite hard.

'No, he works for, uh, the government. My parents are posted in Indore at the moment, actually. I'm staying with my mama in Bombay.'

'Your mama?'

'Yes, he's a — writer.'

'Oh, a writer! Very good.' And, obviously dismissing Ashish and all his race, Sunder's father rose and stalked towards the huge, polished dining table. Sunder beckoned to Ashish to follow. On the way, Ashish spotted his flowers on a side table; they looked stringy and underequipped for the occasion in a large vase.

Sunder's mother appeared, smiled distractedly in Ashish's direction, and issued instructions to one of the servants. Lunch was brought by a white-clad Maharaj, who pointed out what the various dishes were before leaving the bearer to serve them. Ashish ate a lot. Sunder's father ignored the enchiladas and pasta in favour of the standard food, which was vegetarian and excellent.

Ashish was still putting his best foot

forward. 'So aunty, Sunder said you all had a great holiday in Switzerland; what was your favourite part?'

Sunder's mother had to have the question repeated. By way of apology, she told the bearer to give Ashish more pasta. 'Switzerland, yes,' she said, her uncertain face showing some enthusiasm. 'Very good shopping and then, you know, all the lakes. We went to Berne, a lovely medieval town. Have you been to Switzerland?'

I haven't even been, Ashish silently wanted to say, to KuluManali, but he smiled, kept his end up, and said, 'Not yet.'

'Oh, you must go,' Sunder's father said suddenly and firmly. 'Travel is very important, it broadens the mind.' He stared pointedly at Ashish as though he'd said something very original, and Ashish, unsure of what to do, tittered politely. 'Besides, there are a lot of things to do in Switzerland, walking and boating, cities. It's also,' he went on thoughtfully, 'a popular place for people to move to from Europe, because it's central and has good tax arrangements.' Again he made eye contact with Ashish. 'One of the things wrong with this country, Ashish, is that we don't reward entrepreneurs. The government, bureaucrats, politicians, they all want a cut. Finally, there is little incentive to develop

127

industries. Abroad it's different.'

Ashish nodded frantically. Sunder's father continued to chomp; then he picked up a remote control from a silver dish next to him. He raised it commandingly and pressed a button. An enormous plasma television behind Ashish lit up, showing the business channel CNBC. The remainder of the meal passed in bug-like silence.

'We'll go and chat now,' Sunder told his mother after dessert. She smiled vaguely, yes, whoever the hell you are, go ahead. They went into Sunder's room where they played computer games and then lay apathetically on the bed. Ashish, still in social mode, felt obliged to do something, whether that was jump on Sunder (unlikely) or at least make conversation; he must be here for a purpose, the invitation must have meant something. He leaned on his elbows and looked towards the darkened windows, where the blinds were pulled down against the afternoon heat; the air conditioner was blasting again, and a lamp was on.

'So what do you think you'll do after, you know, we finish college?' Ashish looked across at Sunder, who scowled.

'Who cares? College is a total hassle,' said Sunder darkly. 'If I feel like it I might drop out.'

'Without a degree?' It was as though he had suggested jumping off the edge of the map.

'What does it matter? I'll join the business anyway, work for a year or two, do an MBA in America, get married.'

Ashish stared at his hands. 'You want to get married? Don't you feel too — young?'

Sunder looked into the middle distance, which happened to be the direction of the No Fear poster. He shrugged. 'People in our community always marry early. My dad says it keeps you out of trouble but it's not like it stops you doing what you want,' he said.

Ashish examined his fingers. 'Right.'

★　★　★

When he got home, no one had the time to ask him how his lunch had been. His uncle cocked an eye at him from the book he was reading; his aunt was bustling around getting ready for the wedding.

'We should go soon — are you ready?' Lakshmi mami was becoming nervous already, or irritated, it was hard to tell. Ashish glanced up, then back to the newspaper he'd picked up.

Mohan mama was immoveable in his chair, a book in his hand. 'We have to be there at seven, it's four now,' he said.

'We have to be there at six thirty and,' Lakshmi moved over to peer at the clock as though she had not already just done so, 'it's nearly four thirty now.'

Ashish darted a glance at the clock. It was slightly after four fifteen. There was a brief lull.

'Well, *I'm* going to be ready to leave by five, anyway,' announced his aunt, rustling towards the bedroom. She wore a silk sari and her good jewellery; the dot of vermilion on her forehead marked her readiness for a celebration.

Mohan turned a page; the fan rotated quietly above him and Ashish; below, the lane was still. In half an hour or so children from the surrounding buildings would emerge from enforced naps and begin to play cricket, football, or another game that gave them a pretext to shout and break loose from the good behaviour demanded in afternoon hours.

'Do you want to take a bath before we go?' came the cry from the bedroom.

Mohan read attentively, holding down the page with his hand. The other side of the book stirred under the fan.

'If you want to have a bath I'll fill up the hot water,' the voice persisted.

There was no answer.

Ashish read the same paragraph in the newspaper for the third time and thought about going to his room before the conversation between his aunt and uncle took its usual turn. Tardiness was the one thing his aunt couldn't bear; she would, he knew, become more and more importunate, her bossiness disguising distress at his uncle's inaction, and perhaps also at the fact that she was obliged to wait for him. She would continue to hustle, he would continue to resist, until they were actually on the point of being late; then he would snap at her, telling her that she was becoming neurotic and it wouldn't take them more than twenty minutes to reach the wedding. She would mention the Sunday evening traffic and burst into tears of frustration; he would stomp off to get ready. Then, a little late, flustered and chastened like children, they would set out in their best clothes, making a distinguished couple.

Ashish was looking forward to a few hours alone. He wanted to lie on his bed without his clothes, thinking about exactly what had gone on between him and Sunder for fifteen feverish minutes that afternoon, when the door of Sunder's bedroom had been not just shut, but locked, and only the orange glow of the light above the desk interrupted the near-freezing darkness of the air-conditioned room. Right afterwards, Sunder had darted into the adjacent bathroom and Ashish, disoriented, had wiped his thigh with the nearest thing to hand, a pair of socks (made by the family firm?) and checked his clothes and hair. Then his friend had emerged from the bathroom, looked at him impassively and said, 'Do you mind, I've got to go out with my parents in half an hour', and Ashish had been, on the whole, relieved to leave. He could have the actual enjoyment of the moment now, if his aunt and uncle would only finish their Laurel and Hardy routine and be gone; he looked forward to lying in his room while outside birds cried at the dusk, and his physical sensation of emptiness found its counterpart in the movement of Sunday afternoon into Sunday evening, that most depressing of times. He listened now to the rain. It fell soft and thick, and the air cooled and, in turn, became damp and tender.

8

Mohan came home one evening to find unusual smells in the house. His wife raised an eyebrow at him. 'Ashish is cooking,' she announced.

'Cooking! Very good!' He went to change his sandals and wash, and a little later ventured to the kitchen. Ashish was busy stirring milk into something lumpy and white in a saucepan on the stove top.

Mohan smiled and raised his eyebrows at the boy. No response. He cleared his throat. 'What are you making?' he enquired.

'Baked vegetables,' said Ashish tersely. 'Can you pass me the book there?' He pointed with one floury hand. Mohan picked up *Thirty Recipes for Everyday Cooking* and handed it to him.

'Damn,' muttered Ashish.

'Carrotshalfcuppeashalfcupbabycornhalfcup-mushroomshalfpacket*optional . . . half cook the vegetables until blah blah,* heat the butter until — hmm — fry the flour until cooking smell is perceptible — ' he gave the air a strong sniff and regarded his uncle suspiciously.

'I think it's burning,' Mohan said.

'Damn!'

Ashish turned off the stove, moved the saucepan with an ill-tempered clatter, and wiped his hands on his t-shirt. He marched out of the kitchen.

'Eh, Ashish,' his uncle began to protest. But Ashish was intent. He returned almost immediately, carrying the cordless telephone. He flipped to the back of the book. 'It says here that if you have any problem with the recipe you can call Yezdi Sodawaterbottlewala himself, between 5 p.m. and 7 p.m. at the *Indian Record* office — 2287,' he began murmuring to himself.

'Yezdi Sodawaterbottlewala! Oh, this is his book.' Mohan reached out a hand for the book; the boy must have found it wherever he'd wedged it into the shelf.

Ashish made a reproving noise and twitched the volume out of reach. 'Mohan mama.'

'I know him, you know. We were at school together.'

'Really?' Ashish looked up; he had a flour smear on his cheek. 'You never said,' he observed, returning to the page with the number on it. 'His columns are always in the newspaper.'

'We didn't really keep in touch, something happened,' Mohan was saying, almost to

134

himself, as Ashish dialled and then listened.

'Hello, may I speak to Mr Sodawaterbottle-wala please. This is Ashish Datye.' A pause, then: 'Sir, I'm calling about your baked vegetable recipe. From *Thirty Recipes for Everyday*. Sir. Sir, it's the white sauce, it's very lumpy. You say cook till you smell the — sir. No, I — sir. Okay sirthangyousir. Sir onemorething sir,' Ashish was, Mohan could see, quite enjoying himself, 'sir, my uncle says you were at school with him sir? Mohan Vithal Karekar. Yes, he's right here. Yes, he said. Yes hold on sir.'

Ashish held out the cordless phone. Mohan was appalled. 'He wants to speak to you, Mohan mama.' The boy shoved the white handset at Mohan and returned to the stove.

Mohan coughed. 'Hello?'

'Hello, Mohan?' The voice, high-pitched and ridiculous, hadn't changed. Despite himself he grinned. 'Yezdi.'

'How are you, Mohan? It's such a long time since we've spoken. I wasn't sure if you were even still in Bombay.'

'Yes, I'm still here,' he said, wondering if Yezdi meant that he thought he, Mohan, might have died or something.

'We should meet. That was your nephew I spoke to?'

'My sister's son. He, uh, likes cooking.'

'Very good,' said Yezdi. 'So let's meet, Mohan. How is your schedule these days?'

'Well — '

'Do you know the *Indian Record* office?' This was another irritating question; everyone knew the *Indian Record* office, which was opposite VT.

'Obviously,' said Mohan, slightly tetchily.

'How about tea tomorrow?'

'Tomorrow — tomorrow I can't.' This was untrue.

'Friday?'

'All right.'

'Will you come to the office? At five, say? I'll come downstairs.'

'All right.'

'See you on Friday then.' Yezdi hung up.

Mohan stood looking at the handset. He sighed, and felt a vague sense of unease.

Ashish had taken the saucepan off the fire and was looking at it with triumph. 'He said wait for it to cool and *then* add the milk,' he explained happily.

Mohan went outside to replace the receiver.

'*Why* is he cooking?' he asked his wife.

'He wants to invite one of his friends tomorrow. I asked him what he wanted me to make and he suddenly got very excited about this recipe. He said he wanted to make it himself.'

Mohan raised an eyebrow. 'He's using a book written by Yezdi, you know, who I went to school with.'

'Of course.'

'Ashish rang up, for the recipe, and I spoke to Yezdi as well,' he went on, frowning and rearranging some jars on the table. 'We may meet — ah, for tea.' He didn't look at her, but picked up and examined a jar, and felt the coating of rust on its lid.

'Good,' she said absently. It was getting to be time for one of her serials; she made purposefully for the television, a cup of tea in her hand, and began to unzip its plastic cover. 'Your tea's in the pan on the stove,' she said, a last bulletin to him. The television came on, with a possessive little buzz, and after a tiny silence the insanely enthusiastic voices of actors in commercials began to spill from the set. Mohan moved towards the living room window.

At first the television had been on only in the evenings, when the serials she followed were screened at eight or nine. There'd been one, to begin with; now there were at least two. When she was in communion with the set he sat near the window, reading; he would look back to see the flickering light, and her face rapt. From time to time he rose, and went to stand behind her; he never sat down, even if he watched for a few minutes continuously, because that would have indicated submission to the foolishness on screen.

'So that's why you kept coming home late?' a horrified woman said. She put her hand to her face and gasped. It was hard to tell her age because she wore so much make-up; however, it was certain that she was a virtuous character, because her eye make-up didn't make her look like a female demon: the villains always had absurd and frightening eyeliner. Her gasp replayed itself three or four times from different camera angles; one shot went close to her face in staggered degrees that rhymed with the music's exaggerated horror.

'They spin out one incident for a long time,' Mohan remarked.

His wife was hooked, but she smiled and said calmly, 'Yes, that way the script lasts longer.'

He returned to the chair.

Some time ago, Lakshmi had begun to turn on the television in the morning too. It began with the news, which included updates on the weather; that made sense in the rains, although the television often announced a rainfall more dramatic than the one actually taking place. 'City paralysed by heavy rains' ran the ticker at the bottom of the screen, which showed a familiar photograph of a flooded, low-lying subway. But the photograph was from a month earlier; that day the rain, although heavy, was normal: the trains continued to run.

Then there was, on a Hindi channel, the television astrologer. 'Today is not a good day for Virgos,' he said calmly. He wore a kurta with gold buttons. 'Virgos in advanced age may face severe health problems because of Rahu. Those who have been unwell for some time could pass away today or between today and Thursday.'

'And Libras?' the newsreader asked helpfully. This man, one of Mohan's favourite television personalities, was almost definitely wearing a toupee. His hair was improbably thick and dark; it sat in a fat cushion above his forehead. He wore spectacles, and wrinkled his brow when a serious item came on the schedule.

'Libras — your ruler Venus is in debility so you may experience some tiredness. Avoid heavy food.'

And so the television, and its compelling chatter, had hijacked the morning as well. Ashish would wander in after his bath, take up the remote and flick to a music channel, where the latest English and Hindi tunes blared; his aunt, after a pause, would come and watch half a song with him, then flick back to the news. Mohan, since it would have been too churlish to turn off the television, sometimes changed to a Marathi news channel. But he missed the silence.

The day after was to be a public holiday; already Saraswati Park was in festive mood. From one of the Gogate flats pop music blasted out, the same two or three songs in English, over and over.

The theme tune of *Daughters of the House* began to play. Lakshmi got up; with a yawn of satisfaction she went into the kitchen. Mohan followed her to get a glass of water. Ashish's baked vegetables were safely in the small oven that Megha had brought home once, and which they hardly used. Lakshmi was helping Ashish to clear up the clouds of flour and cheese that had settled.

'I could call Satish tomorrow,' she said to Mohan, but he was feeling irritable, because while sitting in the chair he'd been trying to work out the details of the story he'd begun earlier, and it had been noisy, and he hadn't been able to stop himself from listening to her soap episode; now he had a vague anxiety about whether Aarti, who had murdered her husband and buried him in a chikoo orchard, would be found out by her sisters-in-law, and when the husband's ghost would get around to visiting her. No one should watch television, he thought bitterly. He frowned and knitted his eyebrows in response to her remark.

She was surprised; he was usually encouraging about seeing Satish. 'Otherwise he'll be alone all day,' she pointed out.

'What's the difference with any other day?' asked Mohan, for the sake of argument, thinking more of his story than of his brother-in-law, though a vague unpleasantness remained in his mind from the last time they'd seen Satish.

'Well, I don't have to,' she said sharply. 'I'll call him another time, or I'll go to see him.'

Mohan noticed his nephew giving him a blank look before leaving the room. He sighed. 'How long will dinner be?' he asked, though he wasn't especially hungry.

'Soon,' she said, 'just as soon as I've cleared up this mess.' She turned her back on him.

9

Ashish woke, as usual, to the electronic howl outside. He groaned, and mashed his face a little more into the pillow. Dr Gogate's car alarm went off at the same time every day, prompted by the passing of the milk delivery man on his bicycle. The pealing would continue until everyone in the surrounding buildings had noticed — everyone, apparently, apart from the doctor. Was he in the toilet? Taking a bath? Saying his prayers? Engaging in tantric rituals with Mrs Gogate (her face displaying modest unwillingness, modulated by wifely indulgence)? It was hard to know but impossible not to wonder, and Ashish sat up and yawned just as the alarm was finally deactivated.

The car was a Honda, large and sleek; the doctor kept it parked outside the flats. Ashish feigned a lack of interest, but when he was passing it he experienced conflicting desires: one was to look at it carefully and catalogue its features — power steering, airbags, central locking, hydraulic brakes, and extra-powerful air conditioning; the other was to find something sharp, a key would have been ideal, and make a nice bright scratch along the new paintwork.

But he was happy this morning as he disentangled himself from the sheet. Sunder had come over for dinner yesterday. It had been a little odd, of course; the flat wasn't exactly what Sunder was used to, but Ashish thought it had gone off fairly well. They'd eaten the baked vegetables he'd made, and his aunt and uncle, subdued by an earlier quarrel, hadn't asked too many embarrassing questions. Mohan mama had tried, briefly, to talk to Sunder about books, but Ashish had rounded this off swiftly. Sunder, as ever, hadn't been talkative; he and Ashish had gone up to the terrace after dinner.

The evening was midnight-blue and humidly warm; a single fluorescent light at the other end of the terrace cast a greenish glow that hardly reached to where they stood. Ashish was suddenly conscious of the social niceties; he felt they should converse for a while, and even peered theatrically over the terrace wall, observing to himself that he could see the watchman's hut and the banyan tree. 'It's nice, isn't it?' he said. He wanted Sunder to acknowledge Saraswati Park in some way, at least make the conventional remarks.

Sunder belched slightly, then put his

thumbs in his belt loops and stared into the nightscape of darkness, fluorescent light, unidentified roofs, and old trees that made dark masses near the ground. He obviously had no idea where he was, and, equally plainly, was wondering how long it'd take him to get back to civilization.

'This is a really nice area,' Ashish said, suddenly enthusiastic (to Mayank, earlier, he'd only moaned about how far Saraswati Park was from anything familiar). 'Of course, there's no sea view, but there are a lot of open spaces — old trees, that kind of thing. And my aunt and uncle are nice, aren't they? My mama knows a lot, because he reads so much — '

Wearying, apparently, of these subjects, Sunder came a little closer to Ashish, and kissed him, a perfunctory swoosh around Ashish's mouth by a fat, hot tongue. Then he grabbed one of Ashish's hands and guided it towards his zip, at the same time reaching for Ashish's crotch, which promptly and politely sprang into responsive life. They were safe there for some time; Ashish had half bolted the terrace door so that anyone who came up would have to rattle it and shout to be let in.

He opened the bedroom curtains. This morning it was raining lightly, almost a mist, but the air wasn't dark. He sang to himself as

144

he bumbled into the bathroom, a film tune that mixed Hindi and English, soppy lyrics and pumping beat: 'Dus bahaane kar ke le gaye dil, le gaye dil, dus bahaane kar ke le gaye dil, you stole my heart away.'

The textile company that Satish mama had nearly joined had continued to send him their annual calendar, a mistake of record-keeping that had survived half a century. In years when profits had been high, the calendar had been more lavishly produced; one of these hung in the bathroom. It was a large canvas sheet, printed with a scene from the life of Krishna: the god appeared as an adolescent cowherd, hiding coyly behind a piece of cloth and playing his flute while semi-naked, round-breasted milkmaids took a bath in the river. It was a stock subject, but it had been nicely executed. The year of the calendar was 1969 — the months and dates were printed along the bottom in neat batches — and the painting's clean lines and flat colours had a hint of Pop Art.

The milkmaids covered their mouths, laughingly aghast: their clothes had been thrown into the branches of nearby trees and they'd have to come out of the river naked. The young god smiled naughtily. Ashish, as he brushed his teeth, winked at him.

★ ★ ★

He and Sunder developed a routine. They'd
hang out together in college — Mayank had
now been sidelined — and, after classes
ended, they'd eat cake in a coffee shop in
Colaba; sometimes they'd go to Sunder's flat,
especially if his mother was out.

'Let's go to your place,' said Ashish one
afternoon when they came out of the day's
final lecture.

'Uh . . . ' said Sunder.

'Why, is aunty home?'

'Oye, Sunder, where are you and your
girlfriend off to now?' Someone thumped
Ashish between the shoulder blades.

'Fuck off,' Ashish said.

'Calm down miss, don't get upset.'
Snickers from the other two boys; one was
Ravi, Sunder's friend. They laughed and ran
down the stairs, jostling a caretaker who was
half-heartedly mopping one of the landings.

Sunder looked hangdog.

'Ignore it, they're just idiots,' Ashish said.
He almost enjoyed these small displays of
antagonism; they were what he was used to.
At the gate they got into a taxi. Sunder couldn't
deal with buses; he said they were dirty and
mosquitoes bred under the seats, a claim so
bizarre that Ashish hadn't known how to respond.

'Cuffe Parade,' Ashish told the taxi driver. He put his arm across the back of the seat. Sunder twitched and readjusted himself until Ashish removed his arm.

'What's the matter?'

Sunder looked hassled. 'Nothing. Stop being such a girl.'

'Oh, okay.' Ashish sulked for a bit in his corner of the cab.

Sunder leaned towards the driver. 'Don't go via Causeway, go from outside.' He sat back again and said, without looking at Ashish, 'My dad's on my case, he's told me to get on with studying and make something of myself.'

'Make, like what?'

'You know, do better: pass stuff. He says he can't get me into a good business school just by giving them a donation.'

The cab took the left turn near the Cooperage, honking futilely at a BEST bus ahead to hurry up. Ashish tried to imagine Sunder impressing any business school professors at an interview; he'd look bullish, trussed into smart clothes, and be as inarticulate as ever. The thought brought a rush of affection. He put his arm back around Sunder, who this time didn't resist. 'Chill maaro, you're attending regularly, we'll study together; you'll be fine.'

When they got to Sunder's building, Sunder paid the cab driver (he regularly demanded, and got, chunks of money from his mother) and they sauntered through the cool black lobby. The security guard salaamed. Ashish had nearly forgotten the nerve-racking first few visits. He chattered happily while they waited for the lift. 'So, should we do something after this semester's exams? Maybe get a few people together and go to Lonavala or something, Karjat? Mayank, you don't know Mayank properly but you'd like him, his dad could probably get us a reservation at a circuit house somewhere, what do you think? It'd be fun, waterfalls and everything.'

Sunder stood silently staring at the indicator that showed the lift's descent from each floor to the next. Finally it arrived, levitated for the prescribed instant above the ground floor, then came to earth. The doors parted; the attendant touched his cap to Sunder. 'You again,' his gaze said to Ashish. Being polite to people never worked, they always thought it was because you had no power. Ashish gazed modestly at the floor of the lift, where little mounds of dirt gathered, and then at the shoes of the attendant, who probably lived in a far-away suburb and had a long train journey to get here — he must polish them again after he got to work, otherwise they'd be mud-spattered in this weather. Then they were at the fourteenth floor. They came out on the landing: a window was open in the stairwell. From outside, the smell of salt and the cry of seagulls. Sunder rang his own doorbell.

'Don't you have your key?'

Sunder shrugged. 'Why bother, Hitesh should be there, anyway he doesn't need to sleep all afternoon.'

The servant duly appeared, opened the door, simpered at Sunder and stood aside to let them in. They set off down the corridor. 'Is my mother here?' Sunder asked.

'Gone out.'

In Sunder's room, Ashish threw down his bag. Sunder turned on the light and the air conditioner and half drew the blinds. He kicked off his shoes. Ashish sprawled on the bed, and Sunder came and sat next to him; he sighed.

Just as Ashish was undoing Sunder's belt the door opened noiselessly.

'Madam said to give you this,' Hitesh said. He came in, assessed the situation with sharp eyes, and put down a tray with glasses of juice and a plate of cake on the bedside table. When he went out, eyes lowered, he closed the door properly; the insolent click was a comment.

'Shit.'

'Does it matter?'

Sunder shoved away Ashish's returning hand. 'Obviously, don't be stupid.'

'But why, what could he say? And even if he did — '

'Look, you don't understand,' Sunder spat out.

'Oh, I don't?' Ashish felt a prickle in his eyes. 'Why's that?'

'I have responsibilities to my family, to the business,' Sunder muttered, a line he'd apparently been hearing a lot recently.

'So?'

'I can't just — anyway, my father told me when I didn't clear last year that I have to be more sincere.'

'But you *are* — we've been through this — I thought I explained — '

'No.' Sunder batted Ashish's hand away again, this time from his shoulder. He looked cow-like, miserable, and obstinate. 'Anyway, what's the point? I don't want to be one of those paedo types.' He avoided Ashish's stare. 'I'm not judging you,' he went on, looking shifty.

'Don't talk shit, you're just repeating things you've heard on *Dawson's Creek*.'

'I don't want to deal with all this. I don't want the hassle. I don't feel the same as you.

How do I know you're not just using me?' He lifted his head and gazed securely at Ashish.

'For what?' said Ashish incredulously. His mind went back to all the homework assignments he'd written for Sunder, all the times he'd sat and explained class notes to him.

'For my money, or because my house is in town, or anything — how do I know?'

Ashish bounded up. 'What do you mean!' he found himself yelping, hands on hips, like one of the characters in American soaps.

'You never pay cab fare,' Sunder intoned, 'you never have any money.'

'But you always said it was fine — and you're the one who can't take the bus!'

Sunder looked stubborn. 'I think you should leave.'

'You can't just throw me out!' Actually, of course, he could. Ashish had a mad urge to do something, he didn't know what: break something or run to the kitchen and scream at the servants, Do you even know what we do in the afternoons here? But perhaps that was the point.

Sunder merely slouched on the bed, looking sanctimonious, and slightly anxious. Ashish picked up his bag. 'You're making a mistake,' he said bitterly. 'I'm the only interesting friend you have. And anyway, who'll help you with your work now?' He wanted to cry.

'My parents are getting me a tutor.'

'Oho, so who was using who then? Whom, I mean! Who was using whom, haan?' Ashish's voice was rising.

'Don't shout.'

Ashish stomped towards the door, and looked back, waiting for Sunder to say something else. He didn't. He yanked it open and began the walk down the long, suspiciously quiet corridor towards the front door; he wrestled with it for some time before the servant appeared and, smiling to himself, opened it. He pressed the button for the lift, then, not wanting to wait, began to walk down. The stairwell was surprising for a building like this: bare grey cement and plain tiles, a smell of the sea. Ashish passed a sleeping servant or two and sniffed to himself; he couldn't cry here. Finally he reached the lobby. A man with a briefcase was waiting for the lift; he turned to look at Ashish, who flapped stormily out in his sandals. In the sun, the noise of buses and taxis and the warm air recalled him to the world.

He walked slowly down Cuffe Parade, eyed by a couple of liveried drivers who leaned against shiny cars. In the open air, he felt saner. It couldn't be such a big thing, this argument; maybe it had just been brewing. 'People who are really close to each other always argue,' his mother had told him when he was a small child, after he'd spent an evening huddled on the end of the bed listening to his parents blast each other. He had with relief accepted this as the truth. Most of his friendships puttered along satisfactorily without upheaval; this one was different, that must mean something. Still, he cringed at the things Sunder had said, especially about money and his house; in his mind he'd replayed a thousand times that Sunday lunch, especially the part where he'd walked, apparently for miles, across the white marble floor of the living room towards Sunder's father.

On Cuffe Parade the gulmohars were dropping tiny wet leaves that stuck to the pavement. A man outside a building with an odd, sharply sloping drive was sweeping up; but the leaves kept falling.

★   ★   ★

When he got home he closed the outer door with a quiet click, hoping to slip into his room. But his uncle jumped up from the cane chair. Ashish's heart sank; Mohan mama's face was eager and he held a small sheaf of

153

paper. It was a story he'd written.

'Do you — ahem, you could read it if you want,' Mohan said.

Ashish took the papers from him and smiled. 'I'll just read it,' he said. He went to his room, sat at the desk and puzzled through the thing, written out in his uncle's neat hand. The story seemed to be about a woman who worked as a prostitute, and a day when she realized that she couldn't do it any longer; then she carried on. The turning point was an encounter she had with an old neighbour, who had a discussion with her about freedom. But Ashish found it hard to concentrate. Mohan mama would be waiting in the other room to hear what he thought. He flicked through the book, *Become a Writer*. Surely it had answers for moments like this? Across the lane, the empty apartment which the owls visited was blank. Ashish thought of other afternoons at Sunder's house, in the half-dark, air-conditioned room, and his stomach felt hollow. For the first time he feared that Sunder might tell other people about what had gone on — but no, that would implicate him too. Ashish saw himself, again, walking across the white living room, and the lunch that had followed, with CNBC on the television behind him.

He went back to the living room, holding the paper and *Become a Writer*. 'It's interesting, Mohan mama. It's good — very good,' he said. But his voice was flat. His uncle's face, which had lit up, began to look gloomy. 'No, really. It's good,' Ashish repeated.

'But — I feel,' his uncle began, and stopped.

'Maybe you could put it away for a little while and then look at it again. See, here,' he held out the book. 'There's a chapter on revision, and it says that often the real work isn't the first time you write the story, but when you work on it later and make it better.'

'Hm,' said Mohan, taking the book, which he put beside him, a heavy hand on top of it. He reached out his other hand for the paper.

'And what will you write next?' Ashish hated having to be in this encouraging role.

'Hrrm.' Mohan looked at him, but apparently without recognizing him. Good, now I've also managed to make him miserable, Ashish thought; but he had no energy to find the right thing to say. He went back to his room and sat at the desk to stare into the vacuum of the darkened lane.

If only he had been like his uncle, someone for whom each detail of life had its own significance, revelatory as though it had been a clue in a cosmic detective story. Yet there were moments when the story seemed to go out of life. He only saw his desires clearly in the world, and then the forest of obstacles that would prevent them from being attained. Ah dear Juliet/Why art thou yet so fair? Well, not Juliet exactly, or fair exactly; but there was nothing like deprivation to sharpen longing. Surely Sunder would call?

'Eh.' It was his uncle, bringing him tea. He put the cup on the desk and then lingered to say, 'I got the name and number of an English professor who might give you tuition, from your aunt. Someone Satish mama knows or knows of.'

'Oh, okay,' Ashish said without enthusiasm. Since his uncle still wasn't leaving, he added, 'Good.'

'Call him some time, go and meet him, he might be able to help you.'

'Okay, sure.'

'How's the studying going?'

'Not bad.' He was so tired of life he wanted to cry, quietly, with his face buried in a soft cloth, while someone patted him between the shoulder blades.

'Well, don't stay up late working every night.'

'Okay.'

When his uncle had gone, he shoved the

156

piece of paper under a book, checked his phone again, and returned to staring out of the window.

★ ★ ★

The next day it was easy to be on time for college, since he'd slept only part of the night. At three o'clock, on the dot, he woke with a start, sweating, in the midst of a terrible dream. After that, he couldn't sleep; he rolled over and over, got up, turned off the fan, then turned it on again, tried pushing off the sheet, then swaddling himself in it: nothing was any use. He spent the extra hours thinking about Sunder and what would happen at college in the morning.

In the lecture theatre, he sat three rows from the back, on the same side as the entrance. He tried not to look at the door; he opened his bag, took out his notebook and two pens, stared into the distance, frowned down at his paper. Suddenly he heard the familiar deep voice and laughter, and whipped his head round. Sunder came in, walked past Ashish, and went to sit with Ravi and one of the girls.

Ashish felt the blood rush to his face and neck. He must have gone a dark red, perhaps purple. He began to doodle furiously in the margin of his page. He always drew the same things, he had no idea why: plain, square apartment blocks with darkened windows; palaces with striped domes that looked like ice cream; stars in the sky; palm trees. He was sketching a coconut, and trying not to be aware of the girl who sat next to Sunder pointing at him and whispering, and the two boys laughing, when someone came to sit next to him. A hand nudged his elbow. Mayank.

'Hey!' He smiled.

Right after that, the teacher came in, a predictable mauve cloud of bad sari, bad hair, bad glasses and bad mood. She was dripping wet and extracted her lecture notes from a plastic shopping bag. 'Someone open a window,' she said irritably, and so they had the sound of the rain to listen to as well as her even voice following the familiar headings.

Eventually the bell went. Ashish hadn't known what he'd do in the longer break between classes — he'd thought of walking around the block and returning only for the next class — but Mayank stuck to him. The other boy put an arm around his shoulder when they walked towards the cafeteria.

The stairs were slick with dirty water. Ashish heard Ravi's voice: 'Coming to the dhaba?'

'No, let's go somewhere decent.' They pushed past and went unhurriedly down the stairs, jostling each other and laughing. Ashish caught the eye of one of the cleaners, who was pretending to mop a puddle on the floor; then the whiskery, spectacled face turned away again.

Ashish was so grateful to Mayank he didn't know what to say. He sat in the cafeteria, feeling tender enough to cry, and smiled at his tea, and his potato vada; it lay on his plate, round and fat, smelling of oil.

★   ★   ★

Now he spent the hours outside lectures at home in Saraswati Park, reading old comics and popping comfortingly cardboard-like Marie biscuits into his mouth one after the other. He was exhausted all the time; the three o'clock internal alarm continued to operate, as though the world needed urgently to alert him to the fact that he was still unloved.

One afternoon, a couple of weeks after the last time that he and Sunder had spoken, the old electric doorbell coughed, then trilled. Ashish was lying on his bed, in a small sea of biscuit crumbs, reading an Amar Chitra Katha comic about the life of Bhagat Singh.

His aunt had gone out; he thought about ignoring the bell. It rang again. He sighed loudly, 'Yes, yes, coming at once, heaven forbid you should have to wait', and headed towards the door. At this time of day it was probably someone selling bananas or something.

He opened the door. Madhavi Gogate stood there. 'Hi,' she said cheerfully. She had all the assurance of a married woman in her thirties, he noticed; an aunty-style bearing that it was hard to resist.

'Hello?' he said doubtfully.

'Let me in, donkey.'

'Oh, right.' He opened the outer door. 'My aunt's gone out,' he said. He was aware of how saggy he felt; his shoulders slumped, his chest seemed to have caved in, and he wasn't sure whether he had biscuit crumbs around his mouth. He couldn't imagine what she wanted but doubtless she would now get lost decently.

'No, I came to see you.'

He stared at her. A terrible suspicion was forming in his mind.

Madhavi came into the house. 'Now,' she said pleasantly, as one instructing an idiot, 'you ask me to sit down and offer me something to eat and drink.'

'Look, I don't even know what there is. What do you want?'

She sighed and walked into the living room, where she sat down on the divan. 'Some juice, or sherbet. Anything cold. And could you put on the fan?'

Ashish hurried to the kitchen. He opened a cupboard and started to rummage: here was an old bottle of Roohafza, and a packet of orange squash crystals.

'Ashish!'

He returned to the living room. Was she leaving?

Madhavi was still seated; she waved a plump forearm. 'The fan.'

He turned it on, stared at her, and returned to the kitchen, where he mixed a glass of Roohafza and a glass of squash and put them on a tray with a plate of chaklis.

'Mm, thanks!' Madhavi reached out and helped herself to a chakli and the squash. She crunched, then took a sip of the orangeade. Ashish plonked the glass of Roohafza down on the low table. It immediately began to perspire. He glanced at it sympathetically.

'So, Ashish, what do you do when you're not studying?'

'Well — ' he looked towards the window, which was smeared with rain, as though for inspiration. 'I have various projects,' he said repressively. 'In fact, I'm slightly busy just now. So — '

161

Madhavi leaned towards him. Her face was kind. 'No friends, huh? Don't worry, we can hang out, do stuff together sometimes.'

Ashish was outraged. 'That's not what I meant. I have several friends — at college. It's just that I used to live in town, so — '

She beamed at him. 'Don't worry,' she said. 'We're friends now.' Then her eye fell on his glass. 'You're not having your Roohafza?'

Obediently he lifted it to his mouth; as he drank, the condensation piddled onto his trousers.

'Oh-oh,' said Madhavi sympathetically. And then, 'Well, it's just water, after all.'

10

Noises came differently today to the man in the cramped room. He heard his younger sister's voice, clear and plaintive; the cry of a knife sharpener; then voices in the corridor of the old tenement. What was all the racket? He tried to go to the window, but halfway there, he began to feel lightheaded; he stopped and laughed. The base of his skull throbbed. He put up his left hand — his right seemed to have gone dead — and rubbed his nape. He felt unusual, almost euphoric; tired, too.

There were some things on the bed. He swept them onto the floor and lay down. The light bulb was behaving oddly, moving like a kaleidoscope, the ones they used to have as children. You shook them and the pattern altered but the components remained the same, rearranging themselves as you turned the barrel. He saw a particular corner of the house in Tardeo, always people around, Lakshmi, and their youngest brother, Ravindra, who'd died at a few years old — he'd been a sweet little boy. He felt only happiness now, in bubbles, and smiled watching the blurred, tessellate forms of the light. Again the sounds melted into one humming, but beautifully, with a drum beat — he fancied he heard his own name being called; then it stopped. He started to laugh, then wondered if he would vomit. Not yet. The light was different, like midday, but it was the electric lamp. But how wonderful: it was like sunshine in the courtyard where he played badminton with his sister, the shuttlecock flying into the brightness. You ran, blindly, in what you thought was the right direction, then it came down; you couldn't see it, white falling through white and the sun; finally you lashed out and there was laughter all around if you had missed it. An odd sense of humiliation. He began to shiver. With his toes he felt for the blanket at the foot of the bed. He was shaking as he tore it open; it was heavy, and his fingers slipped on the satin edging. At last he crawled under it. Now, if the light could have been turned off, for it hurt his eyes; but it was a great exertion to envisage this, and instead he drew the blanket over his face; that well-known woolly smell, it smelled of him, ah, who else?

The headache was back; he didn't feel, after all, so well, and the humming from outside and inside resumed, congealed, heard as through a tunnel, or as though the sounds themselves had weight and flight: they rose, then fell, just out of reach.

★ ★ ★

Lakshmi put the receiver down. 'There's no answer.'

Mohan turned. 'I'll go there,' he said. He tried to feel irritated with Satish, but his own guilt about the moment of ill temper had been poisoning his mood for days now. First there had been the argument with his wife, and then this morning he had had an idiotic dream that he couldn't quite remember, about looking for but not finding his brother-in-law in a library; he had woken feeling strangely wistful.

'Shall I ring him one more time?'

'What's the point?' He went to the bedroom to put on his sandals. When he came out she was holding the receiver again. 'There's no answer,' she repeated.

Mohan pocketed his wallet. 'I'll go,' he said, and made for the door.

All the way to Grant Road he didn't have a good feeling. But, he reasoned to himself, there'd been other times when he'd been more worried. Once, Satish had been supposed to turn up at their house, but hadn't — this was years earlier, before mobile phones and the like existed — and Mohan had gone to look for him, in exasperation, because Lakshmi was beginning to panic. Eventually he'd found Satish sitting on a bench on the platform at Grant Road station. 'Satish!' he'd said accusingly, but also with relief.

'Oh, Mohan,' his brother-in-law had greeted him. 'What are you doing here?' and he'd shifted along on the bench to make room. Later he'd explained that the afternoon trains had been full; he'd tried to get on and been pushed out again by the crowd in the second class compartment, so he'd simply sat down to wait for a quieter time. Mohan hadn't recriminated about the lack of even a phone call; it occurred to him that his brother-in-law wasn't used to people worrying about him.

It was a slow train that Mohan took from Dadar. A pair of crows sat in the open door of the compartment, quarrelling over what might have been a piece of fish. They made him smile; they were more human, these Bombay crows, than many Bombayites remembered to be. The elder, fatter one poked his beak reprovingly at the younger, who pretended to turn his back and sulk. Then, inch by inch, the thinner crow wheedled his way back into the affair, and the elder, despite his frock-coated pomposity, made a few gurgling sounds of acceptance.

Mohan was facing the wrong way, next to the window, so that he could watch the crows. In a few stations' time the smell of the sea grew stronger and he jumped off the train at Grant Road, which was quiet today. He looked up and down the platform, but Satish wasn't there.

It was perhaps a fifteen-minute walk from the station. He passed the shacks of a group of Pardhis, those startlingly beautiful tribals who came from elsewhere in the state and always seemed to end up as beggars; they wouldn't settle down for long enough to go to schools or keep jobs, and had a reputation, unfairly, for being thieves. Two children sat outside one of the shacks, which were really just bits of canvas tied against the station fence; they looked up at him with their enormous, inky black eyes and smiled, and he waved to them. But what a life. Something made him walk faster as he neared the road where Satish lived. Whatever it was, it would be good to get the episode over with. He'd been a fool to have that argument with his wife, even though now, as he considered the usual course of a day spent with his brother-in-law, he remembered why he'd been surly about the invitation. But Satish was family; they were all he had. As a young man he had very much admired Satish — he was more brilliant and educated than anyone Mohan had known. How would Mohan have felt, for example, if his own brother had happened to be in a similar position — alone like Satish? Being obliged to spend large amounts of time with Vivek would, in many ways, have been worse. You only saw yourself truly when you met your siblings, was that true or merely half true? It was in any case an exasperating affair, this unavoidable recognition.

When he came to the building he looked up at Satish's window and thought for a moment that he saw movement; he was reassured. But this wasn't the window; Satish's was at the end of the corridor.

At the foot of the stairs two breathless young children were squealing and chasing each other for a red rubber ball that they bounced off the walls of the open corridor. When he reached the first floor he saw a tall young man and a woman he vaguely recognized as the neighbour standing near Satish's door, which was closed. Mohan approached them; they looked relieved.

'Is he here?' the woman asked.

Mohan was bewildered. 'Where else would he be?'

'We thought he might be with you,' she said. 'We knocked earlier and there was no answer. I was a little worried.'

He looked from one to the other of their young, blank faces, and realized that they expected him to have a solution. He went to the door, tried, knocked, and then called Satish's name.

'It's me, Mohan,' he added, feeling foolish; it was a detail for the benefit of the audience. 'Open the door, re,' he said more gruffly.

Still silence in the golden-lit passage, where the early evening light warmed the concrete and stone chip floor tiles and the cement parapet of the open corridor that ran next to all the flats.

The young man spoke. 'Do you think we'd better try to get in?'

Mohan knocked on the door, rattled the bolt again, and called out Satish's name. Despite the noise of a television from somewhere else, they seemed to hear the fan whirr inside the silent flat.

'Yes,' he said.

He and the young man threw their shoulders against the door, and tried kicking it; the bolts were quite solid, though, and Mohan kept imagining the acid remarks his brother-in-law would make when he returned. Finally the young man charged against the door, and there was a tearing sound. They pushed it open.

The tiny apartment was brightly lit and smelled fusty. Mohan went in, and the back of his mind registered that the young man was telling his wife not to follow them. In the electric light, it took Mohan's eyes a moment to travel between the cupboard, the window, the floor, and then the bed, where there was a bundle in a blanket. He heard himself say something and went to pull away the blanket. Then he knelt, listening to see if he could feel a pulse or any breath.

The young man took out his mobile. 'Should I call an ambulance?'

Mohan took off his glasses. 'Yes,' he said. He squatted next to the bed, looking at his brother-in-law's face, which was a strange colour; he was contorted, and part of his gums showed. The ear Mohan could see, though, looked quite normal, and this sight somehow made him feel terrible, and indecent. He was perplexed to find a tear rolling down his face.

The young man was dictating the address to the ambulance service. 'After the post office, take a right — looks like it might have been a stroke. No. No.'

Mohan took out his mobile phone from his pocket. He never used it, and had resisted acquiring it for a long time. He dialled his own number. Ashish picked up.

'Hello?'

'Ashish, I'm going to need you to come here with your aunt. Make sure she's okay.'

'What — '

'Now give her the phone,' Mohan said gently.

His wife came on the line. 'What is it?' she said. 'What's happened?'

Mohan rubbed his forehead, between his eyes. 'There's been an accident,' he heard himself say, as tiredly and resignedly as though he'd been confessing to something.

11

'He was my brother, my only remaining sibling,' Lakshmi said.

It was the first non-functional sentence she'd uttered in days; it had been two and a half weeks since Satish's death. Mohan was in his pyjamas. He paused on the threshold of their room and waited for more, but it didn't come.

'I know,' he said eventually. Still silence, and he resumed the journey into the bathroom. He passed a hand over his recently shaven head; the gesture had become a habit. The new hair, quite grizzled, was surprisingly soft.

As he brushed his teeth in the bathroom's unsympathetic fluorescent light, he considered the cremation. It had been a depressing occasion. Not that these things were ever pleasant, but the continual, drizzling rain hadn't helped. They had had to have it at an actual burning ground, at Banganga, because there were no slots at the electric crematorium. They hadn't been many: the three of them, including Ashish; Vivek and his wife; and the young neighbours, who looked mildly embarrassed. Later, Lakshmi had decided to put a small notice in the afternoon paper and have an informal gathering after the eleventh day. About a dozen people appeared for this; they were elderly men and women, several of them Satish's ex-students. He turned out to have been popular, in his way: he had been the kind of teacher, and certainly the kind of individual, whom few people forgot.

Mohan had found himself offering tea, squash, and snacks to the ageing bachelors and bachelorettes in his house. They in turn proffered their reminiscences.

'He was so witty. Strict, but also fair,' one woman said. She was plump, short and slight, with grey hair and spectacles; she wore a modestly cut salwar kameez. He imagined her, years earlier, slim, with long hair in a neat plait: she would have been one of the keen students. Perhaps she had had a special affection for Satish. There were others, too: a high court judge who'd studied under Satish (his driver and police escort waited downstairs next to a white Ambassador); a neighbour's son whom he'd helped to prepare for the civil service exam; and an earnest, middle-aged woman who had come to Satish for help in writing letters to the municipality about the garden in front of her tenement — a nearby block of apartments was trying to turn it into a parking lot.

Mohan now gargled, spat, used the tongue cleaner and washed his face. He turned out the light and returned to the bedroom, where his wife was a silent mass under the sheet. He shook out his own top sheet, got into bed, and lay quietly for a while, thinking about Ashish. The boy had insisted on shaving his head too. 'You really needn't,' Mohan had pointed out; after all, Satish had been no direct relation of his. 'No, I'm coming with you,' Ashish said. Perhaps it had been a sign of loyalty to his aunt. He'd been odd, a little down in the mouth lately, but that could have been anything: the season, worries about his studies, a quarrel with a friend — they hadn't again seen that rather bovine young man who'd come for dinner. Mohan didn't want to pry. He'd noticed though that Ashish had been good at the condolence meeting; he'd gone about handing out drinks and introducing people to each other as though shyness was the last thing in the world he'd ever suffered from. He was a funny child, not a child at all, really; they should do something for him. Mohan would remind him again to go and see that professor, the one Satish had mentioned, who might give the boy extra tuitions.

Something else went through his mind

— something he'd been supposed to do — he didn't remember, but it would come back.

The fan's rhythm, the rotating blades and the swinging orbit of the hub, hit a groove that seemed inevitable, as though the appliance were repeating the last phrase uttered in a conversation and the sleepy listener was simply trying to grasp this one remark, over and over.

★　★　★

The rain had been uncertain for a while; it began again. Long, cool showers soaked everything in their reach; while they lasted, the only thing to do was take shelter and wait. One morning, in the damp porch of their block, Mohan stared glumly at the weather. The ground floor stairwell had been hollowed out by an earlier genius; it filled with water whenever there was heavy rain. At the far end of the lane, just after the watchman's hut, a patch of sunlight gleamed on newly washed leaves. But Mohan remained stuck where he was — it made no sense to rush through the remaining fifty yards of shower, he'd be drenched.

Ashish went off joylessly every day to college; he returned by early evening. When Mohan asked him if he didn't want to meet his friends any more he just shrugged and carried on drying his head with a towel. His satchel, dripping, was kicked into a corner of his room. 'I have tea with Mayank from school, sometimes, but otherwise what's the point of hanging around in town after classes end? May as well come home,' he said, sounding put-upon in the manner of a much older man.

Mohan tried, in his own way, to cheer Ashish and Lakshmi up. On Sunday morning after breakfast he said robustly, 'What should we do today?'

No one even glanced up. Lakshmi was reading a section of the paper, her morning cup of instant coffee beside her, and Ashish was wandering towards the television. The flat was damp and gloomy, the electric lights were on; outside it was raining steadily.

Mohan repeated, 'Come on, let's do something! How about a trip to Kanheri?' He imagined the park's fresh smell after the morning rain.

His wife merely looked at him, then went back to her paper. Ashish said, 'Don't be funny, Mohan mama, imagine sliding around the caves in this weather.'

Nothing could be done with people like this. Mohan retreated to his chair to fume. He cleared his throat. 'Ashish,' he reminded his nephew, 'don't forget to call Professor Narayan this week.'

'Mmh,' said Ashish. He had assumed his preferred Sunday morning pose, stretched out in front of the television with apparently only his upper back still in contact with the chair.

'And sit properly, you'll get a back problem.'

'Hmh.'

★   ★   ★

A month later, after the Ganesh festival, it was time to think about clearing up Satish's flat. They didn't yet know what was to happen with his things, or what the procedure would be about the flat, which might revert to the housing society. But the dusty, untidy room had been on Mohan's mind. It was partly to resolve this discomfort that he told his wife, on Friday night, that he would go and make a start the next day.

Lakshmi, sitting on the bed and plaiting her hair, was silent. Her expressions these days were bruised, as though she existed under a perpetual affront.

'Will you come with me?' he asked.

She shook her head, and began to tie a thread round the end of the plait. He noticed, incongruously, the grey hairs at the side of her head, and that she looked like a little girl in her printed nightdress.

'Don't throw anything away,' she said.

He was stung. 'What makes you think I want to go and destroy your brother's possessions?' But he reminded himself to be calm. 'I'll just go and clean out the cupboards, tidy up a little, and put things in order. Then you can look through his things when you want to, and decide what's to be done,' he said. 'Have you heard from the lawyer?'

It was likely that Satish would have left his things to Lakshmi, but he had little to leave.

'No, I called the office once, but they said that the man he dealt with is away. They said there is a recent copy of the thing,' she said. She put her comb down, swung her legs onto the bed and began to unfold her sheet.

'The will?'

'Yes, from a month or two ago. You are an executor. They said if there's no hurry we can have the will read in a couple of weeks when this fellow comes back, he handled all of Satish's affairs. I don't care, it doesn't make any difference, it's not going to bring him back.'

And she turned onto her side, her back to him.

Mohan stood there, a half-unfolded clean kurta in his hand, feeling unhappy for a variety of reasons: one was that she was so obviously unhappy; another was that she had become sentimental about her brother in a way that was unbounded, impossible to reason with. He sighed, and turned out the light.

★　★　★

The next day, he took a train, changing at Kurla and then at Dadar, and went to Satish's flat. It was odd to leave the station, pass the smiling Pardhi children playing in a puddle next to their tarpaulin shelter, and walk up the same street, where now the gulmohar's red flowers were pasted like frail paper toys against the glistening wet macadam and tiny, petal-like leaves fell onto him. It was stranger still to walk up the same concrete staircase — no children played ball in the corridor today — and past the neighbours' house. He wondered if he should stop and say hello. But their flat was quiet in the fresh, washed morning; they were working young people and probably wanted to sleep late.

Satish's room wasn't as bad as he'd expected. The sheets and blanket lay neatly folded at the foot of the bed. Who had remembered to do that? Maybe Ashish, in an effort to tidy up? Mohan walked around, looking for a cloth to clean with, and picked up things that had rolled onto the floor: a bottle of pills, the case for Satish's spectacles. There was a coating of dust on everything and he began to clean, absent-mindedly, first with the duster and then with the jhadu. He swept up the furry pile of black dust that he garnered from whisking the broom all over the small apartment; he found a pail and the bottle of phenyl and washed the floor, until the familiar chemical smell took over. He opened the windows: the damp, intimate scent of the rain came in; it felt better.

A jar of the health tonic Chyawanaprash stood on the shelf above the electric ring. Mohan unscrewed the lid, brought the bottle near his nose and winced: the chocolatey-looking paste had turned. An old envelope inside the chest of drawers was filled with neatly clipped money-off coupons, in which Satish had written his name and address in his beautiful hand. In the cupboard, the birthday alarm clock, still in its clear packaging, now a little dusty, was ticking away.

Further inside, within an old cigar box, there was a bundle of letters wrapped in a piece of rose-coloured silk that seemed to have come from a wedding sari. Some of them began 'Dearest S' and had the signature 'Vikram'. Mohan wrapped them up without reading more. More researches in the cupboard found Satish's clothes: six white shirts and a raw-silk bush shirt he wore on special occasions; four ordinary pairs of trousers and one good pair; socks and underwear; a stack of handkerchiefs that were much like Mohan's but bare of initials.

Mohan also found the deeds to the flat, which had, after all, belonged to Satish. The apartment, despite its dinginess, was a thing of value: it was in south Bombay, not even far from the sea. It was entirely possible, knowing his brother-in-law, that he had left it to someone they'd never heard of: an ex-student, or some association; all that would become clear only later, when they heard the will.

12

The voice was soft, almost elegantly weary. 'Hell-o.'

'Um, hello?' Ashish said. 'Professor Narayan?'

'Who's this?'

'Uh, this is Ashish Datye. I'm calling, ah, it's, you know Professor Chitale? Who just passed away? I'm his sister's husband's nephew, he might have mentioned me. I'm studying in — '

'He passed away?'

'Yes, three weeks ago. There was a notice in the paper,' Ashish said.

'Oh, I didn't know. I haven't been in touch with him for a little while. I'm very sorry. Was he unwell?'

'No, it was sudden.'

There was a pause. Ashish was home alone; it was about seven in the evening. He regarded one leg of the table, which was beginning to be veiled in shadow. Above him, the gecko that lived in the drawing room darted across the wall with a little rustle.

'So Ashish, tell me,' said the voice, slightly impatient now.

'Well, Professor Chitale, Satish uncle, he

suggested you might be able to give me some tuition. I'm studying English, final year BA.'

'I see.'

Another pause. Ashish felt ridiculous; he glared accusingly at the gecko, which froze in the middle of an old water stain. It may have believed that, here, it was invisible.

A small sigh from the other end of the line. 'Why don't you come and see me one evening and then we can discuss it,' the voice suggested quietly.

'Okay sir, but,' Ashish was beginning. He had no idea what these tuitions were supposed to achieve, or how much they might cost; it seemed gauche to go into all this now, though.

'Take down the address. 17a, it's the top-floor flat, Sadanand Society, Lane number 3, Kalina village. You want to go to Santa Cruz station then take a bus: ask for the Jama Masjid.'

'Okay sir, what time should I?'

'Shall we say Thursday, five o'clock?'

'Yes, I'll — '

'See you then,' murmured the voice, and the call was disconnected.

★ ★ ★

It had been a strange few weeks, Ashish reflected, when he woke the next morning to

183

the usual pealing of Dr Gogate's car alarm. After the whole nightmarish happening with Sunder, Ashish had had to endure college: for almost a week, people pointed him out to their friends and giggled; some story or other was doing the rounds. Ridicule wasn't a new experience, but it was worse because he was bothering to attend lectures, and had to face it in person. Then there'd been Satish uncle's death and the unnamed dark cloud that hung, after it, over his aunt and uncle.

He felt very sorry for his aunt and tried, in his own way, to make her feel better: he talked to her nicely in the morning, and started conversations with her about her favourite television programmes. Her heart wasn't in it, though, he saw; so he removed himself and left her to it. Mohan mama had also been in a funny mood. Yesterday, for example, he had insisted on leaving early, at the same time as Ashish. 'We'll walk to the station together,' he'd said. Ashish, his heart sinking, had agreed.

Mohan wouldn't take the shortest route; whenever he and Ashish went together, the boy found himself following, at a crab-like tangent, his own shadow up the congested little lanes, winding right then straight then right then straight then left, until the junction arrived as if by surprise.

'Can't we take the main road, Mohan mama?' he muttered.

'There's more shade here,' said his uncle doggedly. And they wound their way on. Mohan seemed to like to read the well-known lanes and notice the changes in their life: the gates of metal tubing whose paint flaked and carried a spore of rust, the overgrown small compounds, the cluttered culverts outside bungalows and low apartment blocks, the weeds that sprang up, bright and green, next to the drains. The lanes smelled leafy, but also dank, the early freshness of the rains long gone.

Mohan passed on small facts to Ashish: 'Look, that house has been sold.' A few yards later: 'Son of the man who lives there is getting married, to a dental hygienist. Girl is from Chennai.'

Ashish grunted. The information, he guessed, came from the dosa man, who heard everything that went on in Saraswati Park.

'So, which classes do you have today?'

'French, Shakespeare, history of English literature.' Ashish hated it when adults quarrelled: it was just then that they decided to take an interest in the junior members of the household, as if to prove to themselves that they were indeed good and kind. He remembered a few occasions in his childhood when, after his parents argued, his father had taken him out to play cricket on the maidan. Ashish wanted to bat endlessly; his father had soon tired of bowling him underarm balls. 'Enough,' he'd said irritably after ten or fifteen minutes, 'time to go home.'

They trudged on in silence for a while. Ashish suddenly stopped and began to brush at his shirt pocket. There was a small green caterpillar on it; the animal curled and writhed on the khaki cotton, which seemed to have confused it. In the light and shade under a tree, he tried to get the caterpillar off.

'Here.' Mohan reached out and removed the creature, which continued to wind and unwind; he manoeuvred it onto the pad of his thumb, bent down and put his hand next to a small plant near the rusty gate of a dilapidated house. With the point of his index finger, while Ashish watched, he encouraged the worm onto a leaf. As soon as it attained the familiar surface it hurried away, the shirt experience left behind like a bad dream.

They walked on, Mohan a little straighter, and his eyes brighter than before. Ashish shuffled beside his uncle, breathing in the damp, slightly fetid air. He allowed his satchel to slap against his hip, making a sequence of unpleasing thuds, and remembered the sullen quiet of the morning, with virtually no conversation between his aunt and uncle.

★ ★ ★

On Thursday, after college, Ashish got off a Western Line train at Santa Cruz. Peanut shells littered the floor; a breeze drifted unhindered through the near-empty compartment; outside, he saw palm trees. The small boy who'd begged assiduously all the way till Bandra now sat quietly at the door, his legs hanging into space.

Ashish waited near the station for a bus to the market. He asked for directions to the Jama Masjid and there asked again; he wandered into the network of back lanes where the city forgot itself and became a village. Here was the rich, unwanted smell of cow dung in a small square. Ashish looked around. A concrete bench, painted a violent mint green, encircled a banyan tree. Next to the tree was a small cigarette kiosk. He approached the man behind it.

'Sadanand Society?'

The man jerked his hand behind him and to the left. 'Go down that gully and take the second right.' Ashish, sweating, obeyed. He was beginning to feel exhausted, and thinking that he'd return after all to the Jama Masjid, get a bus and go home, when finally he turned down what he was convinced was the wrong road and saw it: a crackled blue

187

building, five storeys high, labelled on the gatepost: Sadanand Society, Lane 3. He walked past the geriatric watchman, checked the name boards at the bottom of the stairs and began to climb up. In the square stairwell, light and smells of bleach gathered; he watched his feet on each red cement step.

There was a plant in a terracotta pot outside the dark wooden door of apartment 17. Ashish pressed the bell, heard an electronic ding-dong inside, and watched water trickle from the bottom of the pot to fill the pattern of an existing stain. Behind the door footsteps came towards him; inside, there was the sound of a small, practised scuffle with the door catch.

A slim, fair man opened the door and smiled a wide smile. 'Ashish,' he said. He held the door open further and stepped back. 'Come in.' He laughed. 'Oh, I'm Narayan by the way.'

Ashish found himself smiling too, and a little startled. He hadn't expected the other man to be so young. There was something nice about his face, he thought disconcertedly, an openness: in fact he looked more boyish than Ashish himself, although most of his curly hair was grey, and his skin wasn't unlined. Yet his gaze was direct, almost challenging. It was as though he was asking a question of Ashish: probably, the boy thought, 'Are you serious about this?'

He wasn't, but he was prepared to say out of politeness that he was. When unsure how things were going, he typically went along to see where they would take him. He wasn't sure if it was curiosity, a lack of confidence, passivity; at this point he nearly smirked because his thoughts were running away with him and the professor was still saying something; they stood between the hall and the living room. Narayan spoke softly, without emphasis, as though he expected to be listened to. Now he paused, looked at Ashish, smiled a little derisively, and raised his eyebrows.

Ashish heard the fan turn in the living room and a crow arguing outside.

Narayan laughed again. 'So, Ashish? Tell me. What is it you want?'

What a question! Hot and cold running boyfriends, a subscription to satellite television, air conditioning everywhere you could think of and some places you probably couldn't, self-assurance, expensive shoes, to be famous, to be left alone, to be approved of.

Ashish also laughed, but apologetically; he hoped to convey that he was a foolish student, but one with enough self-awareness to recognize the fact. 'Well,' he began, then wondered if he should be more deferential, 'Sir — my mami's uncle thought that you might be able to help me ensure that I — '

'You don't have to call me sir. Call me Narayan.' The other man saw the astonishment in Ashish's face and smiled. His smile was catlike. 'Or if that embarrasses you, don't call me anything at all.' His eyes raked Ashish over.

'Look,' the professor went on. 'I know what your uncle, or your mami's uncle, or whatever the relationship is, I know what he said. But you, I'd like to know what you think about this. Are you interested in reading and talking about books?' Once again, his eyes challenged Ashish, asking a question that didn't seem to be the one he'd spoken aloud.

Narayan repeated, 'Are you interested in that?'

'Yes,' said Ashish quickly.

They remained looking at each other. Then Narayan smiled. Is he going to tell me to leave right now? Ashish wondered.

'Good,' Narayan said casually. 'Then we understand each other. Go, sit, I'll make some tea.'

The light was dim and ill-tempered: one of those monsoon days when the sun is in hiding. Ashish drifted about the living room, while small, methodical noises came out of the kitchen. He didn't want to appear to be snooping, but felt too jittery to sit quietly and wait: instead, he examined the bookshelves, and, conscious of the moment when Narayan would re-enter the room, tried to maintain a critical yet interested expression.

There was a divan, covered in a striped bedspread that seemed deeply familiar. It fitted with the tenor of the room: handloom textiles, terracotta whatnots, a skinny, peculiarly elongated brass figurine made by a canny tribal somewhere in Madhya Pradesh. Ashish was scanning a shelf of DVDs when Narayan came back with two cups; his tread was almost soundless. 'Here,' he said quietly, handing Ashish a red mug without a handle. Ashish looked at it with interest: what was this? But the tea smelled good, with a hint of spice.

Narayan stood right next to Ashish; he was nearly as slim as the boy, and slightly taller.

'Do you like French films?' he asked. He considered his own shelf intently. Ashish got lost studying the grey hairs at the side of Narayan's head, and a small wrinkle in the fair skin behind his ear. He realized he was supposed to make some response. 'Yes,' he said. He began to babble, 'Actually I'm not sure I've ever seen a French film. No, wait, I saw that one about the girl that came out a few years — '

'This one is fabulous,' said Narayan, removing a DVD of *La Belle et la Bête*. He regarded the cover with nostalgia.

Ashish looked, dubiously, at the image of a horned beast and a feral man. The professor turned. 'I think you'd like it,' he remarked. He replaced the DVD with care and, slightly theatrically, went and sat down. Ashish felt obliged to do the same. It was strange, the feeling he laboured under here. It was like a thing seen underwater, which seems to keep moving because of the way the light refracts; he was both indulged and dismissed, pulled and pushed. He found himself behaving oddly, as though enacting a simulacrum of what natural behaviour in this situation would have been.

He took a big glug of tea, noticed how damp the air was, and felt tired, thinking of the journey home and how long it would take; he would be exhausted, in the train.

★ ★ ★

'So how was it? How did it go?' his uncle asked as soon as he came through the door.

'Well, it was good,' Ashish said. 'He's very educated,' he added.

'Of course he is,' his aunt said. 'He's a college professor.'

If I have children, Ashish determined silently, I'm going to tell them every obvious thing that comes into my head. He went to take off his shoes and wash his hands.

When he returned his aunt and uncle were at the table. A plate piled with perfectly round, gold-gleaming puris sat in the middle.

He was hungry and it was good to be home. As he chewed, without noticing the taste of the food, he thought again about the way the professor, or Narayan (Narayan, he told himself), had examined him while they sat talking.

'So do you think it'll be useful?' his uncle asked. 'Seeing the professor? Do you think it'll help?'

'He's very nice,' Ashish said. He tried not to consider how they had had a long and varied conversation in which Narayan had talked about a range of books and films that Ashish didn't know, and, of course, about himself. Now, in the bright pool of light at the dining table, his aunt and uncle asked questions and he, automatically, his mind elsewhere, gave answers. Narayan had said they'd work out the cost of the tuitions later, it would be a belated favour to Satish uncle, who'd been his teacher; he, Narayan, had been teaching at the university, yes, but he had left a couple of years ago, to concentrate on his own research; he didn't know if Narayan gave other tuitions; he didn't think so but he wasn't sure.

Ashish blinked; it seemed unreal to be at home as though nothing had happened in the evening. But nothing had happened, he reminded himself.

'Tired?' said his aunt.

'Don't stay up late studying,' Mohan mama said. 'You need your sleep too.'

Ashish smiled and put down his spoon. He was tired, it was true. 'I think you're right,' he said sleepily. He felt very happy. My luck is changing, he thought, and he left the table, brushed his teeth and went to sleep without even checking to see if the owls were there.

⋆　⋆　⋆

Two days after Ashish's first visit to Narayan, he answered the phone at Saraswati Park. It was a voice he didn't recognize.

'Gautam?'

'No, it's Ashish. Mohan mama's nephew,' he said.

'Is your aunt there?'

'They're both out, can I take a message?'

'Tell her to call her nephew Chintan, in Nagpur. I'll give you the number.' After he had done so, he told Ashish that his father,

Lakshmi's elder brother's son, was unwell. Ashish was slightly confused from trying to remember this relationship, but he recalled that Lakshmi had close relatives in Nagpur; his cousins used to spend summers at what his aunt called 'my brother's house', though her eldest brother had died many years earlier. 'It's quite serious, she might want to come,' the voice finally told Ashish.

'I'll tell her, as soon as she gets home.'

When his aunt and uncle returned in the evening — Mohan from work and Lakshmi from the market — Ashish delivered the news. His uncle, he noticed, looked immediately guilty and glanced at his wife. Lakshmi got on the phone and had a twenty-minute conversation, after which she decided to go to Nagpur the next day. Mohan went out to arrange her ticket — he'd do this through an acquaintance in the railways, who might be able to get a seat in the emergency quota. Lakshmi went to their room and started packing.

13

Mohan sat in the apartment at dusk, exercise book open, pencil in hand and the volume of Mark Twain with the wide margins next to him. Crows screeched; koyals interrogated, whee-*ooo* whee-*ooo*; a brainfever bird made its unsettling rattle and whoop. A car reversed: its klaxon played the undying patriotic hit 'Saare Jahaan Se Achchha'. He tried not to grit his teeth.

Ashish was out; he'd gone for the second time this week to meet his tutor. The arrangement seemed to be working well, so that was one less thing to worry about: now the boy would have a reason to maintain interest in his studies.

The flat was quiet; the living-room gecko, which seemed to have grown much larger, chirruped from time to time, or moved about with a rustle. Mohan found himself looking at his wife's chair, in front of the silent television. It was five days since she'd left for Nagpur; she'd forgotten to take her shawl. It was a large thing, flecked with grey and made of rough wool; a garment intended for a shepherd and cold nights in the desert, not

196

for this temperate city. But she liked to wrap herself in it on cooler monsoon nights. At any given time a long thread dangled from it; he remembered her, the evening before they found out about her cousin's illness, sitting in the chair, wearing the shawl and watching the latest episode of *Daughters of the House*. At an advertisement break, she'd got up for a glass of water and moved out of the patch of light thrown by the set; the loose thread trailed behind her, snagging on a chair arm as she passed, so that it had seemed to try to pull her back.

He got up now, opened the shawl, shook it out and folded it neatly, then hung it again over the back of the chair.

★   ★   ★

On Sunday evening, with dusk in the lane outside and the old sensation of emptiness and mild dread in his stomach, Mohan began to read the essay that harboured his notes: the woman in the green sari, the youngest boy in the ironing hut, and others besides. It was a review of a biography of Shelley, which blamed all the poet's problems on his wife. Mohan read about Harriet and her letter to Shelley's publisher when the young man disappeared for days to visit a woman he'd fallen in love with over Italian lessons. He was always falling in love, and his wife had little to do but sit at home and wait for him to return.

Crickets chirped outside and the lane became quite dormant; sounds came of Sunday evening television and the radio in the ironing boys' hut; Mohan read on in the light of the hundred-watt bulb.

'Mohan mama, it's nine thirty. Should I make some instant noodles?'

He looked up, unmoored. Ashish.

'I'm going to make some instant noodles, you haven't eaten, have you?'

'No, no.' He got up and put the book to one side, hastened out of the circle of light and put on the passage lamp. The boy looked surprised; he must be starving.

'What's the time?'

'Nine thirty,' Ashish repeated.

'Late, you must be hungry. Wait, I'll go and — ' But the shop would be closed at this hour on a Sunday. It would have to be noodles.

In the kitchen, the tube light flickered and its noise joined the thrum of the refrigerator. Mohan found cheese slices, those magical things which, when the plastic wrapping was peeled away, shone as highly as before; tomatoes, a cucumber, and he knew there were onions and potatoes.

'How about toasted sandwiches? And also noodles, if you like.'

'Okay.'

Ashish sliced the tomato and cucumber while Mohan buttered the bread and boiled the potato and water for the noodles.

'How's the study going?'

'Oh — '

But Ashish met his eyes more openly than usual, perhaps because the question was put more casually. He shrugged. 'Oh, you know.' He paused. 'But did you know there are owls in the building opposite? White ones.'

'Really? I haven't seen them.' Their bedroom faced the other way, towards the watchman's hut.

'Yeah, I see them at night — they come out to hunt and they sit in the windowsill of that empty flat.'

'Owls,' Mohan mused. 'They used to come to the other building, the one that got knocked down, near that big banyan tree. They like empty houses.'

'Here.' Ashish passed over the sliced tomato.

★   ★   ★

Mohan remembered now that he hadn't kept his appointment with Yezdi; it had been for

199

the day after Satish's death, a phrase that still seemed wrong. He would ring up and explain, he thought.

Instead, after dinner, when Ashish went to his room, Mohan sharpened his pencils, got out a new notebook, and sat at the table, rearranging some pickle jars and rusted baby food tins to make room. He opened the notebook, laid it on a woven grass table mat, picked up the Mark Twain, rifled through his notes and quickly found the one he was looking for, about the boys in the ironing hut. He wrote a few sentences about the youngest, who'd recently arrived in the city. As he wrote, he looked less at the notes in the margin and thought less often of the real young man. Instead, he found he described a face that mingled the high forehead of a cousin of his with his brother's small mouth; and the way the boy walked reminded him of nothing so much as the jaunty tread of the young kachrawala.

The objects around the letter writer seemed to look on with interest: the pickle jars with their stained and faded labels; the old table mats; the chairs, one of which had a broken seat. It always had to be removed when Satish came for lunch, in case he sat on it and thought, or decided to think, that he had been given it on purpose.

The next day Mohan went to the newspaper building to leave a note for Yezdi. In it, he explained rather stiffly that because of a death in the family he hadn't been able to keep the earlier appointment; but he would be happy to meet Yezdi at another time, if it was convenient. He signed, Mohan; then added his last name and telephone number.

He worked on the stories every day. Ashish came back late, and there was no one at home, a thing he didn't want to think about; he had spoken to Lakshmi once since she reached Nagpur, and she had said that she planned to stay for some time. Her cousin's condition was poor but stable. 'It'll be a help, if I'm here to nurse him. And it's good to spend some time with my family after a long time,' he heard her voice saying on the crackling line. He'd paused, waiting for her to ask him to come, or bring her anything she needed. She hadn't.

'But do you need anything? I could come, if you need more clothes or anything,' he'd finally said.

'No, why would I? I can borrow whatever I need.'

So he'd managed. She'd suggested he ask the maid from the Gogates' to come and clean the floors and cook a little, and he did that. It was an expense, but it was fine, with the money that Megha insisted on sending every month and which had been accumulating pointlessly. It occurred to him only now that they should have done this earlier; then Lakshmi would have had more time to herself.

The maid, with a friendly contempt, would give him orders via Mrs Gogate, with whom he left the key: 'She says buy whole-wheat flour', or 'She asked you to get phenyl for the floor'. Sometimes, in rudimentary handwriting and with poor spelling, she left short, direct notes: *Milk is over*, or *Buy laundry soap*.

If he felt abandoned then he also had the freedom to jettison his old life. So every evening, while waiting for Ashish to return, he'd sit under the lamp and write. He felt a lovely quiet come off the page. It was rich and held the shards of past experiences; a feeling here and there, the sight of a building that one passed every day and yet had never really noticed. Sometimes, he would rush home, thinking, I must write; but when he arrived and sat down, he would feel baffled and absent-minded, wondering what the urgency could have been. When he was unsure what to write and his mind shied from the activity, he'd find himself wandering away from the table, then looking back at it; he'd find something to do near the window, or at the armchair; go to the desk calendar that sat on the dining table, and turn a page.

★   ★   ★

Two days later, at about seven, the telephone rang. He hurried over to it.

'Hello?'

'Hello, Mohan?'

'Yes?'

But it wasn't anyone from Nagpur.

'It's Yezdi,' Yezdi said grandly.

'Oh. You got my note?'

'Yes, you said something had happened in your family?'

'My brother-in-law was taken ill. Actually he passed away,' Mohan said.

'Oh, I see. I'm sorry,' Yezdi said without great interest. There was a pause. 'So are we going to meet?'

Mohan hesitated. After all, their falling-out had been a long time earlier. 'All right,' he said.

'Where do you work now, Mohan?'

He hunched his shoulders. 'I'm a letter writer,' he said. 'At the GPO.'

'A what?'

'Letter writer. I write letters for other people.'

'But how fascinating! Of course, I'd almost forgotten that profession still existed — well, anyway, that must be very interesting. So we're almost neighbours? I can't believe we haven't met all this time. Will you come to the office for tea? How about tomorrow?'

Mohan agreed to meet Yezdi the next afternoon at five in the *Indian Record* office.

★   ★   ★

The next day was sluggish, without customers. Earlier, a day like this would have depressed him; he would have walked up and down the colonnade, talking to the clerks, visiting the philately section, or seeing if anyone in the crowded, confusing main hall of the GPO needed help. Now he just sat and watched the shadows of the banyan tree on the road and the passing faces.

It began to rain. People hurried under their umbrellas, flimsy portable domes, as though each passer-by was trying to carry his shelter along with him.

Mohan thought, *A man goes on a journey* . . . He had no idea what the rest of the sentence was, but a restlessness entered his soul along with the weather and he saw the open windows of a train travelling through the hills, when rain rolls in soft billows through the compartment and the passengers squeal in pleasure. The world outside is green and soft as though it had just appeared from a misty cocoon; even the thought of a state transport bus, doggedly continuing on the highway through the blowing rain, seemed full of mystery and meaning to him now.

The pavements became shamelessly wet, like the cheeks of a movie-goer who cries at a film and makes no attempt to hide it.

★   ★   ★

When Khan heard where Mohan was going he became quite excited. 'You never said! You know him? But he's famous.'

'Well, not famous exactly,' Mohan protested.

Khan became animated. 'Who hasn't heard of Yezdi Sodawaterbottlewala? In Bombay, at least. Who hasn't seen him on television? Who hasn't — '

'Shh, shh,' said Mohan hastily.

'Hey, tell him to send someone to write about our building — it's about to fall down and the landlord isn't doing anything. Also about the drains in Bhendi Bazaar.'

'Yes yes.'

At the *Indian Record* building Mohan insinuated himself into a lobby packed with aggrieved looking people: most seemed to be commercial travellers, men with polycotton shirts, briefcases, and several pens in their shirt pocket. After a few minutes of sweating and waiting for the half-second when the rotating standard fan would blow cool air his way, he went to the counter.

'I'm here to see Yezdi Sodawaterbottlewala,' he said.

'Appointment?' enquired the pert young woman.

'Yes, he asked me to come.'

She flicked through her book and dialled an extension. 'Sir, there's someone to see you — ' she covered the receiver and enquired, 'Name?'

'Karekar.'

'There's a Mr Karekar to see you. Shall I — yes, I'll give him a visitor's pass and send him up.' She hung up. 'Editorial, second floor,' she told Mohan.

He was issued with a nasty piece of plastic. 'Clip this to yourself,' the young woman, probably about his younger daughter's age, told him. He smiled and nodded, wanting to kick Yezdi. At the lift another thin, pinched-looking woman checked his umbrella and demanded in a harsh voice, 'Any electronic items? Camera? Video recorder? Laptop?'

Where, Mohan wondered silently, do you think they are? Down my trousers? 'No,' he said.

'Please wear your visitor's pass.'

He pretended to fumble with it while he waited for the lift. It came, and a jovial man in white uniform asked which floor Mohan wanted.

'Second. Editorial.'

The liftman nodded majestically, as though he'd been a chauffeur told to drive to the Taj Mahal hotel. 'Sir, editorial is to the left,' he said when they reached the second floor. Mohan passed an old linotype machine, a more splendid version of the one they'd had at the printing shop, and entered a vast hall full of desks, computers and people. He wandered slowly, getting a few strange looks. Then he stopped a young man handing out glasses of tea that he carried in a plastic basin.

'Do you know where Mr Sodawaterbottle-wala sits?' Mohan was asking him, just as a familiar voice let out an outraged bray.

'Eh, Sudhir!' The tea boy turned and grinned; he pointed Mohan towards a corner near the window. There was a small glass cabin from which the voice emerged. 'Likes his tea,' he confided. 'Gets very angry if I miss him out. For you?'

'No thanks. I'll take it to him, though.' He relieved the boy of a single glass and went towards the cabin. He pushed open the door.

'Arre, Mohan!' Yezdi, still enormous and now grizzled, thighs spreading across his chair, waved one hand in a gesture of excitement that reminded Mohan of a sea creature he'd seen on the National Geographic channel — one with long whiskers. Sea lion, perhaps, or walrus.

'Ah, and tea's come too! I thought that fellow was going to miss me out again, he's very slack. Two blessings at once!'

Mohan handed him the glass. Yezdi took a large sip before placing it on a coaster atop one of the piles of paper that littered his desk. They shook hands. Yezdi wore a large emerald ring on his right paw. 'Mohan, it's so good to see you, how have you been?'

'Not bad, you tell me,' Mohan said. He sat on the other chair, his back straight.

Below the grand high ceilings in the newsroom, people seemed to be scurrying perpetually. But as he half listened to what Yezdi was saying, Mohan noticed also how the journalists smiled and paused to swing on the edges of the partitions separating desks; they joked and dithered, this was their daily circuit. Like overexcited hummingbirds, they made the rounds from flower to flower, stopping to refuel on gossip and the tea, which was so sweet he could smell the sugar.

From far away in the big room there was a small kerfuffle, then a crash and tinkle: the chai boy had dropped a glass. Immediately there was a cheer; the whole room broke into applause; some whooped, others stamped their feet. The thin chai boy crouched and began to pick up the pieces of glass. Yezdi's face softened with amusement.

Eventually Yezdi had enough of introducing Mohan to people in the office: the chief sub-editor, the news editor, the city editor, all of whom looked harassed and smiled at Mohan before asking Yezdi, 'Are you giving anything today?' As though he'd been a cow dispensing wishes, Mohan thought. Yezdi said no. He winked at Mohan. 'Come, will you walk to Crawford Market with me? I like to go once a day if I can. It's exercise and I also get to buy an apple instead of eating all these greasy snacks.' A uniformed waiter had just appeared, with plates of pohe that glistened with oil, and which he put down at certain seats only. 'You'll have?' Yezdi offered his to Mohan, who said no, thanks.

They set off from the newsroom and waited for the lift. When it came, they descended two floors, and walked out of the grand porch and towards Crawford Market.

'How is your health, anyway?' Mohan felt obliged to ask. It was strange, to see Yezdi, and then to be polite to him, one wonder followed by another.

'Oh, very well. That is, I have some BP and a slight heart murmur,' Yezdi said cheerfully, 'but obviously I'll live to be ninety-four at least, because everyone in my family does.'

'Mm,' Mohan said and nodded.

'And you?'

'Oh, very well, very well. So far,' he added, and his face darkened and then brightened again.

It had rarely taken Mohan longer to walk such a small distance. While Yezdi lumbered along, greeting all kinds of street vendors and other passers-by, Mohan, in the gaps, at Yezdi's request, told Yezdi about his children. 'My younger daughter is in the US, in Iowa, she works for a computer company,' he was saying when they finally reached Crawford Market. Yezdi hailed the proprietor of one of the first fruit stalls, where every kind of fruit shone waxily under the porch; they left again after he'd bought his usual, a single, ruinously expensive imported apple.

'I just don't think our desi ones are as good, Mohan. The bite, the crunch, the sweetness,' he said, and Mohan grinned, and said, 'Hm.'

They walked back again, slowly, alongside the garden of the art school, and Mohan, his attention drifting, looked in at the dusty leaved trees and the old stone buildings and thought, Kipling, his father had worked there and he'd been born in Bombay. Somewhere he'd read a poem about those early days. But he hadn't come back to the city after returning to England.

'Mohan, I feel bad that we haven't been in touch for all these years. It's my fault, in part.' Yezdi paused. They were near the Anjuman-i-Islam school; the front playground was empty — school had been over for some time. The last flare of sun from Mohan's right squeezed through the railings and made him squint. Do you even remember what happened, you fat rascal, he wondered.

'Let's keep in touch now Mohan, it's sad to lose contact with old friends.'

'Yes yes,' Mohan said gently.

'You must come home some time, though my wife doesn't keep very well — but my parents would like to see you, my mother still remembers you — otherwise, let's have lunch together one day.'

Mohan smiled. They shook hands and

Yezdi rolled into the porch of the *Record* building. Mohan thought he'd go home. At the station he realized the plastic visitor's pass was still in his pocket; he surreptitiously left it on a corner seat in the train.

When he got home, both doors were shut: Ashish was still out. The phone began to ring, and he fumbled with the lock, hurrying, and pulled the inner door open. He ran and got to the instrument while it was still ringing.

'Hello?'

'Don't shout,' his sister's precise voice said.

'Oh, it's you.'

'What's that supposed to mean?'

'Nothing. I was expecting a call. How are things?'

'Not bad, except that Indore is very hot, and the flat we've been allocated isn't very convenient, and I don't know anyone, and the shops near here aren't good,' she began. Eventually she broke off to ask to speak to her son.

'He isn't here, I'll tell him you called. He might be out having tuitions with the professor I mentioned to you. But he's fine,' he said, looking about the empty flat. 'Everything is fine.'

There was an uncertain, slightly critical silence at the other end. He waited, but finally reminded himself that it was true: so

212

far, nothing had gone wrong.

'How's Milind?' he asked.

'Oh, *he*'s all right,' his sister said. 'Just goes to work and doesn't notice anything much else.'

'Good. I'll tell Ashish,' he said, and hung up.

★   ★   ★

There was a last stormy day or two, when grit blew half-heartedly through the house and in the air and people wiped their eyes and sighed; one squall, and that was it, the season had changed. It had been a bad monsoon, not in the sense of poor rainfall — there had in fact been more than usual, but oddly distributed in a few days of torrent and floods, and long dry spells.

★   ★   ★

When he opened the notebook again and began to read what he had written he sighed; the pictures in his head were so much more beautiful. Here the words were heavy and the rhythm staccato. It wasn't what it could have been; it wasn't what he had thought.

He put the notebook away.

But later, when he was walking through the

lanes, and after that, at dinner time, and at night when he sat reading in the chair, his mind wandered into the world of the story. The boy from the ironing hut had become a new person, who had a whole life about which Mohan constantly reminded himself: the names of his cousins, his early childhood outside the city, his marriage, even what he thought about when the ironing boys closed the door of the tin hut in the afternoons to sleep. The story had no real shape but he continued to tell it to himself; before he went to bed, he sat at the table, elbows planted amid the different jars of jam and pickle, tins of drinking chocolate and baby milk, and smiled.

He went inside to clean his teeth and the familiar objects in the bathroom were transfigured, and somehow luminous: from his cake of alum in the old soap tin, to the squeezed, half-empty tube of his wife's toothpaste, which was clove-flavoured; she had used it since she was a child and refused to try any other brand. The strange fluorescent light bounced off the white tiles; it seemed to taste metallic in his mouth. He held the toothpaste tube for some time, looking at the wrinkles and minute indentations where it had been crushed (everyone in his household, in response, probably, to the distress they knew it caused him, squeezed toothpaste tubes from the middle). The object appeared to be telling him something. But what? He was tired, he thought finally; he turned out the bathroom light and went into the darkened bedroom. Here there was an absorbed sense of quiet. A diffuse orange glow from the street lamp burnished corners of the well-known furniture: the bevelled edge of the steel cupboard's door, and part of the mirror. The fan hummed, a soothing sound, and air moved impersonally about the room.

14

The credits rolled. Ashish stretched. 'But what does it mean,' he asked, '400 Blows?'

'It's an expression,' Narayan said. 'It can't really be translated.' He got up and watched the rest of the credits intently, ejected the DVD, and replaced it in its case. It was nearly dark; he walked to the window and pulled the half-drawn curtains quite closed. 'But did you like the film?'

'Yes, very much.' Ashish tried to run through the images; the one that stayed with him was the young Antoine, chucked into his bedroom for bad behaviour and daydreaming his way into another world.

Narayan seemed to consider Ashish's face. 'So whom do you like better, Truffaut or Godard?'

Their meetings had found a pattern: when Ashish arrived, there'd be tea, then, shortly afterwards, a discussion, or more often, a film screened in half-darkness. While the television flickered, Ashish was aware not just of the figures on the screen — Antoine, his rebellious face above his white collar and black sweater — but also of the audience, himself and the teacher, bodies silent and warm in the dark.

He thought of *L'Argent de poche* and the young boy taking out his money from a piggy bank to buy flowers for his friend's mother, whom he was a little in love with. She'd assumed they were from his father, a tragedy so minute no one even realized it had taken place. 'Truffaut,' he said.

'Oh no, Godard's the one. Genius, the man's a genius!' Narayan declared. In his fierceness he seemed to stand straighter, his thin shoulders thrown back.

Ashish smiled and was silent. He listened to the train horns outside — the track passed not far from the building — and a murmur of voices in the lane below. It was nearly time to leave.

But Narayan sat down again. He sprawled in his armchair, regarding Ashish.

'Do you believe in fate?' he asked.

Ashish nearly giggled, it was a line from a Hindi film; but he wasn't sure whether Narayan was joking.

'Yes,' he said, eyeing the teacher to work out which would be the answer that produced the right effect. 'Maybe not completely — I don't think everything happens without our being able to control it. Just most things.' He sighed inwardly, thinking, Sunder, and my predicament in general.

Narayan smiled. He looked at Ashish from under half-closed eyes.

'I'm not sure that's quite the way to think about it,' he said. His eyes, both soft and mercenary under the heavy lids, swept Ashish up and down. One eyebrow seemed to lift slightly. Ashish waited. Narayan finally exhaled, and rose. 'I think we can leave it there for today,' he said gently.

'Oh, yes. Sure. Thanks.' Ashish scrambled up.

'See you on Monday?'

Ashish was already at the door, opening the catch. 'Yes, Monday. Thanks,' he repeated, managing to waggle his head at the same time as sliding out of the door.

On the way home, in the train, he sat near the window, leaned his head on the boards behind him and, as so often, replayed the evening that had just taken place, with a few tweaks here and there. What, for instance, had Narayan meant when he'd looked into Ashish's eyes (and up and down the boy's body, but he expunged that bit for now) and said, 'You have a good mind, you think clearly about things'? He must have meant . . . Here the assistant director of Ashish's imagination obligingly set up a scene. Narayan and Ashish sat side by side on the professor's divan, hand

218

in hand, and looked into each other's eyes — or wait, should it be somewhere better by way of location? Goa? Sunset? Night-time? Anyway, looking into each other's eyes — and Narayan rubbed the back of Ashish's neck. He murmured, 'You know, I knew as soon as I met you that this was going to be something special.' Ashish, in this incarnation, was cool. He just smiled.

Fantasy, it appeared, had access only to a limited range of storylines, the point of which was a basic emotional satisfaction that rarely became boring; reality was more inventive, better shaped, he could acknowledge that. But was it better to get what you wanted or to appreciate the complexity of circumstances that continued to frustrate you? The bruised optimism of his uncle's face floated in front of his mind's eye, and that question was despatched for another day.

The train pulled into Parle station; Ashish watched the boy at the glass-fronted snack stall, a lighted oasis of grease and the marks left behind by ritual, repeated wiping with a dirty cloth. In a moment the train set itself into motion once more, and the orangey lit-up kiosk moved behind them to join the blur of lighted spaces that made islands against the night.

After dinner, his uncle descended into one of the infrequent bad moods dreaded by his entire family. Mohan mama's good humour was an act of will for which he had the necessary discipline at least three hundred and fifty days in the year. The other days were not good days. He would get up and, in response to a simple remark at breakfast, snarl suddenly. It was as though dustcovers hung over any part of life that might have been fun. These moods weren't just anger, Ashish recalled Megha telling him. 'It's like the death of everything, it's so depressing.' After a couple of days during which the rest of the family tiptoed around Mohan like silent shadows circling a storm cloud, the tension would usually ease. But this time the bad mood had only just begun; Ashish took cover. He went downstairs, to Madhavi's house.

Hanging out with Madhavi had become a habit: he liked the loud cheerfulness of her house, where the television was usually on, spurting out the news or a comedy programme; Madhavi floated between the college books in her room, and the living room, where a conversation with her mother was always in some stage of unfolding. Ashish would never ordinarily have dreamt of being friends with a girl he wasn't related to, much less one who was younger. But he liked Madhavi: she was practical, down-to-earth, and intelligent. Her house was always open and her mother welcoming — Ashish avoided her father who, distressingly, wore tiny shorts at home; he would smile benevolently at Ashish before returning to doing the crossword with a gold-plated fountain pen.

This evening Ashish clattered and flapped down the stairs and waved to Madhavi's mother through the grille of the inner door before letting himself in.

'Ashish, you'll have ice cream?'

'No thanks aunty. Hello uncle, namaskaar aaji,' Ashish rattled off to Madhavi's father and grandmother, who were in the living room. He strode down the passage towards Madhavi's room. The door was open, and she was lying on the bed, a textbook open in front of her while she yakked on the phone. 'Haan, hahaha, no . . . not really.' She looked up on Ashish's entry and waved at the desk chair. 'Haan, Shilpa, no, Ashish has come. Ha ha, don't be stupid. No he's *not*. Shaddup. Okay, call me later.' She dropped the phone, and sat up. 'Ashish, I spoke to the gardens officer today.'

He sighed. It was one of Madhavi's habits,

housewife-like, to talk to the people in front of her as though they too had been involved in the conversation in her head. 'What?'

She rolled her eyes. 'About the tree, Ashish.'

'Oh, yeah.'

Madhavi's current project was saving the banyan tree in the empty plot from the builders. She had called the ward office a few weeks earlier and found out that, as per the Maharashtra (Urban Areas) Preservation of Trees Act, 1975, it was illegal for anyone to prune, much less cut down, the tree without applying in writing for permission. But since then the rains had started, and it was more commonplace to see fallen branches on the road, or uprooted gulmohar trees that had toppled in a storm. Madhavi had done her research — she'd taken several photographs of the tree, hassled the gardens officer endlessly to come and visit it, and looked up every newspaper article she could find about tree-cutting.

She went to her desk and picked up a sheaf of printouts. 'It says here that contractors will prune trees and cut much more than they're supposed to and sell the extra wood!'

'Hm,' Ashish said. He was now regretting refusing the ice cream, and considered whether to tell Madhavi to ask for some. His eye skated over the pleasant, girly confusion of things in her room — CDs, books, hair clips, notes, magazines — and he wondered where her Calvin and Hobbes collection, a favourite of his, could have got to.

'Also that they'll cut the tree in the night and in the morning claim that it fell in a storm.'

'Yes yes.'

'And that — '

'Look, are you just going to read things out to me now? Don't you have homework to do?'

She put down the clippings and pushed her black-framed glasses up her nose. 'I don't trust the tree officer,' she announced.

'So what?'

'So we'd better do something.'

'Like?'

'Like keep a watch on it, at least.'

'What, you want to mount a vigil for the tree? What do you think this is, Narmada?' Ashish got up and started rifling through her CDs. 'Where's your Kishori Amonkar CD?' He felt like listening to something beautiful and familiar.

'Ashish! Gandhiji said that we have to be the change we want to see in the world.'

In that case, Ashish thought, I'd have to be a very good-looking boy who'd sleep with anyone and make no fuss about it.

'Okay, okay,' he said.

223

15

Mohan held the receiver awkwardly, bending his head as though to catch what a mumbling, irascible person was saying. He didn't understand.

'So when will you come back?' he repeated.

There was an exhalation. Was she angry?

'I can't say,' Lakshmi said.

'All right, well, let me know when you know.' He wished he could be more authoritative; things were getting out of hand. There had been no argument, he reminded himself, even as his stomach pulled away from him into an unending void. If there had been no argument it couldn't be that bad. Therefore, in the course of things, she would come back.

'All right,' she said, while he was still reasoning this. 'I'll call again in a few days, or you have the number.' She hung up.

Mohan sat in the living room in the bluing dusk. He looked at the familiar clutter and ran similar stories through his mind. It could be nothing. She had simply gone to look after a relative who was ill and stayed for a while; these things were normal. He wandered

224

towards the tea chest and noticed that the old alarm clock told the wrong time: it said eleven forty-three. But when he lifted the heavy, rust-spotted thing to his ear he heard a low rumble; it hadn't quite stopped.

One of Ashish's blue rubber chappals protruded from under a chair — he left them here and there at strange, hasty angles as though abandoned in a moment of crisis. The boy's arrival had made more work for Lakshmi; had it been something Mohan had forced on her? But she was so fond of Ashish, more than of his sister, and certainly more than of Vimla. Mohan kicked the slipper back under the chair.

She had left, but not, surely, in real anger. He found himself trailing along, picking up and putting down ornaments, some of which she'd begun to acquire soon after their marriage: a flat brass turtle that she'd bought outside the temple at Alandi; you were supposed to immerse it in the tank. She'd smiled, he remembered, and decided to keep the turtle. He replaced it and sat in an unfamiliar place on the divan; he felt odd, like a stranger in the house.

That trip — it had been after they married, and they'd gone first to a cousin of hers in Pune and then to nearby tourist spots — Saswad, Alandi, Karla. Lakshmi's feet were still reddened from the mehendi; she wore jewellery and a new sari every day. Somewhere — he couldn't remember if it had been Saswad or Alandi — in an alcove in a whitewashed wall near the temple, there had been a man with a yellow songbird that picked fortunes for an anna. Lakshmi, his new wife, was allowed to stroke the silky head of the bird. Its owner prompted it, 'Come, choose a piece of paper.' The small bird hopped on a tray of curled-up notes, looking cross; it eventually pecked at one. The man unrolled it and read, 'When you want to have a child, if you go to a Shiv temple and light a lamp, you'll get a son.' A year later, returning from a Sunday visit to her parents' house, they had remembered and gone into the next temple, which happened to be a Shiv temple, and lit a lamp. The first child had in fact been a son, Gautam; Mohan had secretly hoped for a girl.

That story now seemed to belong to another person. The early complicity and laughter of the marriage, where had it gone? He remembered other things from that time — they'd for some time lived at home with his mother, his sister, who wasn't yet married, and Vivek and his wife. Lakshmi had been happy when the old house was sold and they could move here; for Mohan it had been a wrench to leave. When they were moving out there had been heavy rain for three days, then flooding at high tide, a few hours before the movers arrived. The sky was grey and lightless, frightening; the boxes were ready, crates nailed together, and he and Vivek wrote names and destinations on them with an indelible marker borrowed from the printing shop. The four small children, to their regret, had been sent away with Vimla and Lakshmi; they loved splashing about in the dirty water that came up to their chests, but no one had time to keep an eye on them.

It had been the storm water drains, as usual. The drains, down which everyone in the city throws things they wish to lose forever, from rubbish to the occasional unidentified body; the drains had clogged. When the rainfall and tide rose they could contain no more, and the detritus welled into the streets and gardens; people tutted and waded through the opaque, foul-smelling liquid.

Mohan had thought he would go upstairs one last time, alone, and look at the empty upper floor — the front room now stripped of everything but the patch of sunlight; the passage; the bedrooms. Vivek, though, called out to him, 'Just check those guys have tied the boxes on the last cart properly!' and Mohan ran down to shout after the movers, who waved and nodded to him and carried on.

Vivek came out of the door and locked it. He pocketed the key and looked at Mohan.

'Well,' he said. 'Let's go now.'

Mohan was too embarrassed to ask for the key and return inside while his brother waited, so he followed him down the road, which now resembled nothing so much as a gutter. But a bird broke into song from a peepal tree as they passed the recreation ground, and the house like a person remained in his mind, hurt and still waiting for him to take his leave.

He walked around the room now, trying to remember what life had been like before he'd married. The period was vague; he remembered early childhood, and the painfully sensitive time before adolescence, but it was slightly absurd to think of himself as an adult before he had a family of his own. He glanced at Lakshmi's chair. Had there arisen, in the interval between their wedding and now, demands that he hadn't been able to fulfil? Had she changed? Was he supposed to have changed? Had it been, he wondered darkly, the television? Had their life failed to provide the kind of excitement that she might have enjoyed? He saw her calm face in his mind, and frowned.

He paced in front of the bookshelf; he was, he decided, having some sort of afternoon nightmare, possibly connected with poor digestion or something of the sort. He gazed at the familiar spines but received no consolation. So would it be like this, one of those arrangements where two people live largely apart but continue to be married in name?

He sat down again, and began to wait.

★　★　★

This time it wasn't like the other stories: he saw the whole thing at once. It began with an image of his father's legs from the knee down, a part of his white dhoti visible and his thin calves, which were the colour of toasted bread. He was running down the wide wooden steps of the chawl he'd lived in since he was a young child. From this picture the rest of the story spun out: it was about the moment when everything in Vithal Karekar's life changed. His mother had died when he was still a boy; his father died when he was in his late teens. The only son, he'd been left to arrange the last rites, then make his way in the world. He did that by working in the printing shop where he'd been taken on, and by educating himself, besides, as he could. It was a time of change for the country; at Dandi, in Gujarat, there was a protest against the salt laws, and a hint of this found its way into the story. It wasn't an event Mohan had discussed with his father; he simply knew the cremation must have taken place; as the only son he would have had to carry out the rituals. But he saw it now: the cremation ground high on the promontory, the hot sun, the papery bits of flying ash, the few other grown men — his father's friend Atul, and Atul's father — who had come along from the chawl; even the priest, bare-chested, flabby, with a wily, experienced face, and the driver of the horse cart they must have taken to the cremation ground.

Who knew if the real scenes had been like that? But in Mohan's head they lived this way; he found himself crying for his father, who had then been a young man alone in the world, not much older than Ashish. He'd had no way of knowing what would happen to him; even his dreams, perhaps, weren't quite formed.

Mohan imagined his father raising a sardonic eyebrow — or saying something dismissive — on finding that his younger son was writing this story. Would he have been angry? Mohan had seen little of his writing other than a few pages rescued from the bottom of the tea chest. They were from a story about a water carrier who'd cheated a customer — a Victorian tale with a moral, a little stiff, like a garment rarely worn. When Mohan read it he'd felt vaguely apprehensive, and ashamed, in the same way that he'd worried, when his own children turned eighteen, that he, like his father, would suddenly die and leave them unsupported. There was no reason to suppose that would happen, yet you always expected the pattern of the earlier life to play out in the one that followed.

The crying had exhausted him; he wrote a few paragraphs, then sat in the chair and closed his eyes. Outside, crows were shouting; other birds joined them as evening settled.

When Ashish got back, they ate, then cleared up together. The boy retreated into his room; Mohan went to bed, where he failed to sleep. The street light outside the window glimmered orange through the night: it seemed to glow most brightly just as day was about to break. At this time the crows and other birds of Saraswati Park shouted, sang, and otherwise made their feelings raucously and joyously felt. Mohan got up, feeling insubstantial. The fan turned above him, like a dancer in trance; the sheets made a mocking map of a night spent in sleep.

Morning had come but the street lamp was still on; it made him think of a lantern, and he remembered the holidays were about to start.

★ ★ ★

'Baba.'

He smiled at the voice, high and innocently demanding: Megha. 'Hm, how's everything?' he asked. He held the receiver close and turned into the corner.

'Everything's fine,' she said lazily. 'Work, you know. I don't know when I'll get leave now. I had asked for Diwali, but everyone wants to come back, and now it's so near. I haven't even heard, so that means I won't get it. But they said people who don't get it this year will get leave for Diwali next year. I might come before that, if the project finishes on time. Ba, I had a letter from Satish mama some time ago, I kept meaning to write to him but I didn't get time. He wrote, I'm getting old now, something like that, he wasn't sure if he'd see me again. And he said he met Ashish after a long time, 'That boy seems to have a brain, let's see if he ends up using it', something like that.' She laughed, then sighed.

'Hm,' said Mohan, thinking of the dusty

room in Grant Road. There was a pause.

'And how's Ashish, Ba? Is he bored to death stuck there with just you?'

He smiled. 'Well, he doesn't go out much. Of course, he must be meeting his friends in the daytime at college, and he goes for some extra tuition. But at the weekend he's mostly here. Studies a lot, I think, reads.'

'Ouf. Let me speak to him.'

Mohan called Ashish, who came to the phone with unusual eagerness.

'Hi Meghatai . . . yes, I'm very serious this year, didn't you hear? No, no one but you calls me that any more, call me Ashish . . . so what did he say? When are you coming back with a husband from there, one who dresses like a cowboy and wears one of those hats?'

Ashish was suddenly laughing; his whole body was mobile, his face open. When he'd finished talking to Megha, Mohan took the phone back.

'Your mother's not here of course,' he said. 'It's hot now, even at night — no breeze.'

'October,' his daughter said nostalgically. 'Lucky you. There was a hailstorm here last weekend. They're saying it's going to be a cold winter. I'm sick of the cold now, I want it to get warm. But it's hardly started.'

★ ★ ★

233

After Diwali, Satish's lawyer called; he'd returned, and wanted to organize the reading of the will.

'I'm not sure when my wife will be back — she's gone to look after a relative,' Mohan said.

'Ideally she should be present,' said the quiet, precise voice. 'But it may be better to go ahead anyway. As executor, you're the only person who's required to be there. And your nephew will come?'

'Ashish?'

'Yes, he should be present.'

Three days later, after Ashish's classes had ended for the day, he and Mohan met at the Central Bank building at Fountain. They stood in the paan-stained stairwell, where notices saying Do Not Spit were decorated with gay red spatters, and took the lift to the fifth floor. Here they walked down a dingy, wooden-panelled corridor; the lawyers' office was behind a saloon door that made Mohan think of a John Wayne film. In the reception, they sat under a tiny, hectic fan; Mohan picked up an afternoon tabloid and began to read, passing over the speculation about the affairs of film actors and actresses, and onto the smaller items on the inner pages. One caught his eye: a competition for short stories run by the Asian Council.

The door of a cabin opened. A tall clerk disappeared down a short corridor lined with stacks of paper bound by ribbons; his wire-thin legs moved like a dance through his flapping trousers. He rummaged in one of the stacks and extracted a file.

Soon after, a small young man with a foolish, eager face appeared at the door of the cabin.

'Mr Karekar?'

'Yes.'

'Please come.'

They trooped into his cabin, where the air conditioning was fierce, and he sent the peon out for cold drinks and beamed at them.

'My father was taught by Professor Chitale you know. At Sydenham.'

'Oh?'

'Yes, he was very fond of him.' The round-faced young man, Dhananjay Pingale, smiled, looked abstracted, adjusted his spectacles and fiddled with a paperweight on his desk. 'There, er, may be one or two surprises here,' he said gently.

Mohan squared his shoulders. 'We're not expecting anything,' he began, but the peon now returned with two glasses of pop, one orange, one black. Ashish took the orange one and began to drink thirstily.

'Should we start?' young Mr Pingale asked.

'Hm.'

The quiet, unemphatic voice began to read. Satish had left his books to Mohan, some money and his personal effects to Lakshmi, and an insurance policy in favour of Megha, Uma, Gautam, and Ashok. His apartment was left to Ashish.

The lawyer looked at their astounded faces and said, 'I have a note from him that he wrote when he amended the will in May. It says, 'I am leaving my most financially significant asset to Ashish Datye, who is not a relative of mine but whom I think a promising young man. I encourage him to find and follow his own path in life and to fulfil his hopes as I have not been able to fulfil mine.'

16

In the second half of November, Bombay drifts into its most pleasant season, winter, when as many as three or four times, one shivers in the evening, declares the weather 'really cold' and puts on a light sweater. On such an evening, Narayan and Ashish met to go to the cinema. A newish film, *The Leader*, was still playing; it had opened for the Diwali holidays but neither of them had seen it. At the end of their last tutorial, Narayan had suggested they watch it together.

Ashish got out of a rickshaw at Andheri, his heart racing for no obvious reason. The teacher was waiting outside the cinema. Narayan wore a black sweater; he looked thin and the lines on his boyish face showed under the orange street light. He thought I might not turn up, Ashish realized, and felt both powerful and embarrassed; the teacher appeared bent and pitiable, like a stage villain on the point of defeat. But his face brightened when Ashish approached.

'Ah, you've come. I've got the tickets,' he said.

The seats weren't dirty, as such, but the

darkened hall seemed to contain many suppressed stains. The velour upholstery was dusty and, here and there, a little stiff; the very air was stale — it had passed through a series of audiences: the 12.30, 2.30, 4.30 and now seven o'clock.

People were still coming in — groups of boys, snickering in recently acquired deep voices, and a few couples who looked for the quieter seats at the front. In the dark, Ashish felt self-conscious; he wondered whether Narayan was the sort of man who went to the cinema alone in the afternoons, the man who sat near the aisle and looked with hungry eyes at the people who passed.

The trailers started, and with them the campaign Ashish had been waiting for: an arm snaked its way casually around the back of his seat while an advertisement for an optician's shop at Breach Candy began to play. 'Christian Dior, Versace, Gucci!' What was happening, Ashish wondered. Should he lean back? Or sit up? Where could this go? Was anyone looking? He turned, confronted Narayan's cherubic yet oddly stubborn profile, smiled weakly, and proffered the popcorn.

The feature was about to start; the lights came on. Everyone stood for the national anthem, which was sung, droned, or merely listened to. A grainy film played of the flag, fluttering in a strong breeze. Ashish, his hands decorously at his sides, sneaked another look at Narayan. Would there be a complicit smile? But the professor was loose-limbed, at ease. He adjusted his spectacles and sat down calmly when the music ended. The censor board certificate appeared on the screen, blurred and ghostly, and Ashish noticed that Yezdi Sodawaterbottlewala had been on the panel that had rated the film an 'A'. Then the opening scene began; for a while he didn't think of anything else.

The movie was excellent — it was about a political don and his unruly family. Just as the semi-climactic pre-interval scene ended, the lights came on. Ashish sat up. He had a crazy urge to ensure no one he knew had seen him here.

'I — uh — I'm going to go and — '

'Sure. I'll go out for a smoke.'

Narayan's manner towards him in public was reassuringly normal. They really could have been acquaintances, teacher and student who had decided to pop into a film together. But as Ashish hurried up the plush velvet hill that led to the exit, which was sunk into the bank of seats like a secret door leading out of a cave, he felt a pang of embarrassment. It was easy to find Narayan impressive when he was alone, in the charmed world of his flat.

There, each part of his existence — the pictures, the French films, the handloom sofa covers — dovetailed with the others to appear both pleasing and original. Outside, in the world where Ashish ordinarily lived, he saw Narayan through his contemporaries' eyes, and he cringed.

He took his time in the bathroom, washing his hands and fiddling with his hair so as not to appear in the hall while the lights were still on.

Two boys, a little younger than he, were splashing each other with water from the tap and talking loudly.

'Hey man, Reena's looking hot in that top,' one said. They wore expensive, semi-sporting clothing and swaggered like much older men in front of the mirror.

'Yeah, she's okay. But she's getting fat. I had to tell her not to eat ice cream today.' They smirked, and then, catching Ashish staring, looked at him, then at each other, and snickered.

When Ashish came out of the bathroom the bell sounded. He hurried through the black-painted double doors. When he slipped into his seat Narayan said nothing, merely glanced at him with an easy movement of the head and then leaned back, as though satisfied. Ashish relaxed; he was at home here.

In the blasting air conditioning, the stale scent of the velvet mingled with something synthetic and floral that had been sprayed on the carpet, and the faint odour of cigarette smoke on Narayan's clothes. Ashish leaned back, and thought he felt the warmth of the other man's arm, the smoothness of a cotton shirt sleeve; he closed his eyes.

As the credits rolled the two of them, with the rest of the dazed, blinking audience, allowed themselves to be herded along the plush carpet towards the exit.

The night was warm and moist. It was raining lightly; on the road, headlamps turned the drizzle into shreds of illuminated net. Narayan hovered close to Ashish, and smiled. The light caught his spectacles.

'Well,' he said. 'Which way are you going?'

It was obvious their routes diverged.

'I'll, uh, go to the station,' Ashish said. His voice seemed fake to him, like a much younger boy trying to sound grown-up. He coughed.

'Okay. I'll walk as far as the traffic lights with you then I'll go right.'

'Sure.'

The road was slick with dirt and rain; street lamps and headlights gave the wet surfaces metallic accents. The world around was tired and irritated, trying to get home in a hurry,

241

but Ashish was oblivious, despite the rickshaw driver who honked and missed his foot by inches, or the slowly moving carpet of cars, lorries, and buses that sounded their horns and whose drivers leaned out of the window to swear at each other.

At the junction, Narayan smiled again. 'Well, it was very nice,' he said. He seemed happy; his mood was light, like a child's. Ashish responded equally cheerfully. 'It was good fun,' he said, a phrase dredged from memory; it must, he thought, have been used by someone more consistently chirpy than himself. At that moment he remembered that Sunder liked to say 'good fun'. He felt a strange despair.

'I enjoyed it,' he said emphatically.

'Good. So did I.' For a second Narayan appeared to hover — but what possible salutation could they make, especially here, at the rainy, dirty junction near the flyover? 'Well, see you in a few days,' he said; he raised his hand and walked away. Ashish moved ahead to cross the main road before the station; he was conscious of not looking back, and felt a half-forgotten sentimentality. It *had* been nice, he thought, editing out the feelings of embarrassment. In fact, he couldn't remember the last time he'd enjoyed an evening this way.

'But I don't need anything from the market,' Ashish pointed out. He continued, nonetheless, to trail after Madhavi. As ever, she walked purposefully.

'So come to keep me company then.' She gave him a dazzling grin.

'All right, but just for a bit, I'm not following you round endlessly, I've got lots of study to do.'

'Okay. And we can have coffee before we come back,' she said.

The day was wet and dank-smelling, though it wasn't raining. They scuffled through the inside lanes towards the market, and Madhavi got straight to the point. 'So, it's pretty cool about your uncle leaving you his flat.'

'He's not really my uncle.'

'Who cares?'

'Yeah.' Ashish walked along, staring, out of habit, into the peculiarly dead windows of houses owned by respectable doctors and dentists. 'But the thing is . . . '

'What?'

'It's weird. I don't even know why he left it to me.'

'Oho. You mean he was trying to upset his family?'

'Maybe.' Satish uncle's elegant, malicious

face floated before Ashish's eyes. 'I mean, of course, he was always trying to do that. But why me?'

'Rickshaw!' Madhavi waved at a passing three-wheeler. It slowed and the driver, a thin young man, leered and raised an eyebrow. 'Market?' she enquired.

The khaki-clad driver made a derisory face and accelerated again; he didn't think the short distance worth his while. Madhavi sighed. 'Yeah, so . . . What were you saying?' She pushed Ashish's arm in a friendly way.

'Why me,' repeated Ashish, slightly irritably.

'Yeah, true.' Madhavi giggled. 'Oh, sorry, I didn't mean it that way. Why you . . . hm. Wasn't he close to your cousins?'

'Sort of, he was fond of all of them, especially Megha, but he also had fights with all of them when they got older.'

'Haan.'

'But it's not even really about that. I've met him as a child but recently just once or twice. I don't understand.'

'Does it matter? Are your uncle and aunt upset?'

They had reached the main road, and began to pick their way up it, shimmying closer to the inside edge of the pavement every time a large vehicle approached one of the many puddles.

'No . . . I don't think so . . . ' Ashish didn't know how to express his strongest feeling, which was something like dread at being Satish uncle's chosen heir.

They stopped at a crossing. Madhavi turned to him. 'But Ashish — this is a really lucky thing for you. You could do anything now — you could sell the flat, or live there, or take a loan against it. You don't have to worry about your future. Who does that happen to, at our age?'

'My age,' corrected Ashish, mindful of the two years' difference.

'Whatever. Chal,' and she grabbed his hand, and, to his mortification, dragged him across the road.

They began to stroll up the main market street, pushed against and shoved into by more determined shoppers. Evening, and the various makeshift shops had rigged up their own electricity supplies; illicit wires ran in tangles from the electricity poles to each brightly lit small booth. Ashish, easily distracted, wandered behind Madhavi, gazing at the stall selling imitation, gold-plated jewellery, the stand spread with hair accessories, the pirated DVDs spread on a tarpaulin at the roadside.

'Oh, nail file, I need to go in here,' Madhavi muttered as they approached a brightly lit shop that gave onto the street. Just before she dived in, she turned to Ashish again. 'The main thing is, what's happened to you could only happen to someone really lucky. I hope you realize that.'

He waited for her just outside the shop, and looked into the passing faces, averting his own self-consciously if anyone stared back.

Her shopping done, Madhavi decided they should go for coffee.

'All right. Udupi Cafe?' Ashish said. He liked the dinginess of this establishment, which served south Indian filter coffee and snacks, and was always filled with plump couples, single, self-important old men, and groups of students.

'Yuck, no, let's go to the Idiot-Idiot.' Madhavi was referring to a branch of the popular chain, which served many varieties of flavoured coffee, played loud music, and was the favoured meeting place for youthful couples to flirt tentatively and interminably.

'No!'

'Come on, I'll treat you.'

'That's not the point — '

'Come *on* then.'

'Okay.'

They sat in the Idiot-Idiot, outside, under an umbrella; Ashish stirred three sugars into his cappuccino while Madhavi sucked contentedly at an Iced Coconut Freezz. A light rain fell; at the next table, three teenage boys talked loudly; one of them, who had bad skin, smoked a cigarette. Ashish inhaled the moist, sour-smelling air and remembered Narayan's flat.

'My tutor is really interesting,' he told Madhavi.

'Oh? That guy? How many times a week do you go?'

'Three-four, it depends.' Ashish began to smile.

'Hm. And what does he do the rest of the time? He teaches a lot of other students like you?'

'No, I don't think so.' He pushed a couple of empty sugar packets around on the table. 'He's doing some research, he used to teach in the university.'

'Oh. What's his research?'

'I'm not sure.'

'What's his name again?'

'Professor Narayan.' He felt a pleasurable sense of embarrassment and secrecy just saying it.

She slurped at her shake. 'What's he like? Is he old? Must be married?'

'I don't think he's married. Must be about forty. He's interesting, I like him. I mean, he makes the subject interesting, not like the teachers in college.'

'Achchha.' Madhavi regarded Ashish, put her cheek on one hand, and gazed out at the rain.

★ ★ ★

'No, I don't think you've understood. When Leontes says, 'All this be nothing', the sky, the heaven, the world, he's using the word 'nothing' in a very special sense. In fact, if you check in the Oxford dictionary you see the word 'heaven' also refers to the canopy above the stage in theatres of that period. So actually he's an actor on stage, speaking a part, and pointing out to the audience how unreal the dramatic illusion is.'

Narayan was almost shaking with excitement.

'Oh, okay,' murmured Ashish, interested despite himself. He made a note in the exercise book on the coffee table ('dramatic illusion'), felt thirsty, and wished Narayan would offer him water. The teacher took a sip from a glass on the side table next to him.

'In fact the word 'nothing', if you look it up in the Concordance — you do know what a concordance is?'

'No.'

'It's a book that lists all the instances of each word used, for example in the works of Shakespeare, or in the Bible.'

'Oh.'

'If you look up 'nothing', you'll find many of the other uses of the word in Shakespeare carry a similar double sense. As well as meaning nothing, the word seems to connote that very quality of metatheatricality, dramatic illusion. I've often thought,' he said, a little wistfully, a little proudly, 'of writing a book about Shakespeare's Nothing.'

'Mm.' Water, thought Ashish, perplexed, who didn't offer a guest water? It was just basic manners.

'The last lines of *The Tempest* are another example. 'Oh brave new world, where we may have our music for nothing'. He's talking about something commonplace, not having to pay the players — but I think the playwright's also alluding to that sense of illusion. What would 'music for nothing' be if you consider the phrase as independent?' Narayan stared for a moment out of the window. 'I've always imagined it's something akin to the idea of maya. It's only an illusion, but it has its own texture, its own experiences that are compelling for the souls who are trapped in it.'

Narayan's face lit up, and Ashish smiled. It was hard not to feel that Narayan was talking principally to himself, but there was something sweet about his self-absorption. And he speaks so well, thought the boy affectionately.

Exasperation, followed by a flowering of good humour, passed over the teacher's face. 'But you must be bored,' he said. 'Come, do you want to go up to the roof? We might see the golden eagles. They often appear after sunset.'

On the terrace, Ashish was jittery with adrenaline. Narayan stood quite close; the cotton of his sleeve brushed Ashish's arm. He smelled the teacher: a mild, soapy smell, reassuring, with faint traces of musk and cigarette smoke.

With the twilight the fragrance of champa flowers spread. Something else, too — the heady, sweet scent of parijatak.

Then, with a suddenness that couldn't have been orchestrated, that was wild, two golden eagles alighted on the terrace. They perched atop the water tank, silently watching the city. Ashish craned his neck up. He wondered if something apocalyptic would happen; maybe an eagle would swoop past, taking out one of his eyes with a peck or a grab of those cruel claws. Instead, the birds remained until it was completely dark, and the two men below stayed to watch them, quietly, leaning their backs against the dusty concrete parapet where the yellowing paint flaked. Ashish's arm was touching Narayan's; the smell of the older man mingled with diesel fumes from the road below, something chemical and grainy in the wind, and the fading scent of flowers.

It became cooler; Ashish felt the breeze on his skin and looked at the lights below. Saraswati Park was somewhere down there, but very far away, smaller than a toy.

Narayan touched his arm. 'Should we go inside?' he said.

Ashish nodded. Then he realized it might be too dark for the gesture to be visible. 'Sure,' he whispered. He cleared his throat as they went down the steps. In the passage, the light had gone out.

The flat was a new place, an oasis of electric light. They blinked at each other. Narayan's eyes flickered across Ashish's face.

'I'll make some tea,' he said. He went into the kitchen, and Ashish, after some hesitation, when he stood looking at the large Kal Nirnay calendar pinned up in the hall — big squares and bold black and red numbers for the dates — followed him. A strange thing then happened. When Narayan turned from the stove, where he had put water to boil, he saw Ashish and smiled. He came and stood right in front of the boy. The bright white light of the kitchen tube was hurting Ashish's eyes and made him feel unreal. Narayan was

251

very close. 'So,' he said, 'your first sighting of golden eagles?'

Ashish met his eyes and felt inexplicably excited, as well as alarmed. He opened his mouth, and Narayan bent and kissed him.

17

The sticky man fell, attained a hold, then fell again. He was a creature of nightmare, his torso, arms and legs of blue plastic and his core a feeble string of red gel. When he fell, his jelly hands and feet reattached him, at the last, sickening moment, to the surface of the bookshelf. A little later gravity exerted its implacable pull: he began to topple again, his torso twisting sideways over his legs. Mohan pulled him off the side of the bookshelf and threw him against it once more.

Had it been the same young vendor on the train? In essence the boy was identical: enormous eyes, dusty skin, gummed-up lashes. 'Spiderman, Spiderman,' he'd urged Mohan, throwing the small toy against the wall of the iron compartment, where it began to stick and fall, stick and fall.

'No, no.'

'Spiderman, Spiderman.' The child had looked as though he was about to cry. 'Please take one,' he said ritually. 'It'll be the first sale of the day.'

Mohan had been depressed; the idea that someone else's needs could be fulfilled through him had struck him as pleasant. 'How much is it?' he'd asked.

'Ten rupees. But if you want I'll give it to you for five. Or two for ten.'

'I don't want two.'

The boy immediately detached a clear packet and gave him one of the toys: they came in lime green and bright blue. The one he gave Mohan was green. 'No, give me a blue one,' the letter writer said, for no obvious reason. The boy passed him the blue one. 'Take both, two for ten, two for ten,' he urged.

'No, that's it.'

The child took the note, one of the now rare azure five rupees, and touched it to his forehead, murmuring the name of his own particular saint or god. So the day had begun for him. And Mohan put the sticky man in his pocket and forgot about him, until a couple of days later, when he was throwing that pair of trousers onto the washing pile. He felt a bump and extracted the small packet.

February, and the dosa man in Saraswati Park had stopped wearing a sweater in the mornings and evenings; the watchman had left off the charcoal brazier that in winter glowed in his lap at night. The narrow advertisements under the luggage racks in the train were no longer for cold remedies, tonics and virility potions: now they had returned to offering miracle powders against prickly heat and haemorrhoids.

And Lakshmi had been gone for more than four months. He'd thought, of course, about going to Nagpur to see her; he'd asked her if she wouldn't come home. But she'd explained, in a detached way behind which he wasn't sure if he heard anger or nothing at all, that it was a help to her cousins for her to be there, looking after the sick man. Ashish's exams were getting nearer; Mohan didn't know what to do. He couldn't just leave the boy, even though Ashish seemed well — a little hectic, almost sparkling, sometimes, with a tired happiness — but well on the whole. His tutorials were helping, he said; they were revising the syllabus before the exams started in a few weeks.

The house was running, in its way, with the bai who came to clean and cook. He'd begun to look at the place with new eyes. What *was* all this clutter on the table? What about some of the books, the ones he never looked at? He didn't know what to do with the books — impossible to give them to the wastepaper man, but maybe he could sell them to the few booksellers who had reappeared near the American Express Bank. The table, at least, could be cleared. And by the time Ashish came in one afternoon from college, calling excitedly 'Mohan mama!', he'd done much of the work; the old jars, bottles and tins had been removed, and so had the paper and runners covering the table top. Now you saw its surface: the teak still somewhat silky, glowing reddish brown under scratches and stains.

'What happened?' Ashish asked. He held an afternoon paper in his hand and his face was bright.

'Time to do some cleaning,' Mohan said. He put down the duster and gazed at the field of his surprising victory; he'd made a pile of the leftover bottles and containers which he'd offer first to the bai, then sell to the junk man.

Ashish looked confused. But he persisted, and pushed the paper in front of his uncle. 'See this.'

A small item on page nine said that of the entries in the Asian Council short story competition, one of those to receive a minor award, with a special regional mention, came from Bombay: an M. V. Karekar, for a story called 'The Burning Ground'.

'Isn't this you?'

Mohan stared at the type. More than once he opened his mouth; then he said flatly, 'There must be a mistake, I haven't heard.'

But Ashish ran downstairs to get Madhavi to check on the internet, and they found the list on the Asian Council website. The organizers must have forgotten to get in touch with the entrants before they'd sent out the press release.

The next day at lunch time, Mohan got a call from a lazy, sleepy sounding person who yet managed to appear excited. 'Mr Mohan Karekar?'

'Yes.'

'I'm calling from the *Indian Record*. Mr Yezdi Sodawaterbottlewala gave me your number. It's about the short story prize. We want to do an article on you for our Sunday feature, Hidden Treasures. Have you seen it?' the voice enquired with a note of barely concealed pride.

'Um, I'm not sure.'

'So when can I take your interview? And I'll need to bring a photographer.'

'Well, just cross the road any time, and find me near the kabutar khana.'

'Can I come after lunch?'

'Certainly.'

The excited person turned out to be a young girl, slightly older than Ashish, wearing jeans and a t-shirt. She looks like a child, Mohan thought, and was flummoxed remembering that, when they married, Lakshmi had

257

been younger than this.

The girl said she was a trainee with the newspaper. She asked Mohan a volley of questions, and stared down at her pad, scribbling and tucking away a long strand of hair that had escaped from her pony tail.

'And how old are you?' she enquired.

Mohan was amused to find himself reluctant to answer. 'Fifty-nine,' he said, after a small pause.

The photographer, a middle-aged Marathi man with a hero moustache, took several pictures (he called them 'shots') of Mohan: under the banyan tree, next to the plaque that identified the red and yellow drinking fountain behind the letter writers as a gift from Ma Devidas Purbhodas Tiwari in memory of his late daughter Mrs Lilawati Tribhovandas (on 24 May 1923), and finally — here Mohan looked a little bashful — one next to the gate of the GPO. 'Hey, what about us?' Khan called after the photographer and reporter when they left. 'Don't you want to take our picture?'

The story appeared on Sunday. It was four paragraphs long, misspelled Mohan's name (Kharekar) and said that he was part of a dying breed of letter writers in the city, whose trade had been killed by mobile phones and cheap trunk calls. Still, several people he knew called up to congratulate him, including Yezdi, who said that there had been a couple of calls at the office asking for Mohan's contact details. 'This chap I know from a publishing house wants to meet you for a series of new Bombay writing.' He read out the name, Dharmendra Kapoor, and dictated the telephone number. After Mohan had hung up he looked at the piece of paper for some time. Finally he reached for the receiver again.

★ ★ ★

'Full.'

The lift man, shrunken in his white clothes, looked older than Independence; he pulled shut the concertina door of the lift and it departed without Mohan, who shrugged and began to climb the stairs. These old buildings in Fort had a specific smell that both turned his stomach and made him feel at home: wood shavings, furniture polish, a vestige of incense and betel nut, and of course dust. Spittle stains festooned the walls of the stairwell; the stairs were crumbling at the edges and must have been this way for years. Even inside it was warm: about three o'clock in the afternoon.

At the fourth floor he found the door

labelled Modern Republican (Marxist) Alliance; this had been crossed out, and a piece of paper with New Vista Publishers written on it pasted above the wooden sign. The name of the now-defunct political party was like a very old piece of gossip: it caused a slight current of air to flutter after it, in baffled reminiscence.

'My uncle is the last member of the MR(M)A. This used to be our family business office,' explained the young man who appeared in the shabby reception area, 'I'm Dharmendra Kapoor. Thanks for coming.'

He looked short for a Punjabi, Mohan thought, but he was really more of a Bombayite: he was smiling and fair, with rosy cheeks and conciliating manners. He pointed out the water cooler, turned on the fan, and took the typescript from Mohan. 'I'll get back to you,' he said pleasantly, smiled, and shook Mohan's hand. Then he nodded and went into a smaller office partitioned off from the main room in dark panelling, and where a yellowing sign marked MR(M)A, Secretary General had been scored through by two pencil lines. A piece of paper taped below said Editorial Director.

Mohan, slightly unsure of what to do, sat on the bench in the outer room. He looked up at the dusty framed pictures. One showed

Gandhi and his secretary walking in Bihar; another was a drawing of a spinning wheel. There was an old clock barometer on the reception desk, a thing he hadn't seen for years. A single window, about four by two and a half feet, framed a section of sky and two branches of a budding bhaya tree, a laburnum. When the bench became too noticeably solid, Mohan shifted his weight, and concentrated on the door, which was surely about to open. But it remained shut, while the light at the window changed. The backdrop of the laburnum branches went from white-yellow to deep blue. From the other side of the door he heard a few phone conversations, laughter, and then again silence.

At six o'clock Kapoor came out, humming to himself. Mohan jumped up.

'Oh!'

'I — ah — '

'As a matter of fact I haven't yet had time to read your work. I didn't realize you were still here — that is — if you give me some time,' the young man said, a little reprovingly, 'I could read it and let you know. Leave it with me for a few days — a couple of weeks.' He waited for Mohan to go out of the main door so that he could lock it. 'Not more than a month, hm?' he said when he had done so.

'I'll be in touch. Goodbye!' He ran down the stairs.

★　★　★

When he was home, Mohan wandered near the chair in front of the television, which still had a folded shawl draped neatly over its back. He thought about calling his wife. She knew about the will, but not about the competition; she hadn't reacted much to the news about the will, either. He would call, he decided, when he heard from the publisher. He couldn't rid himself of the thought that it was too late, and she simply wanted him to leave her alone. In the chair near the window he opened the Mark Twain; he began by looking at his notes, but moved onto the essay in defence of Harriet Shelley which he'd started to read weeks earlier.

The printed words reproduced the monotype of the first edition. How beautiful the face was, with its small, human imperfections. Harriet was Shelley's first wife; they had married when they were very young, he was nineteen and she was sixteen; Mohan nodded to himself. Twain was reviewing a biography of Shelley in which the writer put the blame for Shelley's desertion of Harriet onto Harriet herself, a literary sleight of hand that

Twain kept pointing out. Shelley had had to grow up early: 'He was an erratic and fantastic child during eighteen years, then he stepped into manhood, as one steps over a door-sill.' The young couple had been happy at first, though they had little money. 'Harriet sang evenings, or read aloud.' Mohan felt an almost physical pain in the chest, remembering a few early times when Lakshmi had sung, laughing, a song or two for him — nothing complicated, she had no training, but her voice was sweet though not strong. Eventually, after they had been married a year, Shelley became involved with another woman. Twain complained that Harriet's part of the story was never told: 'The young wife is always silent — we are never allowed to hear from her', he wrote. A little later — Mohan was nodding vehemently now — 'surely she would speak if she were allowed'. His eyes skated on, but they had filled and he saw indistinctly. 'We get only the other side, they keep her silent always.' Next to this he saw the start of his notes for the first and second stories. For the first time, it struck him: these stories distilled from the years, where in them was the person who had been there with him? He repeated to himself, 'they keep her silent always'.

It was late; Ashish was still out. Mohan

turned out the bright naked bulb and paused in the dark room, his finger marking his place in the book. He saw something white move opposite. Was it one of the owls Ashish had been talking about? But he didn't see it clearly. He went to bed, and the house seemed to bear witness against him: the fridge murmured reproof, the fan turned like an unceasing background accusation. He lay on his side of the enormous bed, which had been made for his parents. Vivek hadn't wanted it when they had taken the furniture from the old house, and Vimla hadn't had room. It was the size of two single beds, joined, a fact he had always liked; as a child he remembered how, with the mosquito net rising above it like a shamiana, it had been a whole world that he could crawl into and pretend he was in a ship or a caravanserai.

There was no rest tonight. Shadows slid across the room now and again, when movement outside blocked the glow of the street lamp. But the very stillness of the house was a reproach. 'They keep her silent,' he thought, and tears came to his eyes, though the pictures in his mind were confused. He remembered times of humiliation and sadness as a young child, and then how his wife had looked when they were first married. There were things that had been difficult for her, and which he hadn't really noticed, like living with her mother — and sisters-in-law for the first few months, or dealing with a young man who knew nothing about women and yet had firm ideas — he had been an idiot, or worse — about how his wife should behave, what she ought to wear and where she should or should not go alone. Yet he had been so different with his daughters.

He imagined writing her a letter, which was ridiculous. He, who'd turned others' feelings and concerns into more shapely phrases for years, couldn't envisage words fixing anything here. By the time dawn came, his exhaustion was complete; the phrase still repeated in his mind, and his wife was frustratingly just out of reach. A decision came, quite simply. He would be his own messenger; a letter or phone call wouldn't do. Why hadn't he acted earlier? He would go and speak to her, try to persuade her to come home. It was time to make a trip to Nagpur, as soon as Ashish's exams were over.

18

Ashish woke — it had been that intense, dreamful sleep of the evening. The lamp was on near the bed. Narayan sat in the armchair, observing him; his face was half in shadow, his expression hungry, yet analytical. 'Watching me sleep,' Ashish told himself warmly, fuzzily. 'He loves me.'

Narayan's eyes narrowed. 'You're awake? It's probably time for you to go,' he said quietly.

'Should I call my uncle and tell him I'm staying at Mayank's?'

'No, don't do that, he might worry.' But Narayan came to put his arms around the boy for a moment; his skin was warm and dry against Ashish's back. 'Here.' He handed Ashish his clothes.

Ashish got up reluctantly, put on his shirt and then his trousers, wobbling as he stood first on one leg then the other. He stared at a stain on the cream wall, which was in his line of sight from the bed. The stain must have been caused by damp; there was a crack in the plaster and next to it, a baggy patch of dark grey, the colour of a pi-dog that has become wet and miserable in a storm. Then there was a chip in a cement tile near the front left leg of the desk, and the paint on the bookcase was peeling away; it was a simple thing, probably plywood, Narayan might have bought it as a student. And Ashish's mind went down these familiar, not altogether forbidden aisles, but they were places where he wasn't invited. The conversations he and the professor had were brisk in the way they treated the older man's feelings and memories. He would ask Ashish a burst of direct questions that it was hard to imagine not answering, partly because each so quickly succeeded the next; but if Ashish asked a question in return, Narayan just smiled, or answered so lightly that the matter seemed to have been put aside.

In the evening, like today, when it was nearly time to go, Ashish would remain in the bed, wrap himself up to his chin in the sheet, and stare mutinously at the stain on the wall, dim in the half-light. He suspected Narayan was happy enough for him to leave, and the situation was so neatly arranged that he didn't even have to ask Ashish to go, because he had to, in any case: he was expected at home.

This evening Narayan walked Ashish to the door and opened it with one hand. With the other he rubbed Ashish's back between the shoulder blades. 'See you the day after tomorrow,' he said gently.

As Ashish's foot hit the first of the stairs he heard the door click behind him.

In the train on the way home to Saraswati Park, he glanced around the brightly lit, near empty compartment at the dissolute, late-evening faces of the other commuters, middle-aged men, and he felt cheated, as though he had been given nearly the thing he needed to feel complete; but not quite. If he had been able to stay half an hour longer — or if he were able to choose his own moment to exit the cocoon of the cotton sheet in that bed and that oddly depressing room — maybe then it would be different? The afternoons with Sunder seemed like another life, long ago, a period of innocence.

★ ★ ★

But the next time he arrived at Narayan's, the teacher opened the door with a charming smile and even as he was closing it, folded an arm around Ashish and kissed him. 'I was just making some good south Indian coffee,' he said. They took the coffee to bed. Half an hour later, when it was cold, Ashish sat up sipping his cup. Narayan lit a cigarette. 'Does this bother you?' he asked rhetorically. Ashish said no, though he was beginning to hate it. His father had been a smoker for many years, and he knew the matinal coughing fits and yellowed fingertips.

Narayan exhaled. 'So tell me something,' he said lazily, putting one arm behind his head to cradle it.

'Something?'

'A story, about your past.'

'I can't think of anything. Like what, do you mean?'

Narayan turned his head to look at Ashish. 'I don't know,' he said calmly, a little bored. 'About your first relationship, or the first person you ever liked. Or about your parents, your aunt and uncle. Anything.' He propped his head on his elbow, and waited to be entertained.

Ashish was silent for a while. He tried to think of an amusing story. Suddenly he remembered, and it was odd how the years had buried this moment, the early crush he'd had on his cousin Gautam, who was ten years older than him. He'd often shared a bed, of course, with either or both of his male cousins; Ashok, who was much more like Ashish, had never held any attraction for him, not in that way. But Ashish had slightly hero-worshipped Gautam, who was tall, handsome and sporty, devoid of much sense of humour except the gentle and conventional, and yet was always kind to Ashish, the youngest cousin. Gautam would take him along on errands, feed him sweets, and clout Jayant, Vivek mama's son, when he tried to bully Ashish.

Ashish had at the age of eight or nine (he was then a slightly tubby, overserious child) decided that he and Gautam would one day realize they were meant for each other and live together in a state of quasi-erotic, quasi-romantic happiness. He had been so certain this would happen that he had never agonized over it. Gautam had married, years later, in an arranged match that seemed to make him very happy — he was one of those fortunate people whose desires conform almost exactly to those expected by the society they live in. By then, Ashish's childhood crush had long dwindled; he'd almost forgotten it. Now, it was strange to think of Gautam, married for four years, plump and domesticated, sincere about his job in a telecom company in Bangalore, as the object of his cousin's pre-teen romantic flame.

'I used to have a kind of crush on one of my cousins . . . '

Narayan nodded, and allowed half an inch of ash to drop from the end of his cigarette into the ashtray beside him. 'Very normal.'

Ashish laughed, half awkwardly. He felt his efforts to capture the other man's attention fail. 'What about you . . . Who was the first person . . . ?'

'I don't even remember, Ashish. There was a friend of mine whom I felt very strongly about, a childhood friend, in Mangalore. And then as I grew older I just knew — that I wasn't really interested in women. Of course in a way I was far more genuinely interested in them than the other boys around me were.' He laughed.

'And before this — ' Ashish waved vaguely at the rumpled bed, meaning 'before me', ' — was there someone?'

Narayan looked thoughtful. He examined the end of the cigarette, began to bring it to his mouth, and then extinguished it instead. He picked up the packet and flipped it open, as though to inspect those that remained. 'There was,' he said quietly.

'So what happened?'

Narayan smiled. 'I don't really want to go into it. But he's not around any more, here I mean.'

'Was he a student? When you were teaching at the university?' Ashish felt emboldened; these were things he'd wondered about for a long time.

271

'Ashish — ' and Narayan smiled, like a cat. He pulled the boy to him, and put an arm around him. 'You're very young,' he observed.

'What does that mean?'

'It means — ' Narayan laughed. 'Well, it means you're very young. What's the time?' For the light coming under the curtains had dimmed, then become blue; now there was the first, orange glow of a street lamp. A train horn sounded.

'About seven o'clock.' Ashish got up resignedly and began to dress. He looked back at Narayan. 'So you never wanted to live with one person, to settle down?' he asked. He tried to imagine being like Narayan, at Narayan's age.

'No. I'd seen my parents' marriage.' The teacher got up and began to make the bed; he shook the sheet out with a sharp flap.

'But every marriage doesn't have to be like that, every relationship.'

'There are darknesses in every marriage, Ashish, or every relationship that goes on for years.'

'I don't know,' Ashish argued. 'My aunt and uncle, they're happy.'

'Yes?' Narayan's eyes were sharp. 'You think they still sleep together? That they don't wonder, or your uncle doesn't wonder, what it'd be like to sleep with someone else, if they're not doing so already? That they don't have frustrations and hatred that've built up through the years?'

Ashish stood still; he'd been doing up his belt. 'No, no,' he said vehemently. 'They're happy.'

'Good for them. And for you, if it makes you happy to believe that.'

Ashish opened the front door for himself this time; he didn't look back when it closed.

★ ★ ★

At home, he eyed his uncle sidelong, waiting for a bad mood to start. Strangely, it didn't. There was a new, absorbed quality about Mohan. He was actually paying attention most of the time, and he performed many of the household tasks: he checked that the Gogates' maid, Nirmala bai, was doing the household work, he bought vegetables, he kept track of whether the rice or gram flour or ghee was running out. And so things appeared to be fairly normal, and Ashish had a horror of knowing more than he had to about the situation. Privately, he speculated; he even imagined shouting at his uncle, 'You see? How could you let her go? Do something! Take a train and fetch her back!' And he thought of Narayan's remarks, his

273

casual assumption that the family life Ashish had taken for granted was just a sham. He looked at his uncle mistrustfully.

More and more these days he thought of Sunder. When he was coming home from Narayan's, late at night, feeling tired, he'd walk through the lanes of Saraswati Park and begin to relax. Then, he remembered those early days with Sunder: simple pleasures, like being able to go to a cafe together, or meet at college.

The next day, Narayan called. He said, 'Should we have a day off tomorrow?'

'Off?'

'I mean, let's skip our class tomorrow, and meet in a few days' time instead.'

Ashish had been aching not to make the long, tiring, weirdly depressing journey to Kalina, but he agonized. He would, he was sure, die if he didn't get to see Narayan tomorrow; the more he began to feel, with dread, that the teacher was withdrawing, the more it was absolutely necessary that their closeness remain. 'Sure,' he said, determining that he wouldn't call Narayan first.

Three days passed. They settled into a pattern. Days would go by without contact, but suddenly Narayan would call and invite Ashish over. They would watch a film or eat takeaway food before going to bed for a couple of hours. They were having less sex; Ashish had instead to listen to Narayan talk about his life, his ambitions, and his disappointments.

'I thought at one time, when I was about your age, that I'd do a lot of things: write, direct maybe,' Narayan said. They were in the bedroom, and Ashish was twitching and wondering when they would get down to something more interesting than this conversation. The light was already murky and bluish; Narayan hadn't even drawn the curtains. Instead, he was sitting on the bed, his back against the headrest. The fan was on: March, and it was filthily hot again.

'So what happened?' Ashish asked. He lay down, and wondered if he should take off his shirt.

Narayan blew on his tea, then looked at Ashish. 'Well, life, I suppose,' he said. He smiled to himself.

'You could still do all that stuff,' Ashish said.

'Yes. Let's not discuss it, it's boring. What are you going to do, Ashish, when you graduate? Or are you not worrying about that as much after your lucky break?' Ashish had told Narayan about Satish uncle's will, in a moment of expansiveness; since then, he'd felt, oddly enough, as if the teacher liked him less.

He tried to salvage the moment. 'It's really hot,' he sighed, and looked at Narayan from under his eyelashes, his head resting on his elbow.

The eyebrow rose a little. 'Ye-es,' Narayan agreed. He got up. 'I think I want more sugar in my tea. Do you want some?' he said, and went out of the room.

When he returned, Ashish went back to what had lately become his favourite topic. 'We should go away somewhere, while I have study leave,' he suggested.

The eyebrows shot right up. 'What about your revision?'

'Oh, it'll be fine,' Ashish said airily. He hadn't worked seriously in weeks, and didn't want to think about it.

Narayan sat in the chair near the desk. He cradled his re-sweetened cup of tea. 'Do you think it's wise,' he enquired, 'to take it so easy, when after all you're repeating the year?'

Ashish went red. 'Because of attendance,' he said quickly.

'Quite, so perhaps it's a good idea not to have any further slip-ups?'

★ ★ ★

'You've seen them in the daytime? But owls only come out at night.' Late afternoon, a few days later; Ashish and Narayan were drinking coffee in the living room, and Ashish, relaxed for once, had told Narayan about the owls in the empty flat.

'Oh no,' Ashish said. 'I looked it up. That's a common misconception though. It depends on the breed.'

'A 'common misconception', is it?' Narayan's face was distorted; Ashish realized the other man was in a small rage. 'Well, thank goodness you cleared that up,' Narayan said.

Ashish, left in the living room, raised his eyebrows to himself, then dolefully examined his hands. It was getting harder to like Narayan, but that only seemed to make the whole experience more necessary. He was sure, he decided, he was definitely certain that things could and would turn around. After all, they had been so sweet at the beginning. He allowed himself to flip through his memories of the early days, but instead of facts and incidents, it was hazy yet powerful feelings that returned: sitting in the train, after a trip to Kalina, and feeling exalted because of his secret.

Narayan reappeared from the bedroom. He was wearing his glasses, and an unforthcoming expression. He looked older; Ashish almost wanted to giggle. Then he wanted to shout with pique, because the other man just sat down, grunted quietly — now the tiny softness at his stomach was apparent — and began to read a book with several slips of paper protruding from it.

'He's probably stressed,' Ashish told himself. 'With work.' He sat and watched Narayan, who read with almost furious absorption.

Ashish studied the white hairs near Narayan's temple, the lines from his nose down to his mouth, the teacher's slight paunch, his short-sleeve, check shirt and corduroys, and then Narayan's somewhat stubby feet, which were relaxed and propped on the coffee table. While Ashish watched, Narayan took an automatic pencil from the table and began to make notes in an exercise book. When he looked up briefly, Ashish smiled and raised his eyebrows. Narayan glanced abstractedly at Ashish's face then, obviously dismissing it as a problem so minor as to be uninteresting, returned avidly to the book.

Ashish had a terrible thought: he might as well be dating his uncle if this was how Narayan was going to behave. He got up, walked to the window, and stared at the thickening evening. A rickshaw waited at the corner of the lane and a light inside it seemed to gather and hold a delightful mystery. Was it waiting for him? If he ran down now and got into it, without a word to this tiresome man, what would happen? Another chapter in my life, he thought, but without conviction.

He wandered past the shelves, scanned the DVDs — who, anyway, wanted to watch all these French films over and over? He turned around, decided firmly to be suave, and found himself yelping, 'Are you just going to sit there ignoring me all evening?'

Narayan looked up, and put a finger in his book.

'Well?' Ashish said. He felt the blood begin to drum in his ears, yet knew he didn't have the nerve to issue an ultimatum.

'What's the matter?' Narayan was quite calm.

'I thought you wanted to see me. You called, you asked me to come over.'

'Well, I just thought I'd do some work.'

'Then why did you call me over?' Ashish repeated. He'd meant to be authoritative, but his voice sounded as though it was about to dissolve into tears.

Narayan looked blank.

'I'm going to go and meet some of my friends,' Ashish offered defiantly. *Of my own age*, he thought. He waited.

'Okay, sure.'

Ashish stared at him for a moment; now he really hated this man. He grabbed his bag and stormed towards the door, clumsily and slowly enough so that he could be detained. At the door he turned. Narayan was standing, still holding the book, with a finger marking his place. 'I'll call you,' Narayan said vaguely.

'Yeah.' Ashish opened the door and slid out. He would have liked to slam it but the urge to be thought grown-up stopped him. He closed it firmly and ran down the stairs. They smelled as dank as the first day he'd come there.

★ ★ ★

A few days later, he was back. Narayan had called; he said quietly, 'I'm sorry about the other night. You were upset.' He'd sounded sympathetic, as if being upset was a regrettable but understandable weakness.

'No, I just got bored.' As soon as he'd said it Ashish's heart began to thump.

'Well, would you like to come over tomorrow after college? I don't have any work.'

'Okay,' Ashish heard himself say. He stared at his phone when the call ended. It had lasted forty-seven seconds. He threw the mobile onto his bed.

The next afternoon in Kalina Ashish stood looking out of the window and heard a mournful, drawn-out honk in the distance. You couldn't see the railway line from Narayan's flat but you heard the passing trains, which included long-distance ones from Gujarat, making for the terminus at Bombay Central. The sound of the horn always evoked a strange melancholy in Ashish — the sense it brought of endless partings and journeys through the night in disorientation; like the nocturnal howling of pi-dogs when he couldn't sleep, the train horn elicited a luxurious sense of loss.

The same melancholy made him uneasy in the flat, as though everything that took place there was in the process of mourning its own demise. While Narayan sat reading a news magazine and waiting for the water to boil for tea, Ashish wandered restlessly, eyeing the objects in the living room.

'What's this?' he asked. Narayan looked up from his magazine.

'Hm? What have you got there?'

Ashish came nearer; he held in his hand a small pot that made him think of China or Japan. It was rounded and beautifully made, glazed in a dark, almost blue bitumen grey and speckled with brown.

Narayan reached out his hand for the pot.

Ashish let it go, but reluctantly. He waited for his answer. Finally he repeated, 'So what is it?'

Narayan didn't look up. He set the pot carefully down next to him on the small table. 'It's a tea cup, from Japan,' he said.

'You went to Japan?'

Narayan seemed to smile to himself. 'Not yet,' he said.

'Oh.' Ashish wandered towards the sofa, then back again towards Narayan. 'Can I see it again?' he said. Narayan picked up the cup with care and handed it to him; Ashish stood examining it. The glaze was translucent; even the speckles were somehow luminous.

'So where did you get it from?'

'My friend Ritwik gave it to me.'

'Oh.' Ashish put the cup down and stood looking at it. 'Who's Ritwik?'

'Ritwik Bannerjee, a friend of mine.' There was a complacent possessiveness in Narayan's tone that Ashish hated. 'He lives in Japan now, he's teaching there.'

'Oh. What does he teach?' Ashish imagined this Ritwik, handsome as Mandrake the Magician, evil as Ming the Merciless.

Narayan looked up; he seemed amused. 'English,' he said. He smiled to himself and turned a page. One of his legs was tucked under him. The other stretched into a parallelogram of sunshine on the tiled floor. This foot now flexed, in a catlike movement of satisfaction.

Ashish would not, he determined, ask anything else. 'So he used to live in Bombay? Before he taught English in Japan?'

'Yes, he used to live in Bombay.' Narayan looked up. He rose to go to the kitchen and, absent-mindedly, put a hand on Ashish's neck as he passed. Ashish felt the warmth of the touch. Narayan's voice came out of the kitchen. 'Come, shall we have our tea in the bedroom?'

★　★　★

Finally Narayan agreed that they could go away for a weekend soon after classes ended, when study leave began. Ashish told his uncle that Mayank's father had booked a suite for them and three other boys in a conference venue in Lonavala through police connections. 'It'll be ideal, Mohan mama, we can revise in the daytime and go for a swim in the evening. Walking, that kind of thing — healthy body in healthy mind. It's too hot to concentrate in Bombay anyway.'

Mohan had looked as if there were things he wanted to say to this, but instead, after a pause, he'd nodded. 'I don't think it's a good idea for you to be away for long though,' he said.

'Just two nights, I promise.'

Ashish turned up at Narayan's on Friday evening carrying a rucksack and wearing a brightly coloured, flowered short-sleeved shirt that he'd bought on Fashion Street for just such an occasion. He beamed when Narayan opened the door. 'I know we're not leaving till tomorrow but I thought we could get in the mood now,' he chattered as he came in. 'Have you packed? Not that I suppose we'll need much, you know, for two days.'

Narayan looked at him and closed the door. 'Ashish,' he began, and appeared to change his mind. He guided the boy by the elbow. 'Here, come and sit down.'

'Shall I make some tea?' Ashish asked happily. Narayan never allowed him to perform even simple tasks in the house because, the teacher had said, 'I'm used to doing it, and if I let you do it I might miss it when you're not there.' Ashish had decided to interpret this as romantic.

'Here, sit down.' Narayan perched on the arm of a chair. 'I don't think — ' he began and then frowned, darting a quick glance at Ashish. 'This would be easier if you weren't wearing that shirt,' he murmured. Ashish began to feel utterly stupid. 'Ashish — '

'What?'

Narayan had been gazing slightly to the left of Ashish. He now concentrated on Ashish's face. 'I don't think this is a very good idea,' he said.

'What?' Ashish's stomach began to slide away.

'Going away — and everything else. I don't think,' he repeated slowly, 'that we should be involved.' Narayan looked down and examined the palm of his hand. 'You're a wonderful person, Ashish,' he went on, and again Ashish began to experience a terrible sense of betrayal and falsehood. *This is bullshit*, he thought, but for some reason he didn't get up and leave. Narayan continued, 'You're so much younger, and I — in my position as someone elder to you, it's not really right that we should have the kind of — relationship — that we have had — ' He seemed to be talking to himself, or to an invisible judge seated in front of him.

'But you never worried about that before!' Ashish burst out. He felt his voice become gloopy; he was going to cry.

'Well — there was an — attraction. I knew you were attracted to me and I allowed myself to act on that. Perhaps I shouldn't have — '

'Me attracted to you? You hit on me!'

Narayan stood up. 'Ashish. Let's try to keep this civilized.'

Ashish, sniffing back snot and tears, stood up too. 'You don't care any more. Or maybe you never did,' he said. He put his hands to his face. His shoulders shook. He wanted to die, also to lie on the floor and hold Narayan's feet, the kind of abject physical despair he used to experience in childhood and which his mother disapprovingly labelled 'tantrums'. After a pause, Narayan came and put his hands on Ashish's shoulder. Their warmth through the printed cotton was unbearable.

'What'll you do now,' Ashish whimpered, 'without me.' He put his own hands on Narayan's shoulders; the teacher flinched slightly. 'I suppose,' Ashish hissed suddenly, 'you'll be happy, staying here with your DVDs and your Japanese tea cup to jerk off into. Or with whoever else you're seeing.' His voice caught in his throat and he heaved a sob. Narayan drew back.

'Maybe it'd be better if you left now,' he suggested. He folded his arms.

Ashish straightened, sobbed, glared at him, this last look at his favourite face in the world, and stumbled towards the door. Narayan came after him. 'Ashish,' he said.

Ashish turned, ready to forgive all. Narayan

was holding out the rucksack. Ashish snatched it, hiccoughed, slammed the door, and ran down the stairs into the lane.

★　★　★

He had long ago stopped carrying a clean, ironed handkerchief in his pocket; now he regretted it all the way home. He felt an appalling urge to cry; it welled up inside him, and his eyes stung. Of course, he didn't cry — boys never did, and certainly not in public. But the nearness of it was frightening and he wished, often, that he'd had the comforting cotton square with which to pretend to take dust out, or mop his eyes, afflicted with a phantom conjunctivitis that would explain their redness. Instead, he got back to Saraswati Park, ignored the dosa wala who smiled and called out to him, and ran up the stairs of the building.

He unlocked the front door. 'Arre, it's you?' said his uncle. Ashish just had time to see the eagerness on his face alter to surprise. 'What happened?'

'It didn't work out,' he muttered, heading towards the dark passageway. 'The booking.'

★　★　★

He flung the satchel against the bookshelf and closed the door. His copy of *Dubliners* fell onto the bed and opened. A folded, slightly warped piece of paper drifted onto the floor. Ashish picked it up — it was his timetable. There they were, the faded, coloured-in squares: green for baths and teeth-brushing, pink for studying, blue for exercise, yellow for (rare) slices of time off. His first impulse was to avoid looking at it. Then he thought he'd force himself to do so. What had made him think he could control his actions in such minute detail?

He turned over the paper and scanned the lists of topics and books under each heading. He was all right on the Romantics. Shakespeare needed a little work; he hadn't looked at the Modernists; then there was the Indian literature paper, largely untouched. The timetable, so dusty and unloved, represented the shred of him that had wanted to make something of the rest.

Maybe there was a chance . . . but there was so little time now . . . His mind swayed between assertions and negations. Distractedly, he stared out of the window to see if the owls were there. It seemed to have been a long time since he'd checked; he didn't see them. He glanced around the room. How untidy it was. Where had he been? One of

Narayan's dry remarks returned. Ashish had said, enviously, that the other man always appeared at ease. 'I worry about stuff — you don't seem to though, you're always comfortable,' he'd said. They'd been in bed, Narayan's arm around Ashish and the boy eyeing the stain on the cream wall. 'That's because you're in my world,' Narayan had responded, with an irony that wasn't addressed to Ashish.

Now he was back in his own world, or in Saraswati Park at any rate. The room reminded him of his defeats, and the disappointments of the years: the damp marks on the walls, the stains and specks of black on the yellowing paint spoke of lives lived imperfectly. He went to the cupboard and examined himself in the rusty mirror on the door, under the miniature but brave image of Viv Richards and his on-drive. Ashish's eyes had something new about them — maybe recent events had taken the obstinate shine from him. Otherwise, he resembled the boy who'd moved his things in a suitcase and a carton from Esplanade Mansion less than a year ago. Suddenly the floor tiles felt agreeably cold under his feet and he sighed and remembered that first day. Lakshmi mami had made him come in with the right foot first, for good luck. Would things have been worse if he'd put the left foot first? Where was his aunt anyway? When would she return?

The door swung open and his uncle leaned in. 'Go to sleep now, there's a lot to do from tomorrow,' he said. He peered at Ashish. For a moment they regarded each other, one wanting to ask a question that couldn't be asked — is everything going to be all right? — and the other wondering, as ever, what was wrong with the boy and whether it was in some way his fault. Their eyes met; Mohan smiled. 'Good night. Sleep soon,' he said.

Ashish nodded. He went and brushed his teeth and came back to his room to scramble into his nightclothes. The worn cotton felt nice. He turned out the light and lay down, pulling the sheet about him.

He was, he knew, defeated already. Saraswati Park had got him in the end. He was what he was — just a middle-class boy who'd been preoccupied with a sense of his own difference. What made him special? Then there were the exams, a forthcoming trial, and he would again be in a mess — he saw his mother's face, as on the day his parents found out he had to repeat his final year — then he thought irrelevantly that it would be nice to see his parents again, but also that he missed the old house — and he wondered about his aunt — when would she be back — it wasn't the same now she was gone, it was makeshift and sort of fun but ultimately exhausting without her — then about his uncle, what was he up to, how was he coping — then about Megha, when would she come back — and about Sunder, would he have changed the way he wore his hair? It had been so long since they'd seen each other, he couldn't even imagine what it would be like if they met again. But in a weird way he felt he'd always know what was happening in Sunder's life — at a strange, elemental level — perhaps that was nonsense though — and he remembered Narayan's flat, it was the last thing, with a jolt of pain, and then he was dreaming. He was outside a door, ringing the bell, and there were voices inside, laughter too, but they wouldn't let him in.

★ ★ ★

Three weeks later, the night before the first exam. Without knocking, Mohan came into the room. He shut the door behind him and looked around at the piles of notes on the bed, the desk, the bookcases. Ashish cringed, waiting for a rebuke.

But his uncle appeared energized. 'All right,' he said. 'Paper?'

'Yes.' Ashish held up a sheaf.

'Pens?'

'Mm.' He indicated the desk.

'And you know the kind of questions you have to prepare for?'

'Yes, I've got a list.'

'All right. You sit at the desk, begin with the first one. I'm going to make some coffee.'

'Okay.' He sat down, one foot tucked under him, and began with a question about *King Lear*. An unwanted image of Narayan lying back in the bed in Kalina passed through his mind, but he banished it; the heath, instead he would think about the heath. The yellowness of the light bulb had become a line right behind his eyes; just then his uncle appeared with a tray on which there were two cups.

'I made a whole pot of decoction,' Mohan said. And while Ashish wrote, rubbing his forehead from time to time, his uncle moved about behind him, sorting the different papers and clipping them together. It was warm and dry outside; there had been dust storms but the first rain seemed to be holding off. In the intense atmosphere of the electric-lit room, Ashish was suddenly calm. He wrote, and after an hour his uncle removed the paper from the table and said, 'Start the next question.' He put a fresh cup of coffee in front of Ashish, who barely looked up. When he had done one question paper, he leaned back in his chair, stretched, and rubbed at his eyes. He squinted into the darkness; there was a flash of white opposite and one of the owls was sitting in the window in Gopal, winking at him.

'That's good luck,' observed Mohan.

Ashish laughed. 'Some people say owls are bad luck. Anyway, I think I need Saraswati, not Lakshmi, Mohan mama,' he said. The goddesses were sisters. One dispensed wisdom and learning: her familiar was the swan; the other conferred prosperity, and hers was the owl.

'It's all the same thing,' his uncle said calmly. 'Just names for things that don't have names.'

'But Lakshmi and Saraswati don't come to the same house,' Ashish argued. He picked up his coffee cup and stared into the grounds at the bottom.

A hand dropped onto his shoulder. 'That's rubbish. Look — there are owls in Saraswati Park, aren't there?'

An early, deluded bird began to sing.

'Oh god!' said Ashish wildly.

'No no, it's not four o'clock yet. Come,' said Mohan. 'Work for a bit longer, then you can have a bath and breakfast.'

Ashish obediently bent his head again. At five his uncle told him to sleep for an hour; he curled up in bed. He didn't sleep, exactly; his mind had become bruised and seemed to be bashing itself about inside his skull, but he fell into a heavy trance, dry-mouthed, and when there was a brief rain shower outside, his body relaxed under the blanket. Almost immediately, his uncle was saying, 'Six o'clock, get up now,' and Ashish was stumbling into the bathroom towards a bucket of hot water. Grey, early light came in through the modest slatted window. He heard a bird trill — wretched thing, it had no exams to sit — and he soaped himself automatically and found his eye staring overlong at commonplace things: the shine on the chrome-plated tap, and the crusting of minerals on the edge of the copper pipe that ran out of the water heater.

On his bed he saw a clean shirt and a pair of trousers; he smiled at the visit of the phantom valet. When he came into the living room, his rucksack in his hand, his uncle was fully dressed. Breakfast was on the table, and more coffee.

19

The station roared with passengers, porters, valedictory relatives; the train doors hung open and people hurried out with their parcels and luggage. Mohan stood near the bookstall. He clutched his bag and bottle of water, felt dazed, and, like a reformed lecher who sees a girl walk past, covertly eyed the books. A young man came right up to him but it was only when the voice said 'Mohan uncle!' that he blinked.

'Arre, Chintan.' He shook hands briefly with his wife's great-nephew, whom he'd last seen at his wedding, five years earlier. Chintan had been a thin, pale young man; now he'd filled out.

'I wouldn't have recognized you, you've put on weight,' Mohan began to tease, out of form, but Chintan had become more brisk too.

'Let me take your bag, Mohan uncle.'

'No, it's all right.' But Chintan dived around him, wrested the bag away, then set off at a great pace, throwing snatches of conversation over his shoulder. 'Car . . . nightmare to park at this time of day . . . just over here . . . '

Mohan followed him, dodging between passengers and hangers-about, while a nasal female voice announced from the loud-speaker, 'The delayed train for *Bangalore is about to arrive on platform number three.*'

It was blindingly hot and dry, even at five in the evening. Mohan hurried after Chintan through the car park. In the sun, he felt his skin begin to tingle, then give up and yield its life to the unrelenting air; a person could desiccate, simply shrivel away here. When they reached a small, white Maruti, Chintan stopped abruptly. He unlocked the boot — white sun flashed off it into Mohan's tired eyes — stowed the bag, and smiled. 'Atya will be pleased to see you,' he said. 'It's been very nice for us that she could come.'

Mohan got in, banged shut the tinny door and folded his legs; the passenger seat seemed to have been wedged forward. The interior of the car was hot and airless. He tried to wind down the window. It stuck.

'Oh yes, that window doesn't work,' Chintan said. 'Baba's much better, the doctor says he's out of risk.' He shoved five rupees at the parking attendant and shot into the middle of the road, making the good luck charm that hung from the rear-view mirror shake wildly. He honked at a man driving two black water buffalo past the exit. 'These people don't even *look* . . . But he needs rest for some time and, of course,' he turned and beamed, as one who is revealing an insight, 'he's not getting any younger.'

When they got to the house, the door was opened by Malti, Chintan's wife. She looked tired, a little plumper after marriage and her hair was done differently, but she was otherwise the same. She was a bright, capable girl. The child trailed behind her, a little boy — Sachin, hardly three years old. Lakshmi came out. Mohan and she smiled at each other awkwardly. They didn't touch; he stood holding his bottle of water and she said, 'So the train was on time.'

'Yes, only about twenty minutes late.'

'Come, I'll make tea,' Malti said. 'Meet Baba, he's been looking forward to seeing you.'

The invalid's bedroom was just off the living room. This person in the bed, looking frail at the centre of a small galaxy of medicine bottles, glasses, thermometers, magazines, coasters, trays, was Mahesh, Lakshmi's nephew, though he was about her age and more like a cousin. Mohan and he shook hands. The other man's hand was limp and thin; his eyes were rheumy and he coughed uncontrollably; but he knew who Mohan was.

'So, come to take your wife back?' he said straight away, began to laugh, and then coughed instead.

Mohan looked down at the wasted face. The bedside table was crowded with postcards, a packet of playing cards, a small towel, pill bottles. 'And how are you?' he asked.

'I'm all right,' but he started to cough again; spittle flew out and Lakshmi helped him wipe his face. Malti appeared with the tea and they sat around and sipped it. The man in the bed became a sort of polite attraction as he alternately talked, asked questions, and fell silent; perhaps he was dozing.

Chintan had taken Mohan's bag to the room where Lakshmi had been staying. The bungalow, old and reasonably large, was in a part of town that had once been considered far away; it had become more central as the city expanded. Lakshmi's eldest brother Bhaskar had bought a plot of land under a scheme for government employees; as in so many things, he'd been lucky, and the house was now worth much more.

'You can have a bath if you want, I've put the geyser on,' Chintan returned to say.

Mohan went and began to undress in the odd-looking bedroom. It had white panelled

298

cupboards, a dark red plush rug, which should have been the last thing anyone wanted in this climate, and even a fairly old looking air conditioner, as well as highly polished brass ornaments sitting here and there. He wondered if this was the room that had been decorated for Malti and Chintan when they'd married.

The bathroom too had been redone relatively recently, with white fittings and gold trim. The work was slightly shoddy; bits of cement showed, and the large synthetic tiles weren't well grouted, but it was a contemporary idea of luxury. He turned the shower on, watched a stream of hot water come out, stood under it, and felt his skin revive. He lathered himself with the familiar citrus soap and saw his wife's bottle of amla hair oil on the sink; this meeting was both ordinary and utterly strange. There was an unexpected shyness about it, meeting like this in someone else's house, as though they had been a young couple instead of two greying people with four grown-up children (and Ashish, he reminded himself — he must telephone the boy and find out if all was well). And his mind went back to the first time he'd seen Lakshmi. Mohan's reaction to Vivek deciding that he should stop studying and start work had been muted, but suddenly he'd said he wanted to marry. Their mother had agreed; Vivek hadn't felt able to say no. Few girls were suggested; there wasn't much money in the family. Then Vivek had heard of a family living in Tardeo, not the same sub-caste, but there was a girl, a little educated, whose parents were keen to marry her soon. She was just seventeen. Mohan and his brother went to meet her one Sunday. Her parents were there, they talked, and the girl served some tea and food. He saw that she was pretty, but they didn't speak to each other. Her brother had impressed him though; he was so educated — thin, fiery, and contemptuous looking. He was a lecturer in a college. When they went to the door, he'd heard the brother, Satish, murmur something to the girl, who suddenly flashed a grin of pure mischief at Mohan. He'd gaped at her; the grin, when her father turned, had gone completely. But this was the girl, he'd decided then and there.

He turned off the shower, dried himself, came out of the bathroom, and looked in his bag for clean clothes.

'What were you laughing about?' he'd asked her, of course, later, and she'd smiled and said she didn't remember.

He shook out the kurta and slipped it over his head, then stepped into the pyjamas and tightened their drawstring; this was always a comical moment, when one's clothes, apparently designed for an enormous person, were reined into shape. Newly clean, he floated into the corridor, still remembering that day, the light outside the door and how he'd looked back to see if she was still laughing; in the dark passage he hadn't been able to tell. His mother had thought he could have married better. Lakshmi had no dowry to speak of, but he'd been adamant. Vivek had just been relieved that the girl's family were keen and it'd all be simple; Sharmila, Vivek's wife, was happy that it was so easy to dominate the younger sister-in-law.

Mohan went into the living room, where Lakshmi was sitting on the sofa with Sachin. Malti was on her way back to the kitchen. 'I'm making dinner, it won't be long,' she said apologetically. He thought with sympathy that she had a lot to do: the old man; and of course her husband and son; now guests too. His wife looked up when he came in, then back at the television. It was hard to tell what she was thinking. He sat on the velvet sofa, and the child came to him, holding a toy; he began to tell Mohan an incoherent story.

'This is Bhalu, he goes to school . . . ' and he shoved the toy, a faded teddy, at Mohan.

'Does he?' the letter writer said absently. He took the bear and put the child, who wriggled like a puppy, on his knee. Sachin began to climb all over Mohan. 'Which standard is Bhalu in?'

'Tenth!'

'Oh, so old?' He looked across at his wife, to see if she'd smiled, but the light from the television was shining on her face. She turned slightly and met his gaze, then turned back to the television. He felt a moment's panic, and forgot to listen to Sachin who, piqued, got up on Mohan's thigh, held his shoulder, and began to bang on his chest.

'Hm, hm. Gently, gently,' Mohan said, removing him.

'Bhalu's done all his homework!'

'Has he?' What was she thinking, he wondered — she seemed so assimilated here, yet surely that couldn't just have happened. When would they talk? He began to wish Chintan, Sachin, Malti, the old man, all would disappear suddenly, like in the *Arabian Nights*, and he and she find themselves outside the city walls, away from the hubbub and able to speak. This longing, to talk, to not be alone, to explain himself — now he remembered, that had been why he'd wanted to marry. As a child (he didn't recall when the habit dated from, it was so old) he'd kept a running narrative in his head, commenting, explaining the things that happened. But there'd never been an appropriate listener. His sister didn't understand, his brother wasn't interested; friends could only take so much of his thoughts and dreams. It would have been impossible to talk to his father, who was utterly abstracted, or to his mother, down-to-earth and harassed with a thousand things to do. Then his father had died and the future Mohan had silently planned had vanished; he had been going to be some sort of scholar, a person with a great many books who sat at a desk and wrote all day. That was over; he'd decided that at least this loneliness must end. Marriage was surely the answer. Finally there'd be an audience: a sympathetic person to absorb and applaud his ideas, their shape and expression.

But his wife had turned out to be a talker herself. She had her own narration, so confident that he was never sure whether his made any sense to her; then, later, he'd begun to feel that maybe his private thoughts were simply meant to stay that way. This was one of the secret jokes about marriage. People turned out to be exactly the opposite of how they'd seemed at first; they then went on changing randomly, as though enacting a hypothesis of unceasing chaos. He tried again to read Lakshmi's expression in the flickering light of the set, but couldn't. This fugue, for example, and his own ultimate, tardy, but not really reluctant pursuit: could he have predicted it? He softened, thinking that he never would have imagined such distance could grow between him and this simple, engaging girl; he'd been certain she'd always be around, chattering about something, and he'd be smiling, half admiring, half bemused or irritated.

'Bhalu's done his homework and now he wants to tell you a story.'

'Does he? What's the story?' He bent and listened to the child, who stopped kicking, and began to recount something rambling, without sense, but that seemed to comfort him. Mohan held him with one hand and patted his stomach with the other while he prattled.

Dinner was in the same room. Malti reappeared with food and fresh puris; Lakshmi went to help Mahesh with his food. Mohan sat and ate meekly under the tube light, amid the patter of the television. Chintan meanwhile told him about his job, his hopes and plans. He was doing an MBA by correspondence and thought of working abroad. Malti smiled when she heard this familiar conversation; but she was busy, fetching more food and then taking the plates away.

Mohan had begun to fade. Eventually, Lakshmi returned from the kitchen with her own plate, and ate with Malti. She said to him, 'You must be tired.'

'A little,' he admitted. 'I did sleep on the train, but you know how trains are.'

'All the jolting and noise and tamasha!' Chintan said.

'Everyone's so noisy,' Malti agreed.

'Yes,' he said. He looked around at their faces. There was a certain family resemblance, though he thought his wife looked more like Malti than anyone else; there was the same brightness about them.

'We'll sleep,' Lakshmi said.

They got up.

Finally, he closed the door of their room. He put on the light and she turned on the air conditioner, which began to wheeze asthmatically.

'So,' he said.

She sat down on the bed and took out her hairpins. She began to comb and plait her hair, as though this had been any other night. Had she lost weight? He sat nearish her, coughed, and put a hand atop hers. She moved hers and sighed. 'I was very angry with you,' she said.

He stared ahead of him, then squinted at her. 'I'm sorry,' he said stiffly.

'I know,' she said. She smiled suddenly, at the strangeness of this conversation, then glanced down at her comb, where a few erratically curly white strands were tangled. 'My hair's so thin now,' she said irrelevantly.

He scanned the side of her head. 'I can't tell.'

'Of course, don't be stupid, when I was younger my plait used to be this thick,' and she made a circle with her hand. She folded her legs to her chest and put one arm around them. 'So Ashish told me about this competition you won.'

'I didn't win. When did you speak to him?'

'I called — to see how his exams were going.'

'Oh, that. We had quite a time the night before his first paper,' he said.

'But he'll pass this year.'

'Yes, I'm sure,' he said, his mind a haze of nights under the electric light.

'And he'll manage while you're away?'

'I think so. Mrs Gogate said he can go to their house for meals. He and Madhavi have become quite good friends.'

She nodded.

The air conditioner was beginning to bother him. 'You sleep with this on?'

She exhaled irritably. 'It's hot here,' she said.

'All right, I was just wondering.'

'You know, it wasn't just about Satish. Of course that was very bad. I feel awful myself. For him to go like that, completely alone — ' She sighed. 'Still, it wasn't your fault, really. But this other business — you, your writing, that's all you were interested in. And the way you used to behave earlier, as though your whole life had been a tragedy because you didn't get to go to college, become educated, write books. I was so sick of it.'

He frowned, and leaned back on the dreadful pink satin bedcover. 'I never said my life was a tragedy.'

'No, but you always behaved that way. You were distracted, when things were happening — the children's exams, or going away; when the boys and Uma got married. Those things happened and you were there but you were outside it.' She held the comb in one small square hand and waved it like a teacher's pointer for emphasis.

'That's a terrible thing to say,' he said, although, suddenly, he wasn't sure whether she wasn't right.

'No,' she said, and sighed. 'Not really. Not if it's true.' She got up, went into the bathroom, and came out a little later in her nightclothes.

In the morning he slept late, and woke to

find a cup of tea on the table next to him. His wife was dressed; she sat on the bed, reading a section of the newspaper.

'What time is it?' he asked.

'Almost eight o'clock. No hurry — these people all eat breakfast at different times. Chintan has left for work, and Malti's getting Sachin ready for playschool.'

Mohan got up and went to clean his teeth. He came back and sat on the bed drinking the tea, which was hot and had ginger in it. Despite the air conditioner, he had slept deeply for the first time in weeks; he was drowsy and cushioned.

'What do you want to do about the will — Satish's will?' he asked.

'Do? You mean contest it? No no,' she said. She turned the page with a crackle.

He stretched out one leg and winced at the sharp click of the knee. 'But — it's strange the way he managed things in the end. It's good for Ashish, of course. Now if he wants, he could go abroad to study, even if he doesn't get a scholarship. But — '

She lifted her head. 'I don't feel bad about it. I didn't think Satish would have anything to leave, and even if he had, I knew he wouldn't leave it to me. He'd made it clear. In his mind it made sense. He always said, 'I don't have to worry about you, Mohan will

308

be there to look after you and the children', and for him that was good enough. Besides, it's true, we don't need the money; we have the house and the money from your father's business. And anyway, when you write a book we'll become rich. Until then, there's the money Megha's been sending.'

'Book?'

'Yes, aren't you going to write one?'

He found himself blushing and she grinned and took a sip of her coffee. 'Anyway,' she said, 'It's been nice to be here, especially at first, but now I'm a little bored. They don't need me as much now. I've had enough.'

He nodded immediately. Then he couldn't help asking, 'Why?'

She made a face. 'They're good people but they live in a nightmare.'

'What do you mean?'

'Chintan and his wife have so little time for each other. She's exhausted, and he's fed up — work and then his father to worry about. They've been good to me and I've tried to help where I could, but it's not enough.' She looked at him directly. 'I saw him play-fighting with the little one, who of course is horrendously spoilt, and they were hitting each other, but Chintan suddenly started hitting the little boy harder and harder, really hitting him. The child is tough despite everything and he didn't want to give in but his father is so much bigger. Finally he started to bawl.'

Mohan was appalled. 'Did you speak to Chintan?'

She shook her head. 'It was too awkward. Besides, I haven't spent enough time with them over the years. I just tried to look after the child more often.'

'Let's go,' said Mohan decidedly, putting his cup down as if he would set off that instant.

'Arre! At least let's stay for a day or two. They've been asking after you and they were curious to meet you after so long,' she said inconsistently, then laughed.

He smiled too, despite the air conditioner, the pink bedspread, the terrible ornaments, the strangeness of the house. 'So you'll come home?' he asked.

She nodded, and a half-smile broke out on her face.

★　★　★

They had to return by road a day later, a long and tiring journey, because the school and college holidays meant it was impossible to get a reservation on the train. At Dadar they emerged from the bus, an air-conditioned, Hindi-film-music-playing torture chamber,

310

into the sun and humid heat of Bombay. Ashish was there; he wore a clean shirt and held a small bunch of flowers that he presented to his aunt. 'Have you lost a lot of weight?' she asked.

'No no, Madhavi's mother's been feeding me well.' He took her bag and led them towards a taxi.

In the flat, she examined everything. She was bemused to discover the nearly clear table and the cleaned bookshelves, and in the kitchen she said 'Hm', and opened the cupboards. She picked up a packet of tea and turned around, an eyebrow raised. 'We don't buy this kind of tea.'

'Well, they must have run out of the normal one when I went,' her husband said, looking sheepish.

She smiled. Perhaps it was good to be home: the familiar objects sang out to her. 'Get it right next time,' she said severely. 'It's the Red Label.'

★ ★ ★

Although she was tired after the long journey, sleep, normally so ready, was just out of reach in the dim room where the well-known furniture made dark masses. Mohan's breathing and his gentle snoring continued. In the first part of the night he slept on his back; she regarded his unmoving bulk under the sheet while the fan whirled hectically. The usual sighs, followed by the gravelly exhalation every third breath, were at first reassuring; soon after, they began to irritate her. Slightly later, everything oppressive in the room and the world — the dark furniture hulking against the light, the silence outside, the intractability of sleep — all these evils, which might have been minor at another time of day, seemed to emanate from the serene, infuriating exhalations of the figure next to her. She got up and adjusted the fan. There was no satisfactory setting for it. When at a slower speed, it nearly forgot to turn, but at medium it flew into a frenzy.

She lay down again, wrapped the sheet about her, and allowed her feet and arms to escape its confines. Mohan turned to his side; as he settled into the new position, he gave a drawn-out, snuffling sigh. It made her want to scream, the ease with which he had transported himself elsewhere, out of this room and this moment. She rolled over, so that she faced him, and studied the parts of his face that she could see: his straight nose; eyelids secretively closed into tight pockets; the lines that ran between his nose and mouth. It was remarkable that she couldn't feel angry with him; he was so hermetic that it was hard to imagine blaming him for anything. She sighed, rolled onto her back and watched the fan, then turned towards the faded yellow curtains. An orange glimmer found its way under them, from the street lamp at the end of the lane.

Quickly, there came an aggressive wind through the trees; she heard it sweeping the leaves and branches. A storm began and rain lashed the house. But a strange thing happened: the bird whose song she had noticed months earlier started to sing now, in the middle of the night. It trilled through its phrase, ma ga re sa, cheep! in the lustiest, loudest way imaginable. Was it enjoying the storm?

Much later, she was aware of Mohan's movements, though their sequence was unclear — he was up, that much she knew, but she was too tired to tell whether he had just woken or was about to take a bath. Doors opened and closed; shapes of clear morning light printed themselves on her consciousness. Eventually, she rubbed her eyes. She could tell from the warm colour of the sun under the curtains that it was much later than normal. She sat up. When she saw the lukewarm cup of tea at her bedside she prepared herself to be irritated; then she smiled.

20

It was raining; he stalked around the flat. Finally he went to the telephone and dialled.

'Aunty, it's Ashish. How are you, aunty. Aunty, is Mayank there?'

There was a crackle and a yell in the background, then his friend's voice came on the line. It had deepened but in timbre remained unchanged since their childhood.

'Hey, what's up?'

'Look, don't get all American on me,' Ashish snapped.

'What's wrong with you, bhai?'

Ashish clutched the receiver and stared at an old calendar picture of a houseboat in Kashmir that hung on the passage wall. 'I think I'm bored,' he said. 'Wasn't it supposed to be great when we finished exams? Didn't we keep saying, 'I can't wait till the exams are over'?'

'Yeah, I know, now there's nothing to do but wait till the results come out. Already my parents are asking me about jobs, what are my plans. I'm supposed to meet someone my father's friend knows in case he wants to give me a job.'

'Doing what?'

'I don't know. Something. Air conditioning or something.'

'God.'

'Yeah, but still. Or maybe I'll enrol for a master's. I've been telling my dad you can't get a decent job without qualifications these days.'

'Master's in?'

'Mass comm, maybe.'

'Oh . . . yeah.'

'So what have you been doing?'

'Nothing. I think . . . I don't know.'

'Going to see your parents?'

'Yeah, not for a couple of weeks.'

'Let's go see a movie.'

'Yeah. I don't know.'

'What do you want to do then?'

'Something. Nothing. I don't know. I'm *bored*,' Ashish said irritably, as though naming an unarguable medical complaint.

'You want to meet up, at least?'

'Yeah, I suppose.' He didn't want to leave the house and get on the train; on the other hand, what else was he going to do? Home made him twitchy; the thought of going out was tiring.

'Three thirty in the Cafe Idiot-Idiot?'

'Okay. The one at Shivaji Park? Okay.'

*   *   *

'So what are you going to do, Ashish?' Madhavi enquired. They were sitting on the terrace one evening, on a couple of plastic chairs that someone had left there.

'As in?'

'As in with your life. No, as in, in the next year. Now you're fabulously wealthy and everything.' She looked owlishly happy and self-satisfied; Ashish smiled at her plump, intelligent face.

'Oh yeah. No, I don't know. My cousin is saying I should apply to university in the States, see if I can get in last minute to one of those courses, film-making, animation, screenwriting, that type of thing, somewhere in California.'

'Yeah, good idea. Hey!' Madhavi sat up suddenly. 'You should go to one of those agencies, the ones that do applications for you. My friend went and they did all her stuff, she got admitted into three places, one even with scholarship.'

'Yeah? But I doubt my grades are going to be amazing.' He let himself slide further down the plastic chair till his neck rested on the top, and looked into the evening sky, bright with different types of pollution cloud: orange, peach, greyish-purple.

316

'No no, these are all new colleges. Even if you don't get scholarship in the first year, you know, because it's late, you might get some for the next two — three years. And you'd probably like the place as well. You know.'

'As in?'

'As in, you know, it's easier there — to be gay and everything.'

Ashish twisted around. 'What?'

'Oh, come on Ashish.'

He pulled himself up, folded his legs and clutched his knees with one arm. 'What makes you say that?'

'It's obvious, surely. So tell me, what was going on with you and that guy, the tutor? Was something happening?'

'Well — '

She waited, and Ashish began to tell her, in a confused order, all about Narayan. Madhavi interrupted. 'Wait wait. Start at the beginning.'

When he'd finished talking it was pitch dark, and they were surrounded by the usual smells of open-air night in Saraswati Park: traffic fumes, cement, flowers, something chemical in the breeze. The main road, apparently far away, made itself heard now and again in an anguished horn blast or the faint growling of engines.

'Does anyone else know?' Madhavi asked.

317

'No. I mean, I haven't told anyone.'

She nodded. 'I bet your aunt guessed. About you at least.'

'I don't know — she hasn't been here.' Ashish felt relieved, but strange too; he rubbed his stomach and felt his own thinness and insubstantiality.

'Yeah.' The orange light from the street lamp caught the edge of Madhavi's spectacles. She nodded her curly head. 'I didn't know if I should mention this, but I heard something about him — Professor Narayan. About how he had an affair with some post-grad student, some Bengali guy, I don't remember the name, and that's why he had to stop teaching at the university.'

'What?' Ashish felt sick. 'But,' he began to argue, 'people don't just leave jobs because of rumours. If it had really been proved then he would have been disciplined, it'd be common knowledge.'

'No, it depends. One of my friend's mothers teaches there too, she said there was no official complaint but he was warned. Maybe it was office politics and someone used it to get rid of him, but that's what she said.' Madhavi shrugged. 'Don't think about it too much. It's just one of those things. When you've been out of Bombay for a while you'll hardly even remember it.' She tutted.

'Lecherous uncles, the worst possible thing.'

Ashish began to laugh. 'Narayan's not really a lecherous uncle.'

'No?'

'No! Well — '

'Yuck, wait till he's older. So undignified, watch my French films, chhi.'

Ashish giggled, scandalized, but also comforted.

*   *   *

'So you're all packed?'

He and Mayank were eating a farewell custard in the Military Cafe. It had been preceded by a farewell lunch in a tiny diner on Colaba Causeway, and was to be followed by a farewell cup of coffee at the Gateway.

He stirred the last, trembling fragments of custard; it went through his mind that the dessert was suffering as it cringed away from the spoon and he was amused, then appalled at himself. America, what would it be like? There might be men — he hoped there would. He'd be able to replace his present sufferings with new ones, until he could look back at Narayan with only amused nostalgia: oh, I was so young then.

'No, well, sort of. Basically.'

He didn't even know exactly what he had

to pack; he had a few books with him, his new computer, and some clothes. Every day his aunt would appear at the door of his room with something she was sure he would need, from snacks to socks to digestive ayurvedic sweets. Yesterday she had come in looking shy and vaguely sentimental, and given him a small packet wrapped in a handkerchief. He opened it and found a cardboard box; inside was a wristwatch with a leather strap.

'It was my brother's,' she'd said, her face lighting up. 'I thought you should have it because he was obviously fond of you.'

He'd tried to give it back but she'd insisted, and Ashish, bemused and secretly harried, had put the watch, for now, into a dark corner of the cupboard.

'So, California!' Mayank said.

'Yeah, well, nearby anyway.' He'd been accepted into a BA programme in film-making, about which he knew nearly nothing; the efficient woman who'd arranged everything for him at Brite Lites Educational Consultancy said that he was going to have a fantastic time.

'Are you going to come back?' Mayank's round eyes were candid and Ashish was exasperated. If he said no, he'd feel disloyal and irritated with himself; if he said yes, he'd feel unadventurous and therefore still irritated with himself.

He slapped his right hand to his heart. 'My homeland is always with me,' he said in Hindi, in a baritone, film-star voice.

Mayank leaned back and patted his stomach. Ashish looked up at the ceiling, which was roughly the colour of the inside of a teapot, and at the walls, where the usual admonitory signs were displayed; then at the waiter's face, which combined many features of the ceiling (colour, lack of sheen) and the walls (resistance to change, a formal severity) with an elegant boredom all its own.

'Coffee?' Mayank said.

'Sure. You want to go to the Idiot-Idiot near Gateway? Go for a walk first?'

'Okay.'

Ashish settled the bill at the counter and they went out into the sunlight. It felt strange to walk past Esplanade Mansion but Ashish just nodded to the owner of the stationery shop and they continued. He had no desire to go inside and inspect the rotting atrium outside his childhood home again. It was easier to pretend that part of his life was completely over; he felt vindictive, as though Esplanade Mansion had been responsible for the unhappiness in his life. He smiled; they were still under the building, walking in the wide arcade of its cast-iron pillars.

'What?' Mayank said.

'Oh, nothing. Just, for a minute I thought maybe I'll miss Bombay.'

'Hah, miss what! Everything'll be as good in California. Better! Even the weather is good there.'

'Yeah.'

They walked in the colonnade of the Taj Mahal hotel, past the raffish old streets off Apollo Bunder and then back along the promenade, watching the brown sea smack softly against the wall.

'Smells of piss here,' Mayank observed.

'This is a pick-up spot,' Ashish said. 'Apparently.' Even at this hour of the afternoon there were a couple of louche looking men hanging out near the wall, though there were couples too, and a family from out of town; they bought ice cream from the Mewad ice-cream seller and he then took their photograph. It was cloudy, but near the water the reflected light made Ashish's eyes ache.

They loped towards the monument, which always looked oddly decorative and small when you approached it; it had been built as a sort of three-dimensional gift tag and stuck onto the city. The usual vendors were here: the postcard-seller with the dirty red Kathiawadi turban, and the various tight-trousered Polaroid photographers. They smoked cigarettes and frowned into the sun; there wasn't much of a crowd.

'Well,' said Mayank, hands on slightly podgy hips. He resembled his father at this moment; he puffed out his lower lip and squared his shoulders.

'Well.'

They gazed about them, Ashish wondering what the hell he was supposed to be looking for. Was he meant to be feeling sentimental?

'Coffee?' he said.

'Chal.'

A couple of tiny Pardhi kids approached them, with their beautiful faces and dusty hair. They looked cranky, rather than hopeful: it was that time of afternoon.

'Uncle, uncle,' began one, pawing at Mayank's trouser leg.

'Don't touch,' said Mayank sententiously.

'Brother,' tried the other, weaving around Ashish.

'Uncle, we're hungry.'

'Do you want vada pao?' Ashish asked.

'We want pao bhaji!'

'Give us money to buy rice!'

'Come on, fuck off,' Mayank said, removing the hand of the older child from his trousers. The kids followed them to the crossing at Regal, then lost interest and stopped to say hello to a frightening looking

European man whom they seemed to know.

'Hey, look, what are they doing with that guy?' Ashish said.

'What guy?' Mayank was already making purposefully for the cool of the coffee shop.

Ashish slowed down and craned his neck to watch — the man was bending down and telling the kids something, and they were negotiating with him.

Mayank pushed open the door of the coffee shop.

'There are some sick fuckers around,' Ashish said. He followed his friend into the air-conditioned space where, in a strange mock-up of a living room, put-out-looking foreigners and unabashed locals sat drinking enormous cold coffees behind the plate-glass window.

★   ★   ★

When they were leaving the Idiot-Idiot for the station, gulls were crying overhead: that golden hour before sunset when the city looks like a mirage that's about to disappear, leaving behind only a clean beach. Ashish had a sudden longing to do everything — go to Chowpatty, go to Juhu, revisit all his favourite places, go everywhere he had ever had, or expected to have, or nearly had, a good time, and suck what remaining essence of feeling he might out of the places.

They stood at the junction, waiting to cross: behind them the clothing stalls, a Nigerian hustler outside Cafe Leopold, and the smell of the sea. An expensive looking car pulled out smoothly ahead of them. The windows were open. Mayank nudged Ashish.

'What?'

'Wasn't that Sunder?'

Ashish turned towards Mayank, and found the westerly setting sun in his face. He squinted into its warmth and blinding orangeness. 'Was it?' he said.

The traffic light changed.

Ashish looked down the road; he couldn't even see the car any more, though he thought he saw sun glinting off its rear windscreen. But it could have been any car.

'I think his new wife was there with him, there was some girl anyway,' Mayank went on.

'Must be her,' Ashish said.

They crossed the road and paused at the next crossing, opposite the Institute of Science.

Ashish was caught between trying to probe his feelings and not reveal this fact to Mayank. So he kept talking about it.

'Are you still in touch with Sunder?'

'No yaar, not since before he got married.'

'Do you think he saw us?'

'Don't know, maybe.'

They walked on, passing the graceful university gardens.

'It's weird that he didn't even wave or something. If he saw us. Maybe he didn't. Or maybe it wasn't him.'

'Yeah, maybe.'

'Maybe, in the sense?'

'Kya?'

'Maybe . . . ?'

Mayank nearly ground to a halt in front of the high court; the policeman on duty looked at the two of them suspiciously. Mayank stared at Ashish. 'What are you *talking* about?' he enquired.

'Nothing.' Ashish glared at his shoes and they resumed walking. In his head, Ashish continued the conversation; he silently cursed Mayank for not realizing this was all he wanted to talk about. Instead, his friend kept chattering about Ashish's packing and preparations, whether he'd be able to work as a student, and what the course might be like.

As they drifted up the wide road towards Fountain Mayank said suddenly, 'Maybe you should call Sunder before you go.'

Ashish thrilled inside; it must be a sign that Mayank had brought up the name.

'No, no . . . Do you think so?' he said.

'If you want to,' Mayank said.

'Not particularly.'

There were a couple of bookstalls near the odd, witch-like drinking fountain at the American Express Bank, and Ashish looked at them absent-mindedly.

Mayank, annoyingly, seemed to accept that the topic had changed. But it continued to thread through Ashish's mind.

'Do you think I should?' he reprised.

'Maybe, you seem to be thinking about it a lot.'

Ashish glared at Mayank, but the taller boy didn't seem to have meant anything funny.

'Maybe I will, if I have time,' he said finally.

They passed under the shade of the bank porch and strolled through the arcades until they reached VT. The high-ceilinged, light hall of the grand station was more relaxed on this Saturday afternoon, though the five o'clock crowd was beginning to arrive.

'So this is goodbye,' Mayank said.

'Yeah, I guess.' Ashish stared at his shoes, smiled, and then squinted into the sun and at the passers-by; he hated this and wanted it to be over as soon as possible, but knew that he'd feel bad as soon as he'd forced out a brusque goodbye and walked away.

'Take care of yourself,' Mayank said. He

looked concerned, which was depressing, as was the admonition; Ashish couldn't think of anyone he felt less able to take care of. Mayank reached down and embraced him and he tried to enjoy the hug. He didn't know how long it would last, was already beginning to feel sad, and wasn't sure how much to let himself go, so he tensed and waited for it to end. After a time it did, and he stepped back, horrified to find himself slightly teary.

'I'm going to miss you, man,' Mayank said. His big, honest face was sad and earnest. Ashish and he remained looking at each other for a moment.

'You'll miss your train,' Ashish said. Mayank hugged him again, and then cuffed him on the shoulder. 'Stay in touch,' he said, pointing at Ashish.

'Yeah, of course.'

Ashish watched the tall, heavy figure stride away; then he turned and walked, head down, towards his own train. The crowds were intolerable; he felt small and buffeted in the big station. He remembered the Sunday when his uncle and he had taken the train, carrying Ashish's things, and illogically but with the weight of complete emotional certainty he knew that his whole life would be like this: leave-takings with an edge of bitterness, for who knew what was around the corner and who would reappear after a separation? But Mayank, loyal Mayank, he told himself; then he thought again of the expensive beige car gliding down Colaba Causeway into the setting sun.

The train journey brought back the hopeful, depressing trips to Kalina to see Narayan, and he felt melancholic; finally he'd understood what life was like, the meetings and partings it entailed. It was a thought that only made him more attached to his life and the people in it. From his window seat he looked with hungry eyes at the dirty worlds next to the tracks: the brightly painted shacks, the grubby faced children, the ugly concrete tower blocks, the smells. It was his city, his world; it might be imperfect, but it was home. Yet he knew that only his imminent departure nurtured this sudden passion for Bombay, which sometimes was a neutral environment in which he existed, and at other moments felt like a trap he'd never escape. He thought again of Sunder, not the actual Sunder, but a new, strangely compelling person who sat in his car and saw Ashish and glided, nonetheless, serenely on, the sun glinting on his back windscreen as though on a chariot.

Ashish leaned into his sadness. He was almost surprised when his station arrived; he hadn't been expecting it so soon. As he climbed the dirty, crowded steps to the overpass and the exit he reminded himself this was another journey he wouldn't be making for a long time. A tiny middle-aged woman, thin and darkened by the sun, and carrying a large basket of aubergines on her head, bumped into him. She thrust a bony hand hard against his chest so that she wouldn't fall, and glared at Ashish as she recovered her balance; she muttered something, then pushed on into the crowd.

21

'So you came all the way to meet me. I'm touched, yaar.'

The day of Ashish's departure: Madhavi smiled and linked arms with him as they left the cafe and walked to Churchgate. She'd now return to college, and he'd take the train home to finish packing and, later that night, go to the airport. They'd spent the last two hours eating cake and discussing everything. Madhavi had favoured Ashish with some of her theories about life: everything happens for a reason, all events are connected, the right destiny will find you in the end, that sort of thing.

'Well, you'd been reminding me that I promised to take you out, so I thought we'd better do it before I left. And it was all your idea in a way, America and everything. Also, there's something I've been wanting to ask you for a long time,' he said. He stepped away from the crossing, where a bus was hurtling towards them, and pulled her back too. A couple of crows rode atop the bus, which was headed for Colaba.

She looked up at him, her big eyes round. 'What?'

Ashish sighed. 'Your alarm clock. It always goes off at midnight and rings for twelve minutes. Why the hell do you set it if you're not going to get up?'

She started to laugh. 'You can hear that? No, I always think I might do some study for an hour before I sleep.'

'Hm,' he put on his mock-significant face, 'maybe that happens for a reason too.'

Madhavi laughed and rolled her eyes. 'Okay, I have to go. I have to meet Renuka. See you later.' She gave Ashish a sudden hug and left.

He stood watching her, and getting jostled by the people hurrying into the subway; she turned and grinned at him and waved. 'Bye, keep in touch!'

'Yeah yeah!'

★ ★ ★

Ashish went to pack the last odds and ends. There were various pieces of paper strewn around his room: his study timetable, its colours faded; a sheet with a poem he had tried to write; lists and notes to himself. A powerful sense of dread filled him; his chest contracted. He could hardly breathe. Was this a panic attack? He missed everything and everybody in the world so much that he could hardly move for sadness.

He sat on the bed and noted the feeling in his exercise book; his head pounded and he felt slightly queasy. Then he got up and continued stuffing the old papers, and a passport photo of himself that he'd found on the floor, into his bag. He took Satish uncle's watch, still wrapped in a hanky, out of the cupboard, looked at it, then put it in the cupboard again.

There was a sudden flash of white near the window. He ran to it; the owls were back. They sat on the sill of the flat that had been sold, and watched him while he packed.

His aunt called from the passage, 'Leave all the tidying up, Ashu, I'll do it!' In these last days she had returned, apparently without thinking about it, to calling him by his childhood name.

'Coming.' He turned to look at the owls a last time and the nausea, the anxiety and sadness of parting moved through him like a wave. He picked up the cracked cricket bat and, like a batsman who has scored a double century, raised it and smiled at the different corners of the room: the bookshelves, the desk, the window, the bed and the cupboard with its rust-clouded mirror and the sticker of Viv Richards. He waved an imaginary helmet. Applause rang in his ears. He put the bat down, picked up his backpack and left.

The fluorescent light hurt his already tired eyes; he slumped, exhausted, on one of the moulded armchairs in the airport. They were upholstered in maroon velour and obviously dated from the 1970s. This would be his first flight, and he couldn't relax. There'd been long queues in the departure halls while he checked in his baggage and got a boarding pass; he'd watched his suitcase disappear behind the lackadaisical, heavy skirt of rubber panels that covered a mysterious opening.

His aunt and uncle waited with him. They had bought passes that allowed them to stay until he had to go through Immigration, and down a rough carpeted slope into unfamiliar territory. It was all so strange, this new landscape; it was another world, that made him sad and afraid. But he was impatient to experience his emotions in peace. If only they would go; he didn't want them to go, but he looked at their patient, tired, excited faces and felt that they didn't belong in this adventure, which wouldn't be able to start until they had left.

'Don't wait, Mohan mama, it'll get late.'

'*Passengers for the delayed flight AI130 departing for Dubai at 2.45 are kindly requested to proceed to gate number 37 immediately as*

334

the flight is now ready for boarding,' began an announcement.

'Don't be silly,' his aunt said. Her face was a mix of tenderness and tears. 'We're not going to leave you here and go.'

'*Passengers for the delayed flight AI130 . . .*'

'Do you want to eat something?' his uncle asked.

'No, we just had dinner, how can I be hungry.'

'I'll just come,' Mohan said. Lakshmi and Ashish watched him stride into the fluorescent-lit hall. His figure became smaller and the light shone through his hair onto the crown of his head. Bored looking policemen lounged near the barriers at the entrance; they witnessed these separations every day.

Ashish got up and stretched. 'You really don't have to stay,' he repeated to his aunt. To his embarrassment, she looked as if she would cry. She held his hand.

'I know it hasn't been an easy year,' she said. 'But this is your home now, remember that. You can come any time, whether your parents are here or not. Come at Diwali if you like, your cousins will all be here.'

'Okay,' he said. She let go of his hand and he rehoisted the rucksack on his shoulder, uncertain for a moment just which stage in the journey he'd reached.

Mohan mama returned, with a packet of chocolate éclairs, a sweet Ashish had always liked. 'Just in case,' he said, handing them over.

'Thanks,' Ashish muttered. Now he was afraid he'd cry. He'd spotted, out of the corner of his eye, a few other young people, all toting laptops; they must be students too. They were parentless, sitting about and laughing; obviously this wasn't their first year away.

His uncle seemed to read his mood. 'Come,' he said to his wife, 'we'll go now.'

'But there's still time, they said he doesn't have to go yet.'

Mohan put a hand on her shoulder. 'It's time, let him be,' he said.

Ashish's mouth twisted. He dug his nails into his palm. His aunt, then his uncle hugged him. Mohan's embrace was structured, awkward but protective; as ever, it felt like a hug from a well-meaning robot. 'Come back soon,' he said, when he drew away.

Ashish nodded, blurry-eyed. 'Maybe at Diwali,' he said, and a scrap of a smile flew from his face to his aunt's, where it broke out brightly. He stood and watched them go.

He was then excited and desperately lonely after he walked past the immigration counters and towards the darkness that was so close to the windows in the boarding lounge. Here the other passengers' faces had lost their sheen, somewhere in the duty-free shop and the long corridors and stairways between the accessible parts of the terminal and this, the front line of departure.

Another darkness was close. As the time drew nearer, Ashish became choked with tears; his usual, familiar fear returned. It was the one about being alone and abandoned. It was wordless and strong; it pulled him irresistibly. He went to a payphone, put in some change and dialled Narayan's number — he had a powerful urge to tell Narayan that he still loved him — or that he was sorry — something, he couldn't express it. After a few rings he put down the receiver and the coins clinked into the metal tray. Then, again, he looked at the coins in his left palm and put them into the phone. He redialled the number. Nearby, the two girls and a boy he'd seen carrying laptops were sitting together and talking.

'Hello?' That well-known voice, and the soft greeting, slightly bored but inquisitive, that Ashish had so loved. He hesitated.

'Hello?' repeated Narayan, a little less patient.

'H-hello.'

'Yes, hello?'

'It's Ashish.'

'Ashish!' and his heart leapt at the catlike pleasure in Narayan's voice.

'I'm at the airport — I'm leaving a little later. Did I wake you? I'm sorry,' he said with specious formality.

There was an announcement and people began to shove towards the boarding gate now, clutching their passes and their hand luggage and murmuring as though reawakened.

'Is that your flight?' Narayan's voice was sleepy. 'I'm glad you called, Ashish, it's good to hear your voice,' he said.

'It's good to hear yours too,' Ashish whispered. Finally he felt tears running down his face in an unstoppable stream. 'It's just that I'm leaving,' he said nonsensically, and his voice cracked.

There was a small silence. 'I know,' Narayan said.

'I miss you sometimes.'

'I miss you too, Ashish, very often.'

The phone beeped. The money had run out; the line was disconnected. Ashish wiped his face with his hands and joined the boarding queue, which moved through the doors that opened onto the runways. Released once again into the warm, black Bombay night, he smelled the city, its humidity, the scent of rotting flowers, fish, and laundry drying in the breeze; its intimacy.

The little bus took them into the unfamiliar territory of the runway, and he followed the others up the rickety metal staircase to the door of the plane. Inside, the cabin smelled of something minty that caught the back of his throat. He found his seat, stowed his hand luggage in the locker, took out his book, and sat down. When the plane took off half an hour later he was still crying, and remembering the timbre of Narayan's voice.

But he had never taken a flight before, and by the time the 'fasten seat belts' sign was no longer lit, and slender air hostesses handed out small plastic glasses of lemonade, he felt not only better, but like a different person. He hugged the window with his cheek and watched the city, its myriad lights and its pointy sweep into the Arabian Sea. Bombay disappeared behind the plane and they went right into the warm black night; then he relaxed, for everything now was unknown.

22

In the rickshaw, Mohan rested his arm across the back of the seat. His wife was crying openly. Now she smiled. 'Anyway, it'll be good for him,' she said. Then she continued to cry, wiping her face with her dupatta. 'Don't forget to call Vimla when we get home,' she told him. 'You said you'd let her know after we got back from the airport.'

The rickshaw bolted in its unstable way through the quiet roads, the night dark blue and the street lamps sulphur yellow as they left behind the highway, a flyover, a roundabout, buildings under construction. They went first towards Bandra and then in the direction of Sion; it was late, and there was little traffic. Mohan put his hand on his wife's shoulder. 'Less than two months,' he reminded her, 'before the children come for Diwali.' He leaned back, as Bombay passed, and looked forward to the holiday, when the whole family would be together. There was another story he'd been thinking of; he'd meant to discuss it with Ashish, but there hadn't been time. But he'd write, and tell him.

Acknowledgements

Thank you: Christie, Tamsin, Janani, Anna, Jimmy, Claire, Natalie, Ambika and Kannan for reading; Ravi and Velu Palsokar and Mr Shakeel Ahmed for conversations; Stephen Foster for heroism (working-class); Amit Chaudhuri for characteristic kindness; Andrew, Trezza and Giles; Mark Richards at Fourth Estate and V K Karthika at HarperCollins India; Richard Collins for copyediting; Kartikeya, Gargie, and Baba; Nonita; Siddharth; Durva, Kumar; Seema, Sree; Monica, Radha, Nina; Alex, Olivia, Calder, Susannah; Statira, Farrokh, Shirin.

Particular thanks to my agent Peter Straus. Most of all, my parents and Vivan.

We do hope that you have enjoyed reading this large print book.

Did you know that all of our titles are available for purchase?

We publish a wide range of high quality large print books including:
Romances, Mysteries, Classics
General Fiction
Non Fiction and Westerns

Special interest titles available in large print are:
The Little Oxford Dictionary
Music Book
Song Book
Hymn Book
Service Book

Also available from us courtesy of Oxford University Press:
Young Readers' Dictionary
(large print edition)
Young Readers' Thesaurus
(large print edition)

For further information or a free brochure, please contact us at:
Ulverscroft Large Print Books Ltd.,
The Green, Bradgate Road, Anstey,
Leicester, LE7 7FU, England.
Tel: **(00 44) 0116 236 4325**
Fax: **(00 44) 0116 234 0205**

HAND IN THE FIRE

Hugo Hamilton

Vid Cosic is a Serbian immigrant whose friendship with a young Dublin lawyer, Kevin Concannon, is overshadowed by a violent incident ... The legal fallout draws Vid into the heart of the Concannon family, working for them as a carpenter and becoming involved in their troubled story. There, he's compelled to investigate the emerging details of a young woman from Connemara, denounced by the church and whose pregnant body was washed up on the Aran Islands many years ago. Was it murder or suicide? And what dark impact does this event in the past still have on the Concannon family now?

THE PARTICULAR SADNESS
OF LEMON CAKE

Aimee Bender

Just before her ninth birthday, unassuming Rose Edelstein, a girl at the periphery of schoolyard games and her distracted parents' attention, bites into her mother's homemade lemon-chocolate cake and discovers she has a magical gift: she can taste her mother's emotions in the slice. She's horrified to find that this gift reveals that her cheerful can-do mother tastes of despair and desperation. Suddenly, anything can be revealed at any meal. Rose, confronted by the secret knowledge all families keep hidden, finds truths about her mother's life outside the home, her father's strange detachment, her brother Joseph's clash with the world.